CW00501132

# GROOMED FOR MARRIAGE

## By R. Shannon

# COPYRIGHT

This book is a work of fiction. Names, characters, places, and incidents are the product of the author's imagination or are used fictitiously. Any resemblance to actual events, locales, or persons, living or dead, is coincidental.

Copyright © 2020 by R. Shannon
Forward copyright © 2020 by R. Shannon
Preview of this book copyright © 2020 by R. Shannon

All rights reserved. In accordance with the U.S. Copyright Act of 1976, the scanning, uploading, and electronic sharing of any part of this book without the permission of the publisher constitute unlawful piracy and theft of the author's intellectual property. If you would like to use the material from the book (other than for review purposes), prior written permission must be obtained by contacting the publisher at rshannon@gmail.com. Thank you for your support of the author's rights.

White Gothic Publishing
Ocala, FL.

# MAIN CHARACTER LIST

For readers, like me, who find it hard to keep track of characters when there are more than a few, this is for you.

- Colleen Kessler, legal assistant, married to Jacob
- Jacob, stockbroker, married to Colleen
- Fr. Liam, Colleen's uncle, parish priest
- Mike Mullens, retired, Fr. Liam's brother, Colleen's father
- Maria Mullens, retired, Colleen's mother
- Ryan Mallardi, Private Investigator, Fr. Liam's client
- Angelica, Ryan's girlfriend
- Marsha, Colleen's best friend

## MINOR CHARACTORS

- Marie-Louise Lenoir, autistic parishioner
- JF Lenoir, Ryan's new client, Marie-Louise's grandfather
- Alice Brennan, parishioner, obsessed with death

# TABLE OF CONTENTS

# CHAPTER 1

## Monday, April 23rd, 10:30 AM
## Ocala, FL

MOST MONDAYS WERE A bit slow for Fr. Liam after all the weekend weddings and Sunday masses. This Monday in late April, he had been invited to speak at a sister parish, St. Theresa's Parish Retreat. Juanita, his parish secretary, was getting a list of questions she needed answered as Fr. Liam would whisk into the office right after morning mass for just short of an hour. Then he would be gone and incommunicado for the better part of the day. Juanita had to make sure she had all her questions ready because she would only have this one chance to get answers. If she forgot something, she would get stuck waiting for a time she could call or see him.

Even in a world where bosses were one cell phone call away, priests were different. You can't call them during mass, or confessions or when they are comforting people who just lost someone. So it can be tricky. Juanita was already proficient in tackling Fr. Liam as he dashed in and out of the parish office and before he got away for the day. He had been assigned to their parish four years ago after their long-time pastor had passed away. She had been Fr. Liam's parish secretary from his arrival.

Juanita had been with the previous pastor, Pastor McCarthy, until his last day. He died sitting at his desk in the next office. He was 85 years old, still working, but slow-going most of the time. He was a sweet and kind man who Juanita came to love very much. When Fr. Liam was assigned to the parish, and she heard he was an ex-cop who entered the priesthood two years shy of his 60th birthday, she didn't think she would ever adjust.

She liked Fr. Liam well enough, but the first two months were an adjustment because his schedule was three times as busy as Pastor McCarthy's. Fr. Liam's walking and talking pace was also three times as fast as Pastor McCarthy's. In time, Juanita became only too happy to make the adjustment.

As she stacked her work pile with handwritten notes to go over as soon as Fr. Liam swept into the office, Rose Arnett came up to her desk. She handed Juanita another note that was dropped into the poor box. The poor box slot was slightly wider than a half-dollar coin and thick enough to put in only one coin at a time. Someone in the parish was now using it as a suggestion box. '*There is entirely too much talking before mass when people are trying to pray*', '*people need to stop wearing shorts, especially the elderly as they are too wrinkly and disgusting to be out in shorts at*

2

*all'*; every two weeks or so there was some other complaint left for Fr. Liam.

"Look at this one," said Rose as she handed the note to Juanita. Usually the women snickered over the suggestions and more times than not they even agreed with them. *'There is a murderer going to the 11:00 mass on Sundays now'.* Juanita read it out loud and they looked at each other.

"What does this mean? Is this murderer someone we know?" asked Juanita looking at Rose.

Rose raised her shoulders and shook her head. "Just give it to Fr. Liam for his collection." She proceeded to sit at the side of Juanita's desk to count up the money put into the poor box. It would need to be deposited into the bank and a check sent to *Peter's Pantry,* their food ministry.

Fr. Liam walked into the office smiling. "Good morning, ladies."

"Good morning, Father," said Juanita as he walked into his private office. "I have several questions I need to ask you on my work before you leave for your speaking engagement. But Rose gave me another note from the poor box/suggestion box. This one is a bit intriguing."

Fr. Liam came out to Juanita's desk, took the note and read it. He closed his eyes and shook his head. He folded up the note and gave it back to Juanita. "Just add it to the suggestion folder we made for her."

3

"What does it mean? Do you know of a murderer that goes to the 11:00 mass?"

"The whole church is comprised of saints and sinners, so we probably have a murderer or two in the pews, I'm sure. Our suggestion-maker thinks I'm still a cop, which I'm not. I was a cop for 30 years and I was in the criminal-catching business but now I'm a priest and I'm in the soul-saving business. I'll talk to her."

"You know who it is?" asked Juanita and Rose at the same time.

"Yes, I heard her tearing the paper note from a spiral notebook during my homily -- which I don't believe she caught one word of. Then Deacon Bob saw her squeezing the note into the poor box after mass," said Fr. Liam as he went back into his office.

"Who is it?" asked Juanita.

"I would rather not say. If your curiosity is killing you, go to the 11:00 mass on Sundays and linger after mass for a few minutes. You'll see her trying to fit the next note into the coin slot. That's why she has to tear the paper down to as small as she can. She does it right out in the open," said Fr. Liam chuckling.

"Let's go to the 11:00 mass this weekend," said Rose to Juanita.

4

"Okay." Juanita said as she grabbed her pile of work and headed into Fr. Liam's office.

"What time do I have to be over at St. Theresa's? Is the retreat in their parish room, I assume?" asked Fr. Liam.

"Your talk is scheduled for 11:15 and it's in their parish office, yes."

"What questions do you have on your work?"

"I need you to tell me who gets copies of these letters --"

The phone rang. Juanita, sitting in the chair in front of Fr. Liam's desk, handed the four letters to Fr. Liam and he began to read them. She answered the phone on his desk. "Good morning. Our Lady of Mercy Church, this is Juanita, may I help you? ... Hi, Alice ... There's only one so far this week, Mr. Russel. ... His mass is on Wednesday at eleven. ... Kramer Funeral Home. ... Sure, bye now."

"Alice Brennan?" asked Fr. Liam as he put another post-it note on one of the letters with a list of who to copy.

"Yes, she calls every week to see who has died and where the funerals are. She goes to all of them, you know," said Juanita. "Who goes to funerals of people they don't even know?"

"Alice does. That's why they call her *'Madam Macabre'* behind her back," said Fr. Liam smiling.

"But why? Why does she go to all the funerals?"

"She has a fixation, let's call it, on how people die. She works the crowd when she goes to the wakes and finds out how they died and whatever details she can get out of everyone. She's particularly interested in the cause of death, who found them, and what the scene looked like. And let me tell you, she gets more details than a seasoned FBI detective."

"She does?" asked Juanita laughing.

"Oh, yeah. First of all," said Fr. Liam looking up now, "she has a whole mourning wardrobe. If it's a working-class family, she arrives at the wake dressed in a simple black dress with a black lace mantilla and rosaries wrapped around her hand. She walks among the crowd like a grieving relative, touching everyone's forearm and saying, 'I'm so sorry.' That's how each investigation begins. When it's a wealthy family, she arrives dressed in full black designer wear including a velvet pillbox hat with that hanging French netting and she goes into a more formal routine," said Fr. Liam.

Juanita chuckled and took back the letters Fr. Liam had finished putting post-it notes on. She checked her next item.

"Fr. Peter from the seminary called and said he will cover your masses on Saturday and Sunday so you can go away on Mother's Day weekend,"

"Perfect. I can go and visit my brother in Boca Raton for the weekend."

"You miss living close to him, don't you?"

"I do. We've always lived about ten minutes away from each other our entire lives. We're only fourteen months apart; they had no such thing as *child-spacing* back them. We grew up together. We raised our kids together. When I was married, we went out as couples, had holidays together. We've been best friends since we were kids and we're both miserable living so far apart. We're on an organized campaign to talk his wife Maria into moving here to Ocala,"

"Do you think she will?" asked Juanita.

"So far, she's very resistant to it as their only daughter Colleen is recently married. Maria doesn't want to leave her yet. But we're determined not to get discouraged. It's only four hours away. Colleen and her husband can visit Ocala; and Mike and Maria, who are both retired now, can go down and spend time with her."

"Well, good luck on your campaign. I need you to sign these other three letters for the mail. Everything else I can do without you answering any questions. And you better leave for St. Theresa's now."

Fr. Liam finished signing his letters and left for his speaking engagement.

## Later the Same Day - 5:00 PM
## Ocala, FL

The St. Theresa parish retreat talk went well. Fr. Liam got a few laughs during his talk and he felt the group was inspired and hopeful at the end of the day. They had a late luncheon at the retreat and he joined Fr. Dominick for dinner with a couple of his parishioners. From the outside, a priest's job could look very monotonous, but it didn't feel that way to Fr. Liam. The circumstances that surrounded the same rituals or ceremonies were always different. He often felt that certain people were led into his life and he into theirs.

At about twenty-after four, he excused himself from the retreat and said his goodbyes on the way back to the parish office for his 5:00 counseling session. During the years he was on the police force, particularly in his years as a homicide detective, Fr. Liam earned a philosophy and psychology degree in night school. During baptisms, marriages and funerals, Fr. Liam only got to know little snippets about his parishioners. He never spent enough time with them to know them well.

During counseling, he worked with them individually. He helped them with grief issues, addiction issues or moral questions. These were the people he got to know well and even became friendly with. It was more personal. He helped many of them move from a very dark tunnel back into the light of hope. This was a big part of his calling. Little by little this group of strangers became his second family.

He checked his watch and had ten minutes before his session started. He had helped Ryan Mallardi, a young thirty-something parishioner, through the annulment of his first marriage. It was a Las Vegas wedding at some random chapel on the strip. Most of their counseling focused on how a sacramental marriage is different from a civil marriage. As with too many young Catholics today, the concept was all new to Ryan. Although Fr. Liam loved the Church, he had to admit that somehow, in some way, they had completely fallen down on their obligation to catechize an entire generation -- or two. During the last couple of months, Fr. Liam and he had come up against some issues with his mother and girlfriend that he wanted to address. So their counseling sessions continued on a weekly basis.

Ryan Mallardi worked for a private investigator while getting his computer science degree from the University of Florida. He opened his own private investigations and computer security business right out of college. So at the youthful age of thirty-four, he had his own thriving business with three and sometimes four employees. Being an only child of a widowed, still-single mom, he was a self-made man in ways that the coddled youth in America rarely were anymore.

Fr. Liam knew that Ryan, rendered fatherless at the age of eleven, had longed for a father figure all his life. Fr. Liam was only too happy to step in, as his own two sons were both living out of the country.

The door to the parish office opened and Ryan entered. It was 5:15 pm and Juanita was already gone for the day. They shook hands and entered Fr. Liam's office. As Ryan sat down, Fr. Liam said, "Have you received the final annulment papers yet?"

"Not yet. You said it could take up to six weeks, so I'm still waiting," said Ryan. He crossed the ankle of one leg over his thigh and got comfortable. He loosened his tie and opened the top button of his shirt.

"So what's going on in the world of private investigations, beautiful girlfriends and dependent moms?"

"The usual. They're both sniping one another and I'm in the middle and think they're both stubborn and wrong. I have my hands full working investigations and managing my own business. The uninterrupted refereeing is draining me."

"You need to put some boundaries up with both of them. We've talked about this in our previous sessions. Did you ask Angelica to stop making negative comments about your mother?"

"Yeah, I did. So now before she makes negative comments about her, she prefaces each statement with *this may sound negative, but it's not...*"

Fr. Liam half smiled and raised his eyebrows. "What about your mom? Did you tell her you're going to hire a certified nurse's assistant to drive her to doctor appointments and other errands so you can have your time back?"

"I gently told her about wanting my own time and introduced the concept of an assistant to her. I explained that the assistant could drive her wherever she needed or wanted to go. She was insulted and not understanding at all, which was not a surprise. She's now mumbling things under her breath like '*I don't want to be in the way. Why don't you just euthanize me? Then you'll have all your time back,*'" said Ryan with tongue in cheek. "That's an example of the mumblings that are coming. She's got one for every occasion, all guilt-loaded, each one more and more morose."

Fr. Liam chuckled. "Push through and don't allow the guilt-laden mumblings to cause you to change your plans. It's going to take her time to adjust. Guilting you has worked for a long time; she's not going to give it up that easily."

"Yes, it has worked," said Ryan.

"It's going to get better, at least with your mom."

"I hope you're right. It's all exhausting," said Ryan a bit more seriously.

"Don't be hard on yourself, Ryan. This dynamic with your mother becoming overly dependent on you began forming after your father died. You were only eleven and too young to form any defenses to it or even know it was happening. Instead of grieving and finding another husband, or becoming more independent, your mother went into a kind of *professional widowhood*. In that process, she became too dependent upon you. She made you into a *little husband* and this is what has to change. This wasn't done in any sinister way, mind you.

"You can be a good son to her but free enough of your time so you can be a good husband to a wife." Fr. Liam waited to see if this resonated with Ryan.

"I never thought of it that way, but it makes sense, especially the part about not having any defenses to it. I always thought my mother and I had a great relationship," said Ryan, as he looked up and sideways. "I didn't realize how dependent she was on me." Fr. Liam could tell Ryan was looking back in time to see this dependency playing out. He could tell it resonated with him. He knew they were getting somewhere.

"What's the diagnosis with Angelica and me? Do you have any insight into that?" asked Ryan.

"Angelica is a bit demanding, as some very beautiful woman can be. I don't see her as being the most compassionate or sympathetic person, do you?"

"I guess not. She thinks my mother should snap out of it and '*leave you alone*' is how she puts it. But it's all the time," said Ryan as he took a deep breath and exhaled. "She doesn't seem to have any compassion for my mother at all. I mean, not every widow starts rocking the bar scene and gets remarried and moves on. Your church is filled with widows and divorcees that never find anyone else. My mother claims she could never love anyone besides my father. She still has his pictures around the house everywhere. She still wears a gold locket with his picture in it. I think it's a touching love story, but the plot line has drifted entirely over Angelica's head." Ryan took another deep breath and looked at Fr. Liam for some feedback.

"Is her complaint that your mother calls you too much or is her complaint that your mother calls you at all?"

Ryan looked at Fr. Liam and said, "Any time my mother calls me, or if she needs anything, even if it's legitimate, Angelica bitches and moans. She sees every favor I do for my mother as being taken away from her somehow."

"I want you to think this week about what virtues Angelica has and we can discuss that next week, okay?" asked Fr. Liam.

"I can do that," said Ryan. "Virtues, I know a few, but I may have to do an internet search on that."

"The seven virtues are: purity, temperance, charity, diligence, patience, kindness and humility. You can google the seven heavenly virtues and start there. We can talk more next week after you've had a chance to start noticing these. Just look for Angelica's good traits and we'll start discussing them next week."

"Okay. I'll do that."

The session went on for a while longer. Ryan went into some other frustrating instances where he felt caught in the middle of this antagonistic dynamic between Angelica and his mother. Fr. Liam knew he needed to vent so he listened and could see Ryan felt relieved at the end of the session.

Fr. Liam knew as an only child, Ryan had been the head of his little household with his mother most of his life. He wanted to be married without another divorce but somehow this relationship with Angelica kept veering off course. Fr. Liam could see the dynamics between he and his mother and he and his girlfriend. He could also see Ryan didn't have much insight into what was really going on. But he was open to change and Fr. Liam knew that was all that was needed.

From his years studying philosophy and psychology, together with his years working with the criminal classes, Fr. Liam knew that the absence of a father created a myriad of problems. These problems, if left untreated, could create havoc in a young man's life.

Fr. Liam and Ryan talked about boundaries with his mother being essential no matter who he was in relationship with or married to. Once Ryan was assured this dynamic could change, he exhibited signs of hopefulness. This is where the heart of Fr. Liam's work really was.

He had decided to enter the deaconate while still married to his wife, Patty. He was three-quarters of the way through his studies when she got sick with ovarian cancer. She died only four months into her treatment. He was overwhelmed by grief for about six months. At that time, his call to serve went from the deaconate to entering the priesthood. Now he had devoted the rest of his life to working for the Lord's church. He knew it was presently in shambles, but he hoped to be part of the movement to build it back up. It was these moments of helping people like Ryan improve their lives that instilled hope and a sense of purpose into Fr. Liam's heart and soul.

# CHAPTER 2

## One Day Later - 12:00 Noon
## Boca Raton, FL

MARIA MULLENS WAS talking on the phone in her upscale, beautifully-furnished home in Boca Raton. She was drying and putting away dishes with the phone crooked between her head and shoulder. She was fielding another complaint call from her 23-year-old daughter, Colleen, who married almost nine months earlier. Her daughter's complaints were about her husband, Jacob, having to work late all the time. Maria attempted to realign her young daughter's marital expectations. She was convinced Colleen thought the honeymoon would never end. She tried to help her daughter adjust to the changes and compromises demanded by marriage.

"Colleen, a lot of men work longer hours, especially men who make lots of money like Jacob does." Colleen seemed unconvinced, so Maria let her carry on for a few more minutes to vent. In the meantime, she put away the dishes from the dishwasher.

17

"Every marriage has challenges and things we have to get used to. Don't be the type of woman that has to be babysat, Colleen. He's trying to get ahead in his career." Maria had reminded Colleen several times in previous discussions that marriage was a never-ending series of compromises. Obviously, the message wasn't fully absorbed yet.

"Mom, this is the third night this week. He worked Monday and Tuesday until almost eleven o'clock. His hair was a mess and his shirt was a wrinkled mess from sweating. He looked like he was in a wrestling match. Plus he is snapping at me all the time."

"He's probably working under a lot of stress, Colleen. At least he's calling you now by the early afternoon when he has to work late so you don't start cooking. That's a compromise. He's doing that for you, right?"

"Yes, he is. I don't understand. He has the same job that he had before we got married. So why is he now having to work like this?" asked Colleen.

Maria chose not to answer.

"All right. I guess your silence is a non-verbal cue that I'm making too much of it. Is that it?"

Again Maria said nothing.

"I'll stop complaining," said Colleen, unsatisfied with her mother's responses.

"He's still taking you out to a nice restaurant on Saturday nights. He's still talking about having children soon, so it's not all bad, Colleen."

"You're right. I don't want to be a nag or a complainer. I'm worried that he doesn't love me anymore and that's why he's staying away from home."

"I'm sure that's not true," Maria scoffed. "Tell him how you feel. He'll reassure you that this is about his career and then you can let go of that fear. You just got married nine months ago. You're still newlyweds," said Maria, as she walked away from her husband Mike. She saw him approaching with his Ocala homes brochure.

"Your father is approaching me again with that Summer Glen brochure. I told you he's stalking me with that, didn't I?" She looked over her shoulder and glared at Mike. Her husband had been positioning himself behind her to talk as soon as she said goodbye to Colleen.

"Yes, you did. He needs to take a break with that. You need to get that brochure and hide it, Mom."

"He doesn't realize that the country now has stalking laws on the books for this very reason," said Maria, looking at Mike through squinted eyes. Mike dropped his arm holding the brochure and walked with it outside to the pool area.

"Is Uncle Liam coming for Mother's Day?" asked Colleen. "Jacob and I will come at one in the afternoon because we have to go see his mom at four."

"I'll be ready by one. Don't worry. We've compromised and are eating earlier than normal. You see how it works?" asked Maria smiling. "We used to have dinner later in the afternoon. But since you now need to see both moms, I've adjusted. We're having dinner at one o'clock. That's a compromise."

"Okay. You've made your point, Mom," said Colleen, with a tinge of sarcasm. "My lunch break is over. I'll talk to you tomorrow."

"Goodbye, Sweetie. I love you," said Maria. "The first year of marriage can be the hardest so don't be discouraged. You both have to compromise until you reach a happy medium, which you will. It's all going to be okay," said Maria. She looked outside to the pool area and saw Mike sitting by the pool. "I love you, Colleen."

"Love you too, Mom."

Fr. Liam's brother, Mike, after getting busted by his wife, took his Summer Glen brochure out onto the back patio. He sat at the wrought iron table next to their built-in swimming pool. The landscapers had come earlier in the week and the palm trees, the rock garden, and the shrubs were all perfectly coiffed. The pool guy prepared the pool for the start of the swimming season earlier in the day. The pool was spotless and the water was glistening clean. It reflected the sun beautifully.

The swimming season in south Florida was from May to early October. Tourists tended to swim at the beaches into mid-November and later, but the residents of Florida bundled up into sweaters at the first sign of a cool breeze. Mike called his brother, Fr. Liam.

"Hey, Liam, how did your retreat lecture go?"

"It went well. I got some good feedback after it was over, but I think I heard some snoring too. I guess it went as well as could be expected.

"How is the campaign going?" asked Fr. Liam.

"Not too well. I just approached her with the brochure again and she swatted me away like a mosquito," said Mike. He flipped a page or two in the brochure that was now laid out on his pool-side table.

"You better lay low for a while. I think she's onto us and her resistance is too high," said Fr. Liam.

"I think you're right. Did you get the time off to come down for Mother's Day weekend?"

"Yes, I did. I'll come Friday night. We can golf early on Saturday, spend time with Maria on Saturday afternoon and have family dinner on Sunday. We'll both subtly work on Maria a little bit over the weekend."

"Perfect. I'll make sure I have reservations at the golf club for us," said Mike, already planning their weekend in his mind.

"How is Maria and how are Colleen and Jacob?" asked Fr. Liam.

"Apparently, Jacob is working late a lot and Colleen doesn't like it. Maria is trying to tell her she has to be more understanding. This is part of why Maria won't let go of being here. Colleen is calling all the time complaining about every little thing that he says or does. They both analyze everything to death. They're worse than us," said Mike.

"Sometimes the first year of marriage can be a battleground until they work out the kinks," said Fr. Liam.

"We'll see. Colleen isn't a complainer so I'm thinking that maybe there's something going on. Maria keeps telling me we have to support them in the marriage. Between you and me, Liam, when she told us she wouldn't get married in the church because Jacob was an atheist, I was heartsick. Looking back on it now, it's not a church wedding and if it just ended, I think I would be relieved."

"The one reason listed in the letter of St. Paul about leaving a spouse is when they refuse to allow you to practice your faith. She stopped going to mass at his request," said Fr. Liam.

"That's true, but she's giving him cover by saying it was because she wanted to be more interfaith, more spiritual, whatever that means. I better stop talking about it. I can feel my blood pressure going up."

"Don't get mad. Just pray for God's Will, for the truth to emerge. That's all we can do. Because even if it's not a sacramental marriage, once she gets pregnant, they're a family. They're all bound by blood," said Fr. Liam.

"Maria is coming out to the pool now. I have my brochure; I'm going to take another crack at her. I'll keep you posted."

"Good luck," said Fr. Liam.

After her phone call, Maria looked out into the patio area where Mike was sitting at the table by the pool. He was flipping through his Summer Glen brochure again as he talked on his phone. She knew without asking that he was talking to his brother Liam. Since Liam moved up to Ocala four years ago, Mike started moping around the house. He was lost without his golfing buddy, fishing buddy and all-around best friend.

She never saw him as obsessed about anything before he seized on moving up to Ocala. Colleen's sudden and too-short engagement had distracted Mike for about a year. But after Colleen's wedding, Mike had returned to suggesting almost daily that they move up to central Florida. One day he would complain about the brutal summer heat. The next day his complaints were about hurricane season, having to run from pillar to post every time a hurricane swirled off the coast of Africa. And the day after that it was about how crowded the whole area had gotten.

Mike finished his call to Liam and began flipping through the Summer Glen brochure again. Maria came out to sit with him. When she approached, he let go of his brochure, sat back and was just looking at the water.

She wanted to give in to him about the move, but with Colleen calling her every other day and needing guidance, she felt it was too soon to go. She decided she would talk to Mike and Liam on Mother's Day about being open to it maybe next year.

She joined Mike at the table under the umbrella. He smiled up at her and looked over at the water. "How's Colleen?"

"She's okay. They're adjusting to life after the honeymoon is ending, I guess," said Maria.

"What do you mean?" Mike looked into Maria's eyes.

24

"Jacob has started working late a lot; two or three nights a week. Even last Saturday he had to go in for a few hours. She said he never worked like this before they got married, so this is all a surprise to her."

Mike shook his head negatively. Maria could tell he was biting his tongue.

"He wasn't telling her he was going to be late until the last minute. He would call after five, when she had already heated up the oven to make them dinner. Or he would call her when she already picked up take-out for them." Maria raised her eyebrows as she looked at Mike.

"Well, that's ridiculous. He knows he's going to have to work late before dinnertime," said Mike. Maria knew Mike didn't allow Jacob too much wiggle room so she took what he said with a grain of salt.

"What did you tell her?"

"I told her that some men have to work late. I told her you had to work late many nights. There were short stints where you were working almost around the clock. I explained to her that she has to adjust to his schedule," said Maria, waiting for his response.

"He should tell her by two o'clock in the afternoon if he's going to be working late. All men know by two o'clock whether it's going to be an all-nighter. He's being inconsiderate," said Mike.

25

"You think so?" asked Maria.

"Yes, I do. I always gave you a heads-up, didn't I?" asked Mike.

"Yes, you did. You always told me early in the day. I don't think Jacob is as considerate or soft-hearted as you are."

"What do you mean by that?" asked Mike.

"Well, I think Jacob has a good side, but he has a side that can be kind of dark too. It only comes out when he's confronted about something or when things are not going his way," said Maria.

"Do you think we need to be worried about our daughter?" asked Mike. Maria was surprised by his level of seriousness.

A moment of silence passed between them. Maria let it drop because she didn't want to get Mike thinking there was anything sinister going on. Maybe *dark* wasn't the right adjective.

"Elaborate on what you mean by dark side," said Mike.

"Well, when you get mad, you can get loud. You sometimes yell. And sometimes you can go on and on into a bit of a tirade. But you were never mean to me or Colleen. Your anger is outwardly directed. You tend to shout at the world in a way. I've always noticed that this is how you vent your anger. Then when you're done, that's it, you move on. You have no vengeance. You don't seek revenge."

Mike was listening to every word. He was engaged with Maria in intense eye contact.

"But with Jacob, he gets angry, but instead of shouting at the world, he shouts at Colleen. Like he unloads this angst and anger onto her. She has a very sensitive heart and she's always been that way. It's her nature. I worry that this difference in anger expression will lead to bigger problems. She cries and feels blamed and rejected when they fight."

"Do you think he would ever raise a hand to Colleen?"

"No, I don't believe he has that in him. I also notice he has an impatience and an intolerance with people which is harsh. I hope she never has to be on the receiving end of that."

"I better not hear of him ever raising a hand to my daughter. I guarantee his mommy and daddy will not be able to get him out of that kind of trouble," said Mike.

"Now, Mike, I'm only sharing my concerns with you. Don't get mad at him and don't start thinking something has to be done. I'm telling you what is going on with your daughter, keeping you in the loop, that's all. Everything is fine. Every couple has to work out their arguing and discussion styles and put up their own boundaries. Anyway, that's what's going on with them. It's easy at her young age to think the honeymoon will never end." Maria reached over and rubbed Mike on his forearm.

"Okay, I won't shout at the world over it. I'll take your word that everything is fine." He grabbed her hand and they both looked out on the pool. "I never get tired of looking at the pool water glistening in the sun."

"It does look beautiful, especially the first day it's cleaned and open for the season," said Maria.

"You'll keep me posted on Colleen and Jacob?" asked Mike.

"I'm watching the situation as a good mother should. It's a delicate balancing act. I'm monitoring them but trying not to be a meddler. It's a tightrope walk, but I feel confident," said Maria making light of the situation.

"You have to let her grow up too, Maria," said Mike. "We won't always be here and she has to be able to stand on her own two feet."

"'We won't always be here?' Where does that come from? You just retired and neither of us is even 60 yet. We're still young, Mike. We'll be here for a long time."

"I've always had to ride you a little bit about over-spoiling her."

"That's true. I admit I can go a little overboard doting on her. You've pulled me back when I needed it. We're a good balancing act, Mike."

"You're a great mother, Maria."

"It was and is my most important mission – until the grandchildren show up. Which is why we both have to stick around in Boca, just a little longer."

Mike nodded with only a half-hearted grin.

"Couldn't Liam get re-assigned to a church down in Fort Lauderdale?" asked Maria.

"They moved him right into a pastor position and they don't move them too often once they become pastors. Besides, Ocala is more mild, Maria, no hurricanes, and it's out of the city. Boca Raton is no longer the small sleepy little suburb it was when we moved here. It's part of the Miami, Fort Lauderdale metropolis which is getting as busy as New York City. We'll put everything in God's Hands. I understand why you want to be here for Colleen."

Maria knew it was Mike who was compromising this time. She felt Colleen still needed her parents, especially her mother, as she adjusted to married life. Maria could have never known how much she would need her parents.

# CHAPTER 3

### One Day Later - 4:30 PM
### Ocala, FL

FR. LIAM HAD BEEN sitting all afternoon in back-to-back meetings and counseling sessions. He now had fifteen minutes between sessions and needed to stand. As he stood and stretched his legs, he rearranged his desk and put things away for the day. The upcoming marriage counseling appointment would be his last session of the day. It was twenty after five and he could still hear Juanita at her desk as well as the printer.

"Juanita, are you still here?"

"Yes, Father. I'm printing out your schedule for tomorrow. You have two wakes tomorrow." Juanita organized her desk and her list of things to do in the morning.

31

"The baby boomers are dropping like flies. They are dying as quickly as they were all born. I'm beginning to see our parish thinning."

"I know. It's very sad really. By the way, I called Marie-Louise to schedule her for this Friday. She was so alarmed at being contacted by you for a conference that she insisted on coming tomorrow morning. She said she would not be able to think of anything else or sleep and she had to do it tomorrow. I gave in as she is very ... *forceful*? Is that the word I'm looking for?"

"*Insistent*?" asked Fr. Liam.

"*Insistent*, that's the word." Juanita grabbed a copy of the schedule from the printer, put one on her desk and brought one into Father.

"Maybe *strangely insistent* is the most accurate, don't you think?" asked Father.

"That is more accurate. Is she mentally ill or just strange?" asked Juanita, as respectfully as she could.

"Some days I'm not sure. I'll get another chance to analyze her up close tomorrow. What time is she coming?"

"I was only able to squeeze her in before your luncheon, so she's coming at 11:00 tomorrow. I hope that's okay."

"That'll be fine," said Fr. Liam, grinning.

"Are you going to ask her about the notes?"

"We're going to discuss her suggestions, yes."

"Well, good luck, Father," said Juanita as she gathered her keys and her pocketbook to leave.

"Thanks, Juanita. I'll need it. Have a good night. I'll see you tomorrow."

## Ten Minutes Later – 4:40 PM
## Boca Raton, FL

Colleen worked as a legal assistant in Boca Raton and was really good at it. She worked in a worker's compensation legal defense law firm. She left college a few months before getting married but planned to return now that the wedding was over. In the meantime, she decided to switch majors from liberal arts to paralegal studies. Her present plan was to enroll in paralegal courses which were set to begin in September, which was only four months away.

At first, she was worried about going to school while working because she couldn't imagine when she would find the time to study. But having so many free nights lately with Jacob's new schedule, she could use those nights to study.

Jacob said he would be home by six tonight, so she had taken out two freezer meals in the morning. This would allow them to thaw all day in the refrigerator. Once she got home from work, she put them out on the counter, to allow them to come to room temperature. When Jacob came in, she planned to heat them up quickly in the microwave. They would have the rest of the evening together.

As she tidied up the kitchen, she thought back to when she met Jacob. She went to a party given by a college student she knew casually. When she and her friend Marsha walked in, Jacob was engaged in a somewhat heated debate with another guy. The debate was about liberalism. Jacob was a senior in college and he had a bit of a rebellious streak in him. To Colleen, he seemed to be crushing his opponent in the debate. She could tell he was innately smart and self-assured. He was a seasoned debater. He also happened to be tall and handsome.

Graduating later that year from NYU with a finance degree, Jacob walked into a job in a trading and investment firm in Coral Springs. Now making great money, he held his future by the horns. No one was more self-assured and confident than Jacob was. These traits were assets in the finance business. Using his own words, he told her *they were selling themselves as investors.*

She thought back to how much she began to change as soon as they started dating. To her parents' horror, she decided to stop practicing Catholicism. She proclaimed to be more of a *spiritual person* now. She didn't believe anymore in organized religion. She told them about how religion had caused so many of the wars in the world. She waved off how organized religions were more about rules and rituals. Her parents knew she absorbed these beliefs from Jacob Kessler, her new boyfriend. He was a self-described Jewish atheist and proud of it.

She cringed a little when she thought about how combative she became with them over this. She knew she disappointed them. She told herself at the time that she couldn't help who she fell in love with. When two people have different religions, it requires compromise. She figured her parents would come around and understand in time. After all, her mother was always telling her how important compromise was in marriage. She just wished this guilt she still felt would go away.

She walked into her bedroom and undressed from the office. Once in a t-shirt and jeans, she looked over to her mirror. She had souvenirs from the whirlwind romance with Jacob. She decided to marry only four months after meeting. They were madly in love.

While dating, they travelled to Las Vegas and to the Caribbean. They went often to the local casino in Coral Springs where everyone knew his name. He was so much fun and had a way of meeting and knowing people quickly. She wished she had this personal charisma, but she tended to be quiet and reserved.

Lately, she felt like the whirlwind and the honeymoon was tarnishing. Jacob was now working late at least two to three nights a week. Last week, it was four nights. This was the most they were apart since they met. He seemed more stressed out lately too. When she asked him about it, he said it was the job. He claimed the stress at work was getting worse.

As she walked back to the kitchen, Jacob called. Thinking that he was calling to see if she needed anything on his way home, as he did often, she answered smiling. "Hello, Jacob."

"Listen, Colleen, I'm sorry I didn't get to call you earlier, but I'm not going to be able to come home. I have to stay and work."

"You just found out now, 5:45 pm?" asked Colleen, now with an annoyance in her voice. "All right. Well, what choice do I have?"

"Listen, Colleen, don't be a bitch about it. When I get early notice of these things, I call you. I'm under a lot of pressure at work and I don't need to get verbal bitching from you. I've got to go." He then hung up.

Stunned, Colleen kept the phone to her ear and didn't know what to say or even how to react. He never spoke to her in that tone before. He never cursed like that to her or about her. She put her phone down and stood still wondering what to do. Should she call him and tell him not to speak to me like that? Was she really *verbally bitching him* as he put it? She called her mother.

"Mom, I need to talk to you about Jacob. Are you eating right now?"

"No, we went out for a late lunch and we're only having a small snack later. What's going on?"

"I talked to Jacob earlier today and we had plans to eat dinner and watch a movie, you know, spend the evening together. I have meals thawed out already and he just called at a quarter to six to tell me he has to work late and won't be coming home."

Her mom listened for a punchline or a problem.

"Well, I got mad at the lateness of the notice, I guess you could say. As soon as I said something like *'well, what choice do I have,'* he raised his voice and said *'Don't be a bitch about it, Colleen. I'm under pressure at work and I don't need to be verbally bitched by you.'* and then he hung up."

"Well, that doesn't sound like him. Did he ever say anything like that before?" asked Maria.

"Not that bad or in that tone."

"Did you carry on to him a little more than you're admitting to me? Do you think you were riding him a bit before he exploded like that? Be honest, Colleen."

"No, I really said something like, *'fine, what choice do I have.'* I mean, I was mad, and it is frustrating when I'm cooking for us."

37

"You need to tell him you don't like to be spoken to in that tone of voice and don't like to be cursed at. However, you need to pick your timing on it. Don't call him back right now if he's already stressed out. Pick a time when he's relaxed. Tell him you want to bring something up and tell him then. Let him defend himself or apologize when he's more relaxed."

"Okay. He's changing. He's working late, now he's cursing me," said Colleen. "There's something wrong."

"Colleen, don't over-dramatize this. Don't blow this up any bigger than it is, okay? He's not cursing you. He said you were 'verbally bitching him' which I have never heard before, but your generation uses a lot of words and phrases I've never heard before. Don't stew in this, Honey. Let it go. Make yourself something to eat. Watch the movie yourself, call your friends, and amuse yourself. Many successful men work long arduous hours, all right?"

"Okay, Mom. I guess you're right. I'm going to let go of it. Maybe I was snarkier than I thought. I'm letting it go."

"That's a good plan. Bring up the subject of how he spoke to you another night when he isn't stressed and angry."

"All right. I'm compromising. But it seems like I'm the one compromising all the time."

Maria didn't take the bait but instead changed the subject. "Are you still looking for a paralegal course to go to in September? You don't want to forget about going back to school. This may be the best time. If he's in a busy working phase, you'll have plenty of time to do schoolwork. Try to make this work for you, Colleen."

"I'm still looking, but I'm on it, Mom. I was thinking the same thing about having time to study."

"It's part of my mothering job to make sure you're on it." whispered Maria.

"Right, I get it. Okay, Mom, thanks. I feel better now. I love you."

"I love you too, Colleen. We'll talk tomorrow."

# CHAPTER 4

### One Day Later - 10:45AM
### Ocala, FL

MARIE-LOUISE ARRIVED for her conference with Fr. Liam Thursday at 10:45 sharp. She came up to the counter in the parish office and looked intensely at Juanita. "I'm Marie-Louise Lenoir. I have a meeting with Fr. Liam at 11:00."

"Hello, Marie-Louise. Fr. Liam is still on a conference call but he'll be with you shortly. You can have a seat." Juanita smiled at Marie-Louise who looked *a little off* as usual.

"Is the phone call about me?" asked Marie-Louise.

"Oh, no. He's talking to the bishop about parish matters. I'm sure he'll be off by 11:00. There's coffee over there if you would like to help yourself to a cup." Juanita smiled trying to relax Marie-Louise. She didn't smile back. As a matter of fact, no change in demeanor registered at all.

Juanita's section of the parish office was only about five foot wide and ten foot long. It included her desk, a coffee/brochure table and four waiting chairs. Marie-Louise began to pace back and forth, still holding her purse over her shoulder. Back and forth, back and forth for ten minutes. On the back end of her pace, when she came face-to-face with Juanita, she maintained the same intense look. Juanita was praying for Fr. Liam to finish his call. God must have had mercy on her because just as she ended a Hail Mary, the light on Fr. Liam's line went out. His call had ended.

Fr. Liam came out to Juanita's desk with paperwork. Upon seeing Marie-Louise, he said, "Good morning, Marie-Louise. I'll be right with you." She stopped, looked at Fr. Liam as he spoke to her, but then continued to pace.

Fr. Liam handed his secretary a letter. "Juanita, can you add the dates from this letter into my schedule?" He could tell his secretary was flustered from Marie-Louise' presence. He smiled at her first and then smiled over towards Marie-Louise.

"Okay, Marie-Louise. Thank you for coming. Come with me and we'll have a little chat." Marie-Louise immediately marched right behind Fr. Liam into his office. Normally, Fr. Liam would close the door for his conferences, but he left the door open this time. Juanita was tempted to take the phone off the hook. She was dying to know what Fr. Liam was going to say.

"Have a seat here in one of the chairs. I wanted to talk to you about some of these suggestions you have addressed to me. Would that be okay?"

"Okay." She sat rigidly in the chair, with her purse still on her shoulder. She crossed her hands in her lap. "How did you know they were from me?"

"Deacon Bill saw you putting the last note into the poor box and he mentioned it to me."

Marie-Louise's eyes began darting back and forth in thought.

Fr. Liam took out his folder where he was keeping her suggestions. "Let's start with the first one about people talking before mass and disturbing others who are praying. First of all, let me say, I agree with you. Mass is not a social gathering. Since the Lord is present in the Tabernacle, people should be conducting themselves very respectfully."

"Exactly," said Marie-Louise, without a moment's hesitation. She put her purse on the floor. It seemed Fr. Liam's agreement allowed her to relax a bit.

He continued more gingerly. "However, what I have found, having gotten to know some of the parishioners, is that many live alone and they're very lonely. The little bit of interaction they have before mass can be the only human interaction or attention they get all week. So I must confess, I've gotten a bit lax with them because of that."

43

Marie-Louise did not seem impressed but she listened, without shifting her eye contact even by a hair.

"So I have adjusted my expectations of people. As long as they are only whispering, I tend to not say anything. I think it's best to allow them to have this interaction because I believe they need it."

Marie-Louise didn't speak. She continued to listen.

"I've noticed that you are no longer going to mass with your Uncle Francois and Aunt Nicole. Is there a reason for that?"

"Nicole and I don't get along. She thinks I killed her dog," said Marie-Louise like it was nothing.

"When did her dog die and why did she think you were responsible?"

"Well, the dog was old. Back in January, one day when Nicole got up in the morning, he was laying on the floor in the kitchen. He usually stayed by her feet in the bedroom. He was laying on the kitchen floor and he was dead. He had eaten just before he died and because I was in the kitchen, she thinks I put something in his food."

"Did she have any evidence to think that?" asked Fr. Liam, who realized he just opened a whole can of worms.

"No. The dog was already dead on the floor when I went into the kitchen. I didn't like the dog because he smelled awful and he never listened. She thought that because I

44

didn't like him, that I wanted him dead so I must have killed him."

Marie-Louise became very animated as she relayed more of the story to Fr. Liam. "He was never properly trained. So when anyone ate in the kitchen, he continually begged. He would jump up onto your thighs and make begging noises. It was horrible. He barked at everyone coming into the house, even people he knew. Nicole never trained him. She hated me because I complained the dog wasn't trained properly.

"Then she started complaining about me to my Uncle Francois all the time. So my uncle said there was too much tension and we needed to separate a little." Marie-Louise acted annoyed, but Fr. Liam could detect there was hurt underneath the annoyance.

"It must have been quite an argument if it resulted in you now going to church alone." Fr. Liam knew her suggestions only started after Marie-Louise showed up at church alone.

"There were lots of fights as the dog got older because the smell got worse and worse. Nicole felt that we should all just put up with it. Uncle Francois said he didn't want to be a referee between us. He wanted me to be more understanding about the dog."

"I see. So the dog died about 4 months ago?" asked Fr. Liam.

"Yes, he died in January."

"And you haven't resumed going to church with Francois and Nicole?"

"No, Uncle Francois hasn't said anything, so I'm still going by myself. I'm supposed to be going with Adam, my brother, but he keeps making excuses for why he can't go. That's really why I go alone. All his excuses are lame."

"Lame excuses, I get a lot of those from people too," said Fr. Liam smiling. Trying to lift the mood a bit, he said, "I hear confessions, I hear all kinds of lame excuses."

Marie-Louise half smiled.

"Now, let's talk about the note about what people are wearing in church. Again, I agree with you on this when I see some of the clothing the parishioners wear to church --
"

"They're disgusting! Dirty Sneakers? And they shouldn't be wearing shorts at all, ever, in their lives. I don't mean just to church, but ever, anywhere. They have sores on their legs and bulging veins. And then they wear sleeveless tops and their arms are as disgusting as their legs." Marie-Louise was most vehement over this one. "Uncle Francois told me people used to wear their Sunday best to church but the church got lax with them. You should tell them from the pulpit to cover themselves and dress respectfully."

"Well, as we age, we do begin to wear out, I guess you could say. You're a very young woman and this process can be seen as disgusting, to your young eyes. But telling people that they are too disgusting to show themselves at church? That would fall under *meanness and cruelty* in the sin department, so I can't tell them that. But I'll tell you what, I'm going to weave into one of my homilies something about dressing more respectfully for our Lord. How about that?" asked Fr. Liam.

"That would be good." Marie-Louise actually smiled. Fr. Liam had heard she was diagnosed as high-functioning autistic. However, this additional show of emotion made him question the diagnosis. There was something definitely off about her, but he wasn't sure it was autism. He wondered whether this diagnosis was given to a wealthy family about one of their own for reasons of respectability. The Lenoir family was most likely the richest and most influential family in all of Ocala. They held their own in the international community as well.

"Now, let's talk about this last note from you about there being a murderer at the 11:00 mass."

"I heard that the guy with the silver hair and the really old wife, that he's a murderer."

"Who told you that?" asked Fr. Liam.

"My brother, Adam. He has a friend who used to live in New York and he said that's where the murder took place."

47

"Is that right?" asked Fr. Liam. Fr. Liam already knew about the parishioner mentioned from the confessional, but he was bound to secrecy. "Well, first of all --"

"Adam said he went to jail in NY for like 10 years," said Marie-Louise. "He's a murderer."

"Well, first of all, this is a rumor, I assume. Secondly, we don't know if it was first degree or second degree --"

"It was second degree murder because the victim was his wife's boyfriend."

"Did your brother Adam tell you that as well?"

"Yeah, he did. He showed me the story on the internet. I read the whole story."

Fr. Liam folded his hands on his desk. He took a deep breath and said, "Marie-Louise, the church is made up of saints and sinners alike, and even the saints among us are not sin-free. If this man killed someone, was convicted and did his time, he's now out and free to resume his life. I cannot keep him out of church because of his past. Jesus came for the sinners among us. As Christians, we believe no sin is unforgivable. Redemption is for all of us. He has the same freedoms now as the rest of us. Wouldn't you agree with that?"

"But he could be dangerous."

"Well, Marie-Louise, as you may or may not know, I worked as a homicide detective for many years."

"I heard that."

"Most murders are committed by one-time-only murderers who murder under a specific set of circumstances. Not every murderer is a serial killer. So that's number one.

"Number two, I want you to know that we may have other potential murderers among us that are more dangerous because they haven't committed their one-and-only murder yet. So it's best to put yourself in the Hands of God and not worry about the guy with the silver hair. I don't believe you have anything to worry about."

"I guess, but there are shootings all the time now."

"This is the world we now live in. Generations before us had to worry about plagues, polio, measles. Before antibiotics were discovered, people had to worry about dying from all kinds of infections, even the flu. Today we have much better medicine and don't worry about those ailments. But now our worry is crime. So there will always be things to worry about in our fallen world.

"However, if we all live each day like it may be our last, then we're ready whenever the Lord calls us home, right?"

Marie-Louise took a deep breath and let it out. She seemed to settle a bit with his explanation but he could tell she wasn't fully satisfied.

"Do you think that's true, that we have different worries today?"

"Yes, I do." She began to rub the chair rails up and down.

"Well, I've finished with the suggestions you've left me so far. Do you have any others that you would like to discuss?"

"No, not today."

"Would you like to be an usher at the 11:00 mass and help us out?"

Marie-Louise's eyes got very wide and she seemed frightened. "An usher? I don't know if I can do that."

"I want you to watch the ushers this Sunday and see if it's something you can help with. Maybe you can help us if someone calls in sick?" asked Fr. Liam. "The ushers pass the collection basket and help to seat people. It's easy and I think you would be good at it. We need the help."

Marie-Louise seemed to go into deep thought, her eyes darting again. "I'll watch them this Sunday. I know they pass the collection baskets from pew to pew. Is that all they do?" Marie-Louise had stiffened in fear.

"Yes, that's what we would need help with. You don't need to give me an answer today. Watch them this Sunday when they pass the baskets and if you feel you can help us with that, that would be great."

"Okay." Marie-Louise continued to sit and wait with her eyes still on Fr. Liam.

Father knew she needed direction. "So if there are no further suggestions today, Marie-Louise, you're free to leave. I'll see you at mass on Sunday, okay?"

"Okay." Marie-Louise got up, put her shoulder bag on and began to leave. She stopped short at Juanita's desk. "Thank you. Goodbye." Then she left.

"Goodbye, Marie-Louise," said Juanita.

Marie-Louise marched out of the office and off into the parking lot. Fr. Liam came out of his office and walked over to Juanita's desk.

"She's going to be an usher?" asked Juanita. "I couldn't help overhear what you were talking about."

"I think these notes are a cry for some kind of help or attention. She hasn't said yes, but she'll think about it."

"She's autistic," said Juanita.

"She allegedly has Asperger's but they are high-functioning autistics. She can handle taking up the collection. Actually, I think it would be perfect for her. We'll see if she goes along with it."

"And by the way, she's right about what people wear to church," said Juanita.

"I know she is. We have the 1960s to thank for that thinking: '*God doesn't care about what we wear to church*', mimicked Fr. Liam. Of course, these same people get dressed to the nines to go to a concert or a political dinner. I try to keep my expectations low in today's world, Juanita. Like I was taught in the seminary, you have to accept people where they're at."

### One Hour Later - 12:00 PM
### Boca Raton, FL

Colleen raced into Town Center Mall walking as fast as she could. She knew Marsha was always either early or on time. She was too usually, but today she got caught in more cross-town traffic than normal. As she approached Grand Lux Cafe, she spotted Marsha. She was already teasing about her being late by tapping her watch. Both having gone to Catholic schools; they would mimic the nuns looking at their watches when either of them was late.

"Sorry, Sister Marsha, there was more traffic than I was expecting," said Colleen.

"You should have left earlier," growled Marsha in her harshest nun voice.

They hugged hello and waited to be seated.

"How's everything?" asked Colleen.

"It's okay. I need a better job, and this online dating is killing me. Wait until I tell you about my last adventure," said Marsha. "How's your life?"

"It's good but I think my husband is already tired of me. He's staying at work and he's barely talking to me when he comes home. I've caught him rolling his eyes a few times. And I detected a scoff or two when I was telling him something."

"Come this way," said their twenty-something server. She led them to their table and handed them menus. "I'm Gretchen and I'll be your server tonight. Would you like something from the bar?"

"I'll have a margarita, because I deserve one," said Marsha.

"She's online dating, so make it a strong one. I'll have a margarita too, but a light one, no salt," said Colleen.

Marsha opened the menu to decide what to have. Colleen had been in this restaurant so many times with Jacob that she knew the menu by heart.

"So why do you think your husband no longer loves you?" asked Marsha, as she reviewed the menu.

"Well, before we were married, he worked pretty regular hours. He worked from about 9:30 to 6:00, Monday through Friday. Now that we've been married going on ten months, suddenly he has to work late two and three times a week. Last weekend, he had to go in for a couple of hours on Saturday too. He has the same job. Why the sudden change? So anyway, I think he's just running away from home." Colleen unwrapped her utensils and looked at Marsha for her reaction. She put aside her menu.

"Well, I know that the honeymoon doesn't last forever, so this may be him after the honeymoon. Maybe he was working less time because he was madly in love -- which he was, by the way. I know he was upside down and crazy about you. He couldn't take his eyes or his hands off you. He could be coming down off his cloud and the newlywed bliss is wearing off a little bit."

"That's why I notice it so much because he's so different. My mother tells me I should adjust to his work schedule, that lots of men have to work long hours. She doesn't think this is an indication that he has changed. She said that his circumstances may be changing."

"She's right about the working late. Corporate America gives speeches about how they are all about families, health and the environment, but they're slavedrivers in disguise. If they could legally get away with whipping us to be more efficient, they would. Does he at least tell you when he'll be working late?"

"That's where the fighting and the sniping begins. Last night, he was calling me at six o'clock to tell me he wouldn't be home for a while. I had already thawed out food for us to eat. So I told him to give me a head's up about working late so I'm not standing at the stove heating up food that he won't eat."

Their drinks came. They placed their orders and the server left.

"So did he agree to give you notice?" Marsha looked concerned.

"He finally did, but not until he blasted me about harping on him and being bitchy about it. He was mad that I got annoyed. I think anyone would get annoyed, don't you? After all, I work all day too. I was getting dinner ready for us, and he just calls and cancels at the last minute. I already had the stove preheated and was watching for his car."

"You both have a point. He has to work late and it's annoying to be canceled on at the last minute, so I think you two will work it out with a little tweak on both sides. It doesn't sound like a big problem and I don't see *not loving you anymore* in any of what you just described."

"I guess. It's just the way he talks to me. He has this annoyance that is in his tone that I never heard before. He just seems like a different person," said Colleen.

"Maybe you never noticed it because you were madly in love with him. Maybe all this is about the honeymoon ending and the real marriage starting. Did you ever think of that?" asked Marsha. "I mean, as your best friend, it's incumbent upon me to point these things out to you."

Colleen could tell Marsha was half-kidding her, but it was an interesting concept.

"That could be part of what's happening. I never thought of it from that perspective. Or maybe after nine months of married life, we are both letting our hair down. Maybe he's thinking he never heard me bitchy before this, although I think his bitchy description is way off. I was annoyed but I don't think I was bitchy."

"Men have a much more limited vocabulary regarding relationships so you may have to grade him on a curve on the *bitchy vs. annoyed thing*," said Marsha.

"I think you're right, Marsha. So how was your date with the online Greg?"

"Well, first of all, his username said Greg, but he introduced himself as Gregory. So I guess he prefers to be called Gregory, which I have no problem with. But his pictures online are at least 10 years old, maybe even 15 years old."

"Oh, dear, that sounds scary."

"Now, I must admit the pictures did show him as bald-ing. But the pictures represented him as having about 80 percent of his hair which was brown." Marsha stopped for emphasis.

"And in real life?"

"Eighty percent bald, with only hair on the sides, bozo pattern, gray and white."

"That's a bait and switch if I ever heard of one," said Colleen.

"Exactly. False advertising. Blatant false advertising," said Marsha.

"How did the rest of the date go?" asked Colleen.

"It went okay, I guess. But I couldn't get beyond the false advertising. I had this feeling like I was tricked into the date the whole time. So even though he's nice, he's successful, he had table manners -- he claims to have friends and family -- I got stuck on how he tricked me with the old pictures."

"I'm sorry that happened."

"Why can't he put up the bald pictures? He's not an ugly bald man. As a matter of fact, he's thin. He's a runner. He has a nice physique. He has nice skin, he's healthy and has an overall nice look about him. But the trickery, and hoodwinking with the pictures, it was in the way the entire dinner. Like I said, I tried to let go of it. I told myself it was his insecurity that made him do it. But I saw him as more of a slippery car salesman the whole time," said Marsha. "A better person may have been able to let go of it, but I got stuck."

"This is why I tell you to only go for coffee. If you only went for coffee, you could have gulped the coffee down and been out of there in less than an hour," said Colleen.

"You don't know how lucky you are to have met your husband while you were in college," said Marsha.

"You met Alex in college too," said Colleen.

"Yes and married him and he went on to have an affair right from day one. Which is why I also had to divorce him as soon as I got out of college," said Marsha smirking. "I thought we went over all of this."

Colleen chuckled. "We analyzed that relationship to death, I remember. We've been all over that."

"My point is when you meet someone when you're young and in college or on your first job, there's something spontaneous and romantic about it. When you have to start rummaging around in these online dating bins, it's like trying to find a husband at the Salvation Army. All dignity and spontaneity are removed from it. It's on par with other acts of desperation," said Marsha.

"It's only temporary, Marsha. So many people meet online and they go on to have successful marriages. There's a lot of men who are not good at dating and they're online looking for a spouse." Colleen was good at building up Marsha's confidence and giving her a more hopeful look at things.

"Besides, you only have to find one really decent guy. So even if you have to drink coffee with 10 losers -- or liars in the case of Gregory who was hiding the extent of his baldness -- once you find that one person, you're set for life. You won't even remember the names of the other dates."

"You're right. I only have to find one. That does put it in a more balanced and hopeful perspective. I tend to keep going over all the losers like somehow, I deserved each of them for different reasons; like I was a war criminal in a past life."

"No, no. My father and uncle used to tell me all the time that there are a lot of men who never grow up and to stay away from them. They told me they'll never be good husbands. You need a mature man who can be a good husband. I'll never forget that. After they pointed it out, I did see a difference in the different men I met. Some men were mature and some weren't," said Colleen.

"That makes sense. So you think Jacob is mature?" asked Marsha.

"Jacob is responsible and mature in most ways, but I do believe he's spoiled by his parents who dote on him. But my parents, especially my mother, dotes on me too, so we're about the same in that department. I'm responsible, but I guess a little too sheltered or pampered? Jacob is the same. We both need to grow up a little, I guess."

"What does your mom say about all this with Jacob?" asked Marsha. "I'm sure you've told her about this."

"She tells me about having to accept his working late because some men have to work late, period. But my mother grew up in another generation. I know my father would never talk to my mother in the same condescending tone that Jacob uses with me sometimes."

"You didn't mention anything about a condescending tone earlier," said Marsha, now more serious. She took a long and hard sip of her margarita.

"I couldn't put my finger on how to describe it before now, but that's it. He's curt and condescending, a combination of both. Like he's annoyed he even has to address this with me and then he's sharp and condescending about it. I hate the delivery more than what he's even saying," said Colleen, as she finished her margarita.

"Huh, that's why we need to have these sessions where we can dissect and examine all this under the proper lighting," said Marsha. "It's important for our future strategies."

"Exactly."

Their food came and they finished their dinners. Marsha felt better about online dating, knowing she only needed to find one decent guy. And Colleen felt empowered and better able to verbally describe the changes with Jacob. After dinner, they were ready for the next leg of their separate journeys.

## Six Hours Later - 5:45 PM
## Ocala, FL

As Fr. Liam waited for Ryan, he thought about how he would bring up the subject of compatibility between him and Angelica. They fought all the time and nothing seemed right except the sexual chemistry. Ryan seemed determined to make it work, but Fr. Liam had his doubts about whether that was even possible.

Ryan entered his office. They shook hands and Fr. Liam sat down. Before sitting, Ryan removed his jacket and laid it across the seat next to him. He sat down, loosened his necktie and crossed his lower leg over his thigh. Fr. Liam could see him letting go, relaxing.

Not much guidance was needed today because his mother was on the back burner and Ryan was focused instead on Angelica. He wanted to discuss why they had this up-and-down pattern -- one day up, the next day down.

"It's either everything feels perfect or we're fighting like cats and dogs and one of us wants to break up. I've never fought with any woman so much in my life. It's exhausting."

Fr. Liam asked, "Is it lust or love that you feel for Angelica?"

Ryan thought a moment and said, "I think it's both, but maybe we can analyze it more. We spent a lot of time together recently. We spent the entire weekend together last week and I wound up with very mixed feelings about her. I think she has mixed feelings about me too."

Fr. Liam asked, "What do you love about her?"

Ryan smiled and said, "She's beautiful, of course. She's smart. She can be very sweet sometimes and ... um, she's really sexy. You were married so you understand what I'm talking about."

They both smiled.

Fr. Liam said, "What do you have in common?"

Ryan thought a moment. "Well, this is where it gets a little tricky. I basically dislike all of her friends, and she's attached to them like sisters. They're all catty and negative, especially towards men in general. There's some sort of rabid feminist thing hanging in the air at all times, at least when she's with her friends. I don't notice it as much when we're alone together.

"She likes to party and go to bars. Although that can be fun in small doses, I prefer to be sober and alone together. I would rather do other more meaningful or constructive things. That's one area that we fight about, going out and partying all the time."

Fr. Liam asked, "Does she drink a lot? Do you both drink a lot?"

"Well, she does get drunk whenever we go out. This is one of the reasons I try to think of other things to do because the drunkenness can go either way. It can make her passionate, loving and sexual and that I have no problem with. But it can go in the opposite direction, where I do one little thing, like ask her to leave before she's ready and she flies into a rage and it's game on. Then she's nothing but hostile and wants to fight. The alcohol even makes her a bit physical."

"Does she cook?" asks Fr. Liam.

"Cook?" Ryan asked, with a dumbfounded look, "She kind of brags about not cooking actually. It sounds more liberated to her, I think. What makes you ask that?"

"Well, if you're planning to get married and have a family, which is what you've told me is your ultimate goal, it helps if the woman can cook so the kids can eat. Unless you plan on working and then cooking yourself, but with the 12-hour days I know you work, that would be a little hard to pull off.

"I know in a world ruled by feminists that question is forbidden to even ask, but for any marriage, and yours in particular, it would be good if you found a woman who can cook or provide food in some way, especially for small kids. They are still domestic skills crucial for the survival of a family. Woman still look for men who can financially provide for a family. And most men still look for a woman who can bring things to the table too, no pun intended. I was curious if Angelica has any traditional mothering skills." Fr. Liam shared a knowing smirk.

"She says she doesn't cook, but I don't know if she says this for some feminist points around her girlfriends or whether she really doesn't cook. She's Italian, I guess I assumed she can cook."

"Has she ever cooked dinner for you?" asked Fr. Liam.

"Come to think of it, when I eat there, she brings in restaurant-bought food or makes grilled cheese or something from the freezer. But I don't believe I've ever actually seen her cooking like my mother cooks."

Fr Liam asked, "So she's a food provider, but you're not sure if she can actually cook. You can work around a food provider.

"What else do you fight about?"

"Well, we fight a lot about me working long hours. Any time I need to help my mother, that's either a full fight or a sniping session. She keeps telling me I'm married to my job or married to my mother and not available to her. I think she has no compassion for the fact that my mother is a widow. You and I have talked about this. This is an ongoing battle."

"How often do you help your mom and what kind of things do you do for her?"

"Well, you already know I go there almost every day either at lunchtime or after work to drop things off that she needs from the store or drive her somewhere. She doesn't drive, which makes it hard for her."

"Hard for her and hard for you. And how often do you see Angelica during the week?"

"We usually see each other about twice a week. I also see her on weekends, although she still loves to go out with her girlfriends on Friday night for happy hour. I usually meet her around 7:00 or 8:00 depending upon my work schedule."

"Where does she go when she goes out with her friends?"

Ryan hesitated a minute and said, "She usually goes to a bar drinking, happy hour. Occasionally they'll go to the mall or to lunch on a Saturday. But they usually go out at night. Angelica loves the nightlife."

"I see." Fr. Liam was raising his eyebrows punctuating their conversation with a bit of lightness. But he could see the bigger picture registering with Ryan.

Ryan chuckled and said, "So what do you think?"

Smiling, Fr. Liam said: "I think you have yourself a girlfriend who has a drinking problem -- or the start of one at least. She's also not preparing herself one bit for any kind of domestic life with a husband and kids. I think she's captured you lustfully and sexually and you're telling yourself this is a relationship." Fr. Liam paused to give

65

Ryan a chance to speak. He was silent but raised his eyebrows.

Fr. Liam continued. "This fighting seems to occur when you try to redirect her attention from going out drinking to something healthier. Also, your mom seems to be an inconvenient real-life situation she wishes would go away. I must tell you, this shows a lack of understanding at best, or it may be a lack of compassion and empathy, which is even worse. That's what I think; that's what I see."

Ryan took a moment to absorb what he knew and recognized as the truth. It was the whole truth, a no-holds-barred truth. He took a deep breath. "Wow, that's quite an assessment, but something about it rings true. I wasn't ready for all that."

Fr. Liam went on. "Start thinking about what you would like your married life to look like. Think about how your life would look with kids, and what kind of woman would you want and need for that kind of life. They make pretty girls who want marriage and kids too, you know. You need to think with your heart and soul and not with only your emotions and sexual passions." Fr. Liam raised his eyebrows again and smirked. "I was married and I know we both know what I'm really talking about."

Ryan reluctantly said, "I fell in love with Angelica instantly without knowing anything about her. I was instantly attracted to her. My feelings drove me to want to know everything about her, but maybe it was only lust and passion that drove me … at least at the beginning."

"You've told me you want to get married and have kids, so this is your relationship goal. When you got to know Angelica, this should have been the focus of your questions and where you were focused. Do you think it was?"

A moment of silence passed between them.

"No, I wasn't thinking practically. I was focused on how things felt between us. I don't believe I was motivated or directed by any relationship goals. I don't even think I ever heard that term. I will have to reflect on that for a while," said Ryan.

"Not all liberated women are feminists or hostile to traditional life. Many women know and can speak their own minds, but they still want to get married and have kids. You're not looking for anything unusual, Ryan."

The conference went on for another 30 minutes and they discussed how focusing only on his feelings or impulses was not getting him to his goal.

They both paused a moment and Fr. Liam noticed they only had a few minutes left.

"Well, it's about that time. I have a lot to think about. Thanks for giving it to me straight. You know I like your style."

Fr. Liam said smiling, "I know you can handle it. I can dance around the mulberry bush when I need to, but why waste your time? It's best to get to the truth in the shortest amount of time. It's the truth that sets us free. Why dawdle, right?"

Ryan grinned and picked up his jacket laying on the chair and stood up to leave. "How is your brother Mike doing? Has he talked his wife into moving to Ocala?"

Fr. Liam stood and walked him out to the front door of the parish office. "Well, my sister-in-law is onto him right now, so he's laying low for a few days, waiting for another chance to ambush her. I'll be visiting them over Mother's Day weekend, so we can both work on her together. She's a tough opponent, but we haven't given up yet."

Fr. Liam and Ryan shook hands and parted. Fr. Liam opened the door and let Ryan out. He watched as he walked to his car. He was a tall, attractive young guy with his own business but he needed his own Maria. Somehow Fr. Liam didn't see Angelica as being the one.

Maria was the type of woman who built a successful life around his brother Mike who could barely manage anything in his life except his business. Looking from the outside, most people would think Mike provided Maria with a successful life. But the opposite was true. Maria built a loving family around Mike and gave him the stability and balance he needed to excel in his business. He said a silent prayer that Ryan would meet his Maria soon. First, of course, he had to face the truth about him and Angelica.

# CHAPTER 5

### One Day Later, Friday - 5:00 PM
### Ocala, FL

TAKING FR. LIAM'S advice, Ryan hired a caretaker to check in on his mother so he could go on a weekend trip with Angelica. The CNA would drive his mom to pick up whatever she needed and offer general help. His mother was resistant and guilted Ryan about leaving her alone. She claimed she would probably be dead when he came back but Ryan pushed forward anyway.

Ryan and Angelica were packed and ready to go to the airport for their weekend together. Ryan wanted to stop by his mother's house to meet the CNA. Angelica turned it into another opportunity to complain about his mother.

"Angelica, you're already starting a fight and we're not even on the road," said Ryan in an exasperated tone. "Relax, I just want to stop by to see who this caretaker is and say goodbye. Chill out for God's sake."

"Why does a 34-year-old guy have to check in and out with his mother like he's ten years old? Why can't you just call her and ask her how the caretaker is? This is another example of how all our plans have to weave in and around her. It's ridiculous."

Ryan pulled into his mother's driveway and said, "Let's not fight, Angelica, okay?"

"I'm going to read my Facebook page and pretend we're in traffic. I'm waiting in the car."

"That's fine. I'll be three minutes -- maybe five. Don't get mad. We're going away. We're twenty minutes away from sheer romance." Ryan leaned over and kissed Angelica. She kissed him back but then pulled away with the slightest of dirty looks.

"Hurry up," she said. She attempted to appear positive and patient.

Lydia, Ryan's mom, was sitting on her living room couch glaring at the forty-year-old Jamaican caretaker when Ryan came in.

"Thank Heaven you're here," exclaimed Lydia, rising quickly and grabbing her heart.

"You must be Ryan. I'm Nadia, from Helping Angels." Nadia smiled and extended her hand to Ryan.

72

"Yes, I'm Ryan, the son she'll be swearing about under her breath for the next three days." He shook hands with Nadia. She seemed like a pleasant and sweet woman.

His mother, now up from the couch, grabbing the fabric of the top of her dress and scowling, asked Ryan to come with her into the bedroom. He followed her in, still running the three-minute clock in his head to keep the peace with Angelica.

Once inside her bedroom, she closed the door and whispered, "How can you leave me with this woman? I get a very bad feeling about her. I've loved you all your life. How can you do this to me?"

"First of all, I'm not leaving you with this woman. She'll be stopping in once a day to see if you need anything. She's going to make sure you're taking your medications and see if you need a ride anywhere."

"She'll steal all of my stuff," said Lydia, now reaching a melodrama range.

"You know I already have cameras around the house. I'll be checking on the computer to make sure you're okay. I'll check to make sure she's not stealing your stuff, which I'm sure she won't be."

"I'm sleeping on the couch then in case anything happens," said Lydia.

"Mom, these people all pass background checks. I've just met her, and she seems lovely." Ryan installed the cameras because he fully expected his mother, resistant to being left alone, would claim that Nadia tried to kill her, never mind steal her stuff.

"Why do you have to go away?" Lydia was pleading with him, but Ryan knew it was part fear of being alone and part performance.

"Angelica wants to go away for the weekend. We both want to go away for the weekend."

"Where is she? Why isn't she coming in?"

"She needed to make a call or two for work."

"Who doesn't come in to say goodbye to her boyfriend's mother? What kind of person is she? This is how atheists act," said Lydia pointing at him.

"All right, Mom. I've got to go now. I'll see you when I get back."

"If I haven't been murdered." scolded Lydia.

"You won't be murdered. You'll be fine."

"What am I going to do here for three days?"

"You'll go to church in the morning on the shuttle, watch TV in the afternoon and snoop through the windows at the neighbors, like you do every day. And Nadia will bring you to the store when you want something. She'll bring you to church on Sunday. I need some of my own personal time, Mom. We talked about this."

"Personal time? What does that even mean? Personal time for what? You can't take your girlfriend to Disney World, it's an hour away".

"Okay, you've made your point. I've got to go."

Ryan kissed his mom and she grabbed him into a mom hug. After a minute of rocking back and forth, he peeled her arms off and said, "I'll see you in three days." He walked back out into the living room on his way to the front door.

"Goodbye, Nadia. Here's my card if you need to get in touch with me." He whispered to her: "Don't take anything she does or says personal. She's suspicious of everyone." Ryan smiled at her.

Nadia smiled back, "I won't."

As he was leaving the house, he glanced back and saw his mother slowly walking back to the couch and looking at Nadia through narrowed eyes. No subtleties with mom.

Ryan opened the car door and he got blasted by Angelica. "Three minutes? It's ten minutes by my clock."

Ryan took a deep breath but didn't take the bait for a fight over an extra seven minutes.

"Was she mad that I didn't come in?"

"No, she was fine with it," lied Ryan.

## Three Hours Later – 8:00 PM
## Boca Raton, FL

It was Monday night at 8:00 PM. Jacob had called by noon to let Colleen know he wouldn't be home until around eight o'clock. He offered to stop and pick up a pizza for them and they could still watch a movie together. He had been getting better at letting her know that he had to work. It was getting to the point where the norm was working late and occasionally, he would come home early.

Colleen watched out the window every few minutes to see when he arrived. As he approached their door, he appeared angry or frustrated. He was frowning and seemed deep in thought. She was hoping this wasn't going to be another mood swing he was having.

As he came in holding the Domino's Pizza, he had a stack of mail on top of the pizza box. He put the pizza down and hugged and kissed her hello. She immediately relaxed as he now seemed very happy.

"Are you hungry? I am," said Jacob, as he started thumbing through the mail.

"I am hungry. Let me get plates and set up an area for us to eat." Colleen reached for the paper plates and napkins. "So how was work?"

"Do you know that our postman has lost two checks I've been waiting for? We're not getting the correct mail or all of our mail. I've gotten mail from other neighbors a few times already. We either have a drunk for a mailman or something sinister is going on. I'm having the mail redirected to me at work. I'll file the postal form tomorrow, so it'll come to me from now on, okay?"

"What about my bills, will you bring them home?" asked Colleen.

"I'll bring them home, or we can work it out where you can do an online transfer and I'll pay them all from my account. We'll work it out," said Jacob. "You only have your car insurance and phone bill, right?"

"Yes, and my health insurance. I believe that's all I have since we got married."

"Do you have any other credit cards or anything like that?" asked Jacob.

"No, I use the one debit card for everything but no credit card. That's it. Everything else you're paying already, the rent, the electric, water --"

"So it'll be an easy switch. It'll be seamless. I'll take care of it tomorrow."

"All right. It sounds easy enough. Just let me know when you get my bills," said Colleen. "I'm never late, so don't forget."

"I won't. We should pay them all from my account. We're a married couple now. You can take out weekly cash and just transfer your check. I'll start putting money aside into the house account. We'll figure out how it's easiest over the next week. I'll file the form tomorrow. We'll then compare notes on bills and set everything up so it runs on autopilot. How does that sound?" asked Jacob as he put the mail aside and hugged Colleen.

"That sounds great." She wrapped her arms around him.

"I'll get undressed while you get the sodas ready. It's movie night for us, right, Sweetheart?" Jacob kissed her on both cheeks and was all smiles as he left the room to undress from work.

The honeymoon seemed back on. Colleen felt wonderful. She was glad her mother talked her off the wall the other night about him working late. She was glad she let go of what now seemed like pettiness.

Jacob came out to the living room dressed in shorts and a t-shirt. He already had a five o'clock shadow that Colleen found so masculine and attractive. Sitting on the sofa, they ate pizza and settled in for a couple's night at home.

"So how is work. What's going on? You never told me what's going on that has caused this surge in working more hours. Are there new clients?"

"There's a lot of new clients. We merged with a smaller outfit and they're bringing in some big clients. We have to sort of wine and dine them so they don't decide to move on to other firms. So there's a lot of that going on. We're taking them to dinner, having them over for drinks at the office, schmoozing, I guess you could say."

"I pictured you having to do more work at your computer for some reason," said Colleen.

"Well, the market closes at four and although there's some afterhours action, we do a lot of phone calling and client courting in the evening hours. Sometimes when we need to sign a contract, that's when it can get late. Once the lawyers enter the scene, they never shut up and it goes on and on. They tend to talk and talk until they tire everyone out. They're usually the ones who push the clock to ten or eleven at night," said Jacob. "You work for lawyers; you should know how they are."

"Surprisingly enough, they're pretty quiet in the office. They only start talking when they're on the clock or in active-lawyer mode, I guess. And they do tend to focus on the importance of every word and can analyze things to death. There's almost a paranoia that takes hold of them.

"Everything at my job is going well. We'll be getting a little slower as summer approaches, but I'll enjoy the easier pace. I cannot get any filing or organizing done when the lawyers are going from trial to trial. I do all my organizing and office-keeping during the summer months," said Colleen.

"Good idea." Jacob's attention was pulled away to look at the movie lineup. "What would you like to watch tonight?"

"After I have the wine, I'll probably fall asleep, so it's your choice," said Colleen.

"We almost forgot the wine." Jacob jumped up, went into the kitchen and got the bottle out of the refrigerator. He grabbed two wine glasses out of the China cabinet on the way back to the sofa. He poured the wine into the glasses and handed one to Colleen. He held his own glass to make a toast.

"What are we toasting?" asked Colleen.

"Here's to a great merger which means more business and more money for me. And here's to you getting time over the summer to organize your office. And here's to us as newlyweds. How about that?"

"I like the second one. Here's to us as newlyweds."

They drank their wine and ate the pizza. Jacob picked a guy flick. Colleen snuggled up and, true to form, was asleep by eight o'clock. She woke up after the movie and they moved into the bedroom for another night of bonding and marital romance. Things were looking up, or so Colleen thought.

## Three Hours Later - 8:30 PM
## St. Thomas, US Virgin Islands

It was Friday night around 8:30 when Ryan and Angelica arrived at their hotel in St. Thomas. The flight itself was short, but the hassle of flying was long and frustrating. Angelica was stressed out by the routine; this line, that line, shoes on, shoes off, it was an obstacle course for her. Ryan was a more seasoned traveler and didn't mind the security hurdles. Managing Angelica was the challenge.

By the time they arrived in St. Thomas, took a cab to the hotel and checked in, Ryan was ready to spend some alone time in the room. Angelica was excited to go and check out the nightclub in their hotel. They were engaged in a debate about whether to go out or stay in. Angelica continued dressing as they discussed the pros and cons. As she did her hair and makeup, his arguments got weaker and weaker. Once she slipped into a sexy black dress and told him how much fun it would be, his defenses completely collapsed. Seeing her dressed up he suddenly got in the mood to do whatever she wanted. Her beauty and sexual prowess were her greatest weapons against Ryan's will. He quickly dressed for the nightclub and they went out together.

Tall and thin, Angelica was a statuesque beauty. Her perfectly hi-lighted hair cascaded halfway down her back. Her facial features were classically Roman and her ability to enhance her looks with cosmetics was on par or better than any professional makeup artist. She looked amazing. They walked around the club and then stopped at the bar and had drinks. They met and talked with another two couples who were also on vacation. They all wound up partying until the wee hours of the morning. After the third drink, Ryan's relationship goals went out the window and he and Angelica enjoyed talking and dancing with the other couples. Later on, fueled by the alcohol, they made love passionately before falling asleep in one another's arms. They both felt that things couldn't be better.

# CHAPTER 6

## One Day Later - 10:30 AM
## St. Thomas, US Virgin Islands

RYAN AND ANGELICA woke up a bit groggy and slow moving – you could even say hung over. Their drinking and partying went into the wee hours of the morning. They decided to spend the day resting and napping in the sun. It was the perfect day for it. It was sunny, warm and there was only a slight breeze. The beaches attached to the hotel had spotless white sand and plenty of room to sunbathe. There were several couple lounges with umbrellas along the sand. They found one and soon cuddled together in it. It was perfect for sunbathing. The umbrella shaded their heads but the sun could still bake their bodies from the waist down. It was perfect for a long day of relaxation.

Ryan thought about what Fr. Liam told him about his relationship goals. He decided to steer their conversation in that direction. This was the perfect time. They were wallowing in the Caribbean sun, laying side by side and facing one another. "Angelica, do you think about having kids? Is that something you want?"

"Ryan, you never asked me that before. You're so sweet." She thought a minute before speaking. "I want kids, yes, but I'm just not ready to have them right now. I feel like I'm still striving for things and not ready to settle down yet. When you have kids, you have to settle your life down, don't you think?"

"Yeah, I do. So how far off do you see this time period of settling down? I'm almost 34 and I want to have kids soon," said Ryan.

Angelica looked at Ryan and raised her eyebrows. "Is this a proposal, Ryan?"

"No, it's not a formal proposal. I just want to talk about what your goals are for our relationship."

"My goals? I don't know. I think we get along great. But you know my issues with that umbilical cord between you and your mother. I think I would like to move in together first and see how things worked out."

"If we had kids, would you be able to cook for them?" asked Ryan chuckling.

"Did your mother put you up to this? I bet she put you up to this. I know how to cook. But to be honest, I want to be successful enough or you to be successful enough that I can have a nanny or housekeeper. I find working all day very hard. And the thought of then having to be a full time cook and housekeeper on top of that? Forget it. I don't think I can do it. And you work too many hours." Angelica suddenly sat halfway up and started waving over one of the walking bartenders to order a drink.

"Let's not drink today, Angelica, okay?" asked Ryan.

"Let's not drink? We're on vacation. Are you crazy? You can *not drink* if you want, but I'm drinking," said Angelica firmly.

"Order me a bottle of water."

The bartender came over with his tray and order pad. Angelica ordered a margarita and a bottle of mineral water. The bartender left with their order.

"Would you want to be a stay-at-home mom?" asked Ryan.

"I'm too afraid of that. Too many guys leave their wives after a few years. Then you're out of the work force and suddenly you're poor and forgotten. Maybe I would work part time."

Ryan took it all in but had no verbal response.

"So what do you want, Ryan?"

"I want a pretty traditional marriage, I guess. I would like to have a wife that stayed at home with our kids and I worked and supported everyone. I believe that situation would be the easiest for everyone."

"I don't know; that lifestyle scares me. I think I would find it too boring being home with babies all the time," said Angelica, as she settled back into Ryan's arms waiting for her drink. "Oh, look, there's Gary and Sue from last night." Angelica sat up and waved trying to get their attention.

"Maybe we want different things, Angelica," said Ryan.

"Don't be silly, Ryan. We're perfect together. We'll work everything out, don't worry," said Angelica.

She kept waving to the couple from last night. Gary and Sue finally saw her and came over. They pulled over another couple's chaise lounge and the party began. Ryan knew he would have a lot to discuss with Fr. Liam. He wondered whether it was just the wrong place to discuss things this serious. Or did he and Angelica not have that much in common? Did they just have different goals?

Gary and Sue invited Ryan and Angelica to join them at the casino for dinner and suggested they do some gambling later on. Angelica was all excited to go. Ryan went along with things but he saw how easily Angelica was able to pull things her way. He thought about Fr. Liam's suggestion to picture what he wanted his married life to look like. Partying all day and night was not it. This would be fun once a year, but Ryan was afraid this was what Angelica craved on a weekly basis.

## One Hour Later – 11:30 AM
## Boca Raton, FL

After a wonderful romantic Friday night, Colleen got up in the morning and prepared for their day. They had an appointment at 1:30 to look at houses with a real estate agent. She still had time to tidy up, do laundry and make sure her work clothing was all set for next week.

Jacob was still lounging in bed with his cell phone, looking at news sites and videos. At about 11:30, he got up and took a shower. Colleen finished tidying up and sat at the kitchen table waiting for Jacob. She looked through the MLS listings they would be looking at today with Rachel, the real estate agent. It was exciting to look for a new house with a baby in mind.

As Jacob came into the kitchen, he saw her looking at the MLS sheets. He went over to pour himself coffee and said, "What are you looking at?"

"The MLS sheets. You remember we're meeting with Rachel today to look at the houses."

"Is that today? Oh, I'm not in the mood to look at houses, are you?"

"Yes, I am. I'm excited. Our lease runs out in a few months, Jacob. We agreed not to sign another year-long lease so if we're going to get a house, we have to start looking. You'll feel better after you finish your coffee." Colleen was highlighting some information on each of the MLS sheets and writing questions in the margins.

"You're right," said Jacob as he went into the bedroom. Colleen finished her notes and clipped everything together so she would have it all ready. She watched the clock. They had about thirty minutes before it was time to leave.

Jacob came back into the kitchen, leaned up against the counter and smiled at her. He took his last sip of coffee and put his cup into the sink.

"What?" she asked.

"Nothing. You were right. I do feel better."

"I told you," said Colleen, with a gloating smile.

Jacob's phone rang and he answered it. "Hey, what's up?"

Colleen looked at him to see if she could guess who it was. She wondered if it was Rachel confirming their appointment.

"I'm supposed to go and look at houses today. Can't we do this on Monday or even tomorrow?"

Colleen's heart sank. It must be work calling him in on a Saturday.

"All right. My wife is looking at me with daggers in her eyes. You may have to plead my case to her," said Jacob, smiling at Colleen.

She half smiled, but her disappointment was plain to see.

After hanging up, Jacob came up to Colleen and put his arms around her waist. "See if Rachel will reschedule for us."

"I want to go today, Jacob. We're running out of time. We already rescheduled with her two weeks ago because of your work schedule." She tried not to show her disappointment or the frustration she felt with another last-minute cancellation. "I think I should go and look at the four houses today. Then when you're free, we can look at the ones I like."

"That will work actually. That's a good idea. It's going to come down to which one you want anyway, Colleen." He hugged her close and rocked her back and forth. As he kissed her face, he said, "Don't be mad, Colleen. You know I was ready to go. I can't help it if I get called into work. Don't be mad with me, okay?"

"All right." Although her mother was right and men did have to work lots of hours, she still felt that something was wrong. She couldn't point to anything specific. She just felt rejected in some way. This last-minute call seemed all too contrived. She immediately thought she was getting paranoid.

Jacob scurried around grabbing his things and he was out the door in less than ten minutes.

Colleen called her mother mainly to vent her feelings of rejection and disappointment. Her mother listened and let her go on and on and finally said, "Colleen, I know you're disappointed. Your father and I have plans with another couple to go golfing today. But if you want to go another day, we would be happy to go with you if Jacob can't."

"No, Mom, but thanks. I'm going today to look at the four houses by myself and if I like any of them, I'll have Jacob look at the one or two I like. It's just disappointing being trumped by his work all the time. I'm second fiddle to his job now."

"It is very disappointing. I understand. Try not to allow it to ruin your entire day, okay?" Her mother was searching for where her mood was as the call was coming to an end.

"I'll let it go when I meet with the real estate agent. She wanted Jacob there because we haven't even signed with her yet. We both need to sign a contract with her. Our lease runs out by August, so we have to start looking for pre-approval for a mortgage."

"Well, then it's best you go today. Have a look, narrow it down to two houses and then you can look at them with Jacob. The real estate agent will understand. Don't worry, okay?" Maria waited for assurance.

"I won't. You and dad have a great day golfing. I'll talk to you soon.

"Love you, Sweetheart."

"I love you too, Mom."

When Maria put the phone down, Mike asked her, "What was that all about?"

"Jacob was supposed to go with her to look at houses today. He got a last-minute call to come into work and had to cancel, again at the last minute. She keeps saying he's changed. I'm beginning to wonder if she is seeing something deeper. You don't think he could be up to no good in some way, do you?" asked Maria.

"I do believe he is capable of being up to no good," said Mike.

"I should have known you would say that. He's not our choice for her, but he's her choice for a husband and we have to support her marriage, Mike."

"It sounds like she's calling with a lot of complaints. I don't think she's that happy right now, do you?" asked Mike.

"I don't know whether she's just in her first year of marriage, which is all about adjustments, or whether she's detecting something deeper. But so far, her complaints are that he has to work late and sometimes is called in at the last minute. There are lots of people -- police officers, firemen, doctors, paramedics -- who are on-call almost all the time. So this is not that unusual. You had years where you were working overtime, going to business dinners and spontaneous meetings. It happens," said Maria.

"You're right about that," said Mike.

"She takes every disappointment so personally, like she's being rejected by him. I hope this is only her getting used to marriage," said Maria, with her brows knitted together.

"You don't think he could be gambling again, do you?" asked Mike.

"I wondered about that myself. But she hasn't mentioned one thing about money, so I don't see how working long hours would be an indication of gambling. I would expect gambling to cause arguments and fights over money."

"Is he still going to those gambling meetings?" asked Mike.

"I don't know. I'll have to ask her about that."

Colleen met with Rachel and explained about Jacob being called into work at the last minute.

"That happens all the time," said Rachel. "We'll look at the houses and once you have one or two, then we can schedule when Jacob can make it. Let me drive."

As Colleen got into the passenger seat, she thought back to her mother telling her that lots of men worked late. Here was Rachel saying the same thing. She told herself she had to learn to be more flexible with this kind of thing. She decided to let go of her disappointment and went on to see the four houses.

As they went through each one, it was exciting to see the second bedroom and envision a nursery with a baby that would be theirs. It may have been more romantic seeing the nursery with Jacob, but she decided to let it be okay to experience alone. Rachel had children and pointed out where the crib would go, the changing table, the baby's dresser. It was all very exciting. It would be romantic telling Jacob about it later.

Colleen had one question after another from her research on each house. Rachel had all the answers at her fingertips. She knew about the mortgage insurance as well as the homeowner's maintenance costs on each house. She was familiar with other things about each neighborhood as well.

When they were done, Colleen had two houses that would be great in their own way. As soon as Jacob was available, Rachel said she was a phone call away and to call her anytime. That would make meeting her at the last minute not a problem.

On her way home, Colleen passed St. Joan of Arc Church. This was her church but she hadn't gone in over a year now. She dropped out, so to speak, pretty much since she met and got serious with Jacob. She remembered they had a 24-hour Eucharistic chapel. She pulled in and drove around to the chapel and walked inside.

The chapel was small and intimate. As she sat down, she began to pray in no formal way, just speaking her feelings of insecurity to the Lord. She suddenly felt bad about having completely let go of her faith. She knew she did it to keep the peace and not create a problem with Jacob who hated all organized religions.

The jury was still out as to whether Jacob was too secular to understand how important her faith was to her, or whether he was out and out anti-religious. Her thoughts went one way one day and the other the next day. It really didn't matter because it was her and only her who turned her back on the Lord and his church. If God could forgive the original apostles who abandoned Jesus in his darkest hour, she hoped that she too could be forgiven. She realized having a faith and needing a faith were two completely different things. She needed the Lord now.

She spent about thirty minutes sitting quietly in the presence of the Lord. The chapel was only candle-lit with one spotlight on the monstrance which sat on a small altar in front of the chapel. The subdued lighting created an air of devotion that she missed in her life. Other worshipers were present. There was perfect silence. As she looked around the chapel, she could tell she was also in the presence of true believers. You could spot them by their level of reverence, a virtue that somehow lost its cool, according to Fr. Liam, sometime beginning in the 1960s, which was long before she was even born.

She thought back to serious discussions between her parents and Uncle Liam and Aunt Patty about the state of the church. They were complaining even years earlier about how it had changed since the 1960s. Uncle Liam was the one who said there would always be true believers in Christ but maybe not that many of them. He said the Lord would always raise up enough to keep His church going. She could still hear her mother's voice telling her that the people outside the church were too focused on the hierarchy in the church. She agreed that they were always preening, posing, and too often getting themselves into all kinds of trouble. But she disagreed that it was a reason to leave the church. After all, it was the simple people, the people in the pews, people of devotion, theologians, apologists, writers and teachers who kept the faith alive and passed it on.

As she blessed herself and left the chapel, Colleen felt centered and no longer alone. Once back inside her car, she decided that although she didn't want the difference in beliefs to come between them, she did need to get close to the Lord again. There was an emptiness in this secular life that she wasn't expecting and didn't like. Jacob had changed drastically since they were married. He would need to tolerate her return to her faith. She needed to find a way to be who she authentically was and not create a problem between them.

Around about the same time as Colleen was leaving the chapel, her dad had left a voice mail message for his lawyer. "Hey, Lee, this is Mike Mullens. It's Saturday and I don't know how often you check your messages, but I need the name of a good private investigator. You've mentioned to me you use them on occasion. Can you call me with a name or two?"

# CHAPTER 7

### Two Days Later - 5:30 PM
### Boca Raton, FL

COLLEEN PULLED INTO her apartment complex and parked in her assigned spot. She opened the trunk and grabbed two bags of groceries she picked up on her way home from work. She walked towards her apartment already planning to set up the living room for tonight. She would light a few candles to create a romantic mood for them. Jacob would be home at about 6:15 and he was picking up Lemon Chicken from the Ming Restaurant on his way home. He sounded like he was in a good mood.

As she approached the apartment, she saw a paper taped to her front door. In big bold print, she read: *"Eviction Notice"*. She was startled. She assumed this must have been put on the wrong door. She looked for the proper names, but it said Colleen and Jacob Kessler. Her mind jumped around searching her for some explanation. How can this be? Her, getting an eviction notice? There must

97

be some mistake. She pulled the notice down and went inside. She put the cold groceries into the refrigerator and left the other items on the kitchen island. She called Jacob.

"I just picked up the Chinese food. What's up?"

"Jacob, I came home and there is an eviction notice on our door with our names on it." she said. She could hear the nervousness in her own voice.

"I forgot to send the check on the 1st, so the landlord is just playing chicken. I kept forgetting to send the check but I'll call them and put the check in the mail tomorrow. Don't panic, Colleen. We have a nice evening planned."

"I'm a nervous wreck. I think you should call them and have them do a wire transfer or put it on the credit card so it's fixed. I've never had an eviction notice before. I don't want this to affect my credit rating."

"Oh, here we go. Colleen, you're flying off the handle, over-reacting for no reason. These corporate landlords shoot eviction letters out when the rent is one nanosecond late. Trust me. I will handle this. Just relax."

"I don't like stuff like this. It makes me nervous," said Colleen. "I just want us to pay the rent on time, a day early even."

"Okay. I will. I won't let it happen again. It was an oversight because I was busy and had the mail redirected.

But you've got to relax and not allow this to make you bitchy tonight."

"I'm not bitchy, Jacob. I'm concerned and even anxious, but that's not the same as bitchy. Don't call me a bitch," said Colleen. She was sure about herself since her talk with Marsha.

"Okay, okay. I didn't mean to flip any switches. Please, Colleen. This doesn't have to lead to a fight. We're planning a nice evening. Don't let the corporate landlord's auto-generated eviction notice ruin things for us, okay?"

She took a deep breath and calmed herself. "Okay. I'm not going to let it ruin our night. I trust you'll take care of the rent and I don't have to worry about it." She ended on a bit of a question mark hoping Jacob would give her assurance.

"Yes, I'll take care of it. I'm sorry it happened. It won't happen again. I promise," said Jacob in his pleasant voice.

"I'll set the table for us and get sodas ready," said Colleen trying to sound calm.

"Let's have a glass of wine tonight. Do we have any wine in the refrigerator?" asked Jacob.

Colleen looked in the refrigerator and they did have wine. "We have a half bottle of white wine."

"That'll work. I'll see you in less than ten minutes. I love you, Colleen."

"I love you too, Jacob." She put the eviction notice aside and put the rest of her groceries away. As a legal assistant, she knew that some legal letters were auto-generated based on dates. So what Jacob said could be true. He was very busy with work, so she let go of it. As she went about preparing for their dinner, she felt victorious. She was able to let go of her anxiety and trust her husband to fix things. She could hear her mother's voice telling her to accept things and be flexible. She felt like she was getting the hang of it.

Jacob came home and they had a romantic night together. Eating their take-out Chinese food by candlelight was romantic and fun. Then they snuggled up together to watch a few of their favorite shows. The romance continued until they both fell asleep that night. Things felt and looked wonderful, at least on the surface.

# CHAPTER 8

### Eleven Days Later - Friday Evening
### Mother's Day Weekend
### Ocala, FL

IT WAS FRIDAY EVENING of Mother's Day weekend and Fr. Liam prepared for his four-hour long drive to his brother's house in Boca Raton. He made a play list of his favorite philosophical and theological podcasts to listen to while driving. He was looking forward to a relaxing weekend with family. He bought Maria a box of her favorite chocolates along with a pretty card for Mother's Day. He kept shifting them out of the early evening sun while driving down the turnpike.

Once he arrived in Boca, he really relaxed. He was around family now. He, his brother and his sister-in-law sat in the kitchen catching up on family news and a bit about politics. Maria went to bed around 10:30. The guys went into Mike's office, which was the only room Maria would tolerate Mike smoking his two daily cigarettes in. She made

101

him get a top-of-the-line air filter and a smokeless ashtray. That was their compromise.

His office was part business and part man cave, you could say. There was a conversational seating area, with a chesterfield sofa and two upholstered chairs ,that could accommodate four to six people. Occasionally, Mike had some guy friends over for a game of cards or to analyze the latest news or politics of the day.

Tonight, Mike and Liam caught up as brothers. They also strategized about their campaign to pressure Maria into moving north. They decided in light of Mother's Day, they would not put any pressure on her so as not to ruin her day. But they did decide that if the subject arose organically, they would both seize the moment. It made them both feel like they were doing the right thing.

"Okay, so we'll see if the subject comes up on its own. Otherwise, we won't say anything," said Fr. Liam.

"Exactly. I'm leaving the brochure out on the kitchen counter and maybe Colleen or Jacob will ask about it," said Mike, winking.

"I'm surprised she hasn't torn up that brochure already," said Fr. Liam.

"Me too. She knows I have about three of them, so it would only reappear the next day," said Mike, as he lit his second cigarette for the day.

"Do you want a drink?" asked Mike.

"Yes, I'd like a little scotch and water as a nightcap. What about you?"

"I'll have the same," said Mike.

"I'll get it. I've got to stand up a little bit after that long drive." Fr. Liam rose and took two glasses from the side liquor table and poured two scotch and sodas. "Do you want ice in yours?"

"No, the way you poured it right there is fine," said Mike. "So did you find out who was leaving the notes for you in the poor box?"

"I did. One of our deacons walked into the church after mass and saw the woman squeezing another note into the box. The poor box only has a coin slot opening, so it takes some doing to get the folded note in there."

"Did he say anything to her?"

"No, he told me who it was and I set up a meeting to go over the notes with her."

"How did that go? Wasn't one of them that there was a murderer in your midst?"

"Yes, one note was about a murderer going to the 11:00 mass. Another note was a complaint about people talking before mass. They shouldn't talk because they're disturbing people who are praying. But the best one was that the older

103

people are too disgusting to wear shorts and sleeveless tops to mass. She was particularly appalled by them wearing dirty sneakers." Fr. Liam chuckled as he related the complaints to Mike.

"I don't know anything about the murderer, but I agree with her about the talkers and the dirty-sneaker-wearers."

"Well, I told her I agreed with her on some of it. But I explained that many of the talkers are lonely and the only people they talk to are people they know from church."

"What about the murderer?"

"Apparently, it's someone who murdered his wife's paramour and he went to jail for it and now he's out. I told her that in my experience most murders are committed by one-time-only murderers and that not every murderer is a serial killer. We talked about how we no longer worry about diseases or common ailments, but now our worry today is about crime."

"Did she buy it?" said Mike chuckling as he smoked his cigarette.

"I believe it put her mind to rest a bit. I think the whole thing was and is a cry for help. I've asked her to help us take up the collection at the eleven o'clock mass."

"What did she think about that?"

"She was resistant. She's been diagnosed with Asperger's so she panicked a little bit at first. My request was unexpected so it put her off initially. But I told her to watch the ushers take up the collection this Sunday and then she can tell me yes or no about helping us."

"That's a good idea. Why is she crying for help?" asked Mike taking another drag on his cigarette.

"Her parents both died. Her mother was killed in a car accident while over in France. Her father never adjusted and he committed suicide a year or so later. Her uncle has taken her and her brother in as his own but I think her autism is causing problems with his wife. He had to separate them a bit.

"Apparently, his wife thinks his niece killed her dog. This is only one side of a convoluted story she came out with. But I could tell when she began talking about it that it is its own can of worms." Fr. Liam finished his drink and put the glass on a side table.

"That's very tragic to lose one's parents so close together and on top of it, she's autistic. Poor kid," said Mike.

"Exactly. And with the autism, the chances of her getting married are probably slim to none. So she's really alone. My heart goes out to her. I'm going to lean on her a little bit to become an usher because she needs more community around her. No one should be all alone."

"You're a good man, Liam."

"I try. Everyone needs a family and a community around them. The loneliness that's prevalent today is not to be believed. I have people break down in the confessional and weep about their loneliness and despair."

"What do you tell them?"

"I can't reveal anything because it takes place in the confessional. Of course, even though it starts as a confession, once they break down and reveal their loneliness, it becomes more of a counseling session. But I'm still bound by the confessional.

"I don't know what to tell them. I rely on the biblical teaching that we shouldn't worry about what we'll say, that the Holy Spirit will speak through us and give us the right words. I rely on that teaching. I say whatever comes into my heart. I let them know I'm listening to them. Even that alone makes a difference."

"You're definitely called to this work. I would probably tell everyone to quit blubbering and keep moving," said Mike making light of it.

"No, you wouldn't. These people are brokenhearted. I say whatever the Lord gives me at the moment and use my psych degree where I can. I try to comfort them as best I can and give them hope."

A moment of silence passed as Mike took his last drag and put his cigarette out.

"I'm going to sleep now. Long day, long drive. How about you?" asked Fr. Liam.

"I'm going up too. I'm sure Maria left you everything you need up there but if she forgot anything, call me."

"Do you text yet?"

"No, please. I still hang up on people when I answer the phone. I'm still adjusting to no longer having a secretary and having to answer my own phone. One thing at a time."

"Okay. See you in the morning."

## One Day Later - Saturday
## Boca Raton, FL

The brothers went golfing at eight on Saturday morning. Maria enjoyed a leisurely morning all to herself. She met them both at the Boca Raton Golf Club and they had lunch together. They caught up on more family news and when Maria was talking about Colleen, Fr. Liam got the impression that she was choosing her words carefully. He wondered what that was all about. His brother seemed to be watching her tiptoe through the update as well.

When they were driving home, Maria wanted to stop at the Delray Beach Marketplace, a new outdoor shopping mall. She needed to pick up two gifts. They managed to get a parking space within walking distance to the store. Maria went shopping and the guys sat outside on a bench adjacent to the gift shop.

Alone now, Fr. Liam said, "So what's really going on with Colleen and Jacob? I got the impression Maria was being very careful with her wording and phrasing. What did she mean about adjusting to all the compromises of marriage"?

"Jacob has to work late a lot and he sometimes gives Colleen no notice, which is ridiculous. She keeps telling Maria that he's changing." Mike used air quotes.

"Changing? That could mean a lot of things," said Fr. Liam, still looking at his brother.

Mike looked over to the gift shop to make sure it was safe. "Between you and me, I called a private investigator in Boca to do a background check and a credit check on him. I keep thinking about Maria telling me he had to go to Gamblers Anonymous for a while. Colleen told us he had to go because he felt he had the start of a problem."

"Has Colleen mentioned anything about them fighting about money?" asked Fr. Liam.

"Maria hasn't said anything to me about that specifically. But I get the impression that sometimes one or both of them only give me a half-a-story, like there's some kind of mother-daughter security clearance I'm not entitled to."

108

Fr. Liam chuckled. "I'm sure there is. I hope he doesn't start gambling because that is usually a nightmare. The really bad ones destroy their entire family financially. The only solution is to get away from them legally. That would be a nightmare for Colleen. Let's pray that's not the case."

"The main issue seems to be her adjusting to him working late. But to be on the safe side, I'm having a background and credit check done."

"I hope you don't get caught because that alone will cause a problem. Snooping around her husband's back? I'm sure you don't' have clearance for that either, " said Fr. Liam.

"I know. I'm being very discreet," chuckled Mike. "If he's not doing anything wrong, nothing will show up and I won't have to say anything."

A guy walked by them but stopped in front of them. He pointed at Fr. Liam and asked, "Are you a Catholic priest?"

"Yes, I am."

"You people are a bunch of pedophiles. You should all be shot," he said, and then walked on.

Fr. Liam said nothing. Mike looked at him and said, "You should tell him to go to hell at least."

"I don't engage with people who are spraying hatred. Nothing good ever comes of it," said Fr. Liam.

"You've changed. There was a time when you would have punched a guy who said something like that." Mike shook his head.

"When you wear the priest habit, you're a representative of Christ on earth, and no longer just a private citizen. I can't do anything that would bring disapproval or shame to the church," said Fr. Liam.

"I'm pissed. I'm angry over it and it wasn't even directed at me. I should have punched the guy," said Mike.

"I'm used to it. *'Innocent until proven guilty'* is fading from our culture. We have mob justice now. There are a lot of people who have no problems broad-brushing the whole priesthood. Often, they're the very same people who are screaming about their group being broad-brushed," said Fr. Liam. "You need to let it go. If you get angry, they win. If you let it go and allow it to drift away on the wind, you win."

"You're right, I suppose, in your position at least. I'm a private citizen and I could have gotten into it with the guy,"

"Not really. Guys like that have their lawyers on speed dial. If you laid one finger on him, he would take a picture of you and you would be involved in a lawsuit. And they would sue the church because I was sitting next to you."

"You're right. Unfortunately, I know you're right."

"You keep thinking this is the same country we grew up in. It's not. We're more than halfway to a police state. And unfortunately, the lawyers and judges are on the front line of destroying the country," said Fr. Liam.

"Don't remind me," said Mike shaking his head. "Here's Maria now."

Maria came out with a yellow shopping bag inside of which were two gifts beautifully wrapped. She also had two cards ready to be signed.

"How did you do?" asked Mike, as she came over to the guys sitting on the bench.

"I found two beautiful graduation gifts. They're wrapped and ready to go. That's why I love shopping for gifts here. It's a one-stop shop. When you leave, you're ready to present the gift. Otherwise, it can be three more stops to get the gift wrap, bow, tape and greeting card," said Maria smiling. Fr. Liam could tell Maria enjoyed the efficiency of it all.

"We better start home now. I need to stop at Publix to get our platter of food for tomorrow. Mike, you can get some champagne for our luncheon," said Maria as she began leading the guys back to their car.

## One Day later - Sunday - Mothers' Day
## Boca Raton, FL

It was Sunday morning and they all went to Mass at 9:30. Fr. Liam was the bell of the ball when so many of his ex-parishioners saw him at Mass. After church, he got caught in a big group of people who all wanted to talk to him. They had lots of questions about how things were going since he moved away four years ago. Mike and Maria hung around on the edges of his fan club, happy to see how many people still missed him.

Back home now, Maria finished up setting the dining room table. Mike had a dozen yellow roses delivered to her for Mother's Day. She had them displayed on the buffet table across from their dining table. It added the perfect touch.

Being married to a hobnobbing businessman for thirty years, Maria became a seasoned hostess. Having family over was her favorite type of entertaining. With all the talk about Colleen and Jacob trying to have a child, she couldn't help but envision having grandchildren fill the house with sounds of laughter and love. Even Mike was happy that his brother Liam came down for the weekend.

The guys were watching a ball game on TV as Maria was putting the last touches on her table. She set up the ice bucket for champagne on the side buffet. Now that Colleen was married and there were two mothers they had to visit, she would only get a few hours of their time. She and Jacob would be arriving at 11:00 and would be leaving at 2:30, so there was a lot to get in during the three and a half hours.

The oven was preheating. She prepared fresh rolls to be put into the oven. She glanced out the window and saw Colleen and Jacob's car pull up in front of the house. As they exited the car, they gathered a gift from the back seat. Maria walked to the front door and said to her husband: "Mike, promise me you're not going to make any snide remarks to, at or about Jacob and no dirty looks. I'm serious, Mike."

"I promise," said Mike, silently sneering as if Maria just took all the fun out of the event for him. Fr. Liam chuckled at his brother's non-verbal response.

"I know I don't have to say anything to you, Liam," Maria said, in a teasing way.

"I'll be on my best behavior." Fr. Liam was still chuckling.

Jacob came in the door holding a beautiful multi-plant centerpiece display that Maria knew was for her. Colleen stepped in right behind him and said, "Happy Mother's Day, Mom". Jacob handed Maria the beautiful plant. "This is for you, Mom."

"Oh, it's beautiful. Colleen knows I love a beautiful centerpiece." Maria took the plant into the living room and placed it on a table against the wall. "Thank you both so much."

113

Colleen and Jacob kissed and hugged Mike and Uncle Liam. Everyone had a seat in the living room. As a seasoned host-husband, trained by Maria herself, Mike got everyone a drink. He initiated conversation about work and what was new. Maria put the sliced turkey and side dishes into the oven and set her timer for 20 minutes. She brought it with her into the living room and joined the conversation.

Maria noticed that everything seemed wonderful between her daughter and Jacob. Colleen was all smiles. This was a good sign. She couldn't help but notice that Jacob's knee was jumping up and down like crazy. She wondered if this was nervousness or something. She thought, *'Is it possible he's nervous around us?'* She sat down next to Mike on the couch.

As they finished up some work talk, Colleen looked at Jacob and he nodded, so she handed Maria an envelope. "This is from Jacob and me for Mother's Day."

"You brought me the lovely plant," said Maria. She glanced at Mike and Fr. Liam, who were taking it all in. Fr. Liam retrieved the wrapped chocolates and waited to present his gift next.

"This is the real gift," said Colleen.

"Maria opened the envelope and read it out loud: *A Day of Beauty at the Pink Lady - Massage, Hair Style, Manicure and Pedicure.* Oh, that's so sweet. Thank you both so much!" She handed it off to Mike to have a look.

Mike looked at it and said, "Very nice, very nice." Maria could tell he was still abiding by her reprimand earlier to not make any snide remarks.

Colleen pulled another envelope out of her purse and waved it a bit. "Jacob got me one as a Future Mother's Day gift, so we can go together," said Colleen.

The blood drained from Maria's face for a moment. "Is this a formal announcement of motherhood?" asked Maria with bated breath.

"No, no, not yet, but we're hoping it will be soon," said Colleen, looking over at Jacob.

Jacob laughed and said, "Not yet, but soon."

"We're hoping it will be soon too, aren't we?" Maria glanced at Mike for backup. Mike nodded along.

Fr. Liam gave Maria his card and box of chocolates. She thanked him with a hug. Then her timer sounded.

"I need to put the rolls in for about 10 minutes and then we'll be ready to eat." She left the living room and Colleen followed her.

In the kitchen Maria said, "I hope I'm not rushing things too much. I know we have to eat and visit within the two hours. This is my first time with the time limit. I hope I'm not rushing everyone."

"No, it's fine. We can always sit leisurely at the end of the meal. It's better that way."

"So you seem happy and you both look great," said Maria, as she closed the oven door and set her timer again.

"Yes, he's been less snappy this week and things feel much better," said Colleen.

Maria began passing platters to Colleen to bring into the dining room table.

The guys were alone now in the living room. Mike could see that Jacob seemed anxious with that knee continually bouncing up and down. Mike made small talk by asking Jacob about his job. He didn't remember seeing this nervous behavior on any other occasion. He wondered what Jacob was so anxious about.

It took about fifteen minutes for Maria and Colleen to heat up the bread and move things to the dining room table. Mike saw Jacob check his watch every five minutes. He was dying to ask him if they were keeping him from something but knew that would qualify as a snide remark. He kept his mouth shut.

He and Fr. Liam were talking golf, which Jacob played, and that kept the conversation ball going back and forth with little ease. Jacob and Mike had almost nothing in common other than golf and loving Colleen. With that bouncing knee, Mike wondered if Jacob was taking drugs or was on some anxiety medication.

Mike was glancing back and forth between Jacob and his brother to make sure Fr. Liam noticed the bouncing knee. He saw his brother looking down at the knee every so often, so he knew he saw it. He knew they would discuss this later when they were alone.

Mike and Fr. Liam were carrying the burden of the conversation between the guys. Jacob was answering any question they lobbed to him, but he wasn't making too much of an effort on his end. Mike was suppressing one snide remark after another only because he had sworn to good behavior. He hoped to remember them all later so he could at least share them with his brother.

Fr. Liam got Jacob talking a bit about a merger at work. Jacob became a little more animated talking about that. Mike never liked Jacob as he thought he was too arrogant and too sure of himself for such a young man. He used to get such enjoyment out of pointing out how he was wrong about subjects he felt he knew everything about. That's where the "*No Snide Remarks Edict*" came from. Maria saw him as a young confident man who should be tolerated and even supported as he made his way in the world. Mike didn't see it that way at all.

After the talk about the merger completed, the conversation balls fell to the ground and Mike and Fr. Liam exchanged a little conversation about their golf game yesterday. Jacob didn't weigh in or contribute. He seemed anxious and preoccupied.

Finally, Maria called them to dinner. Fr. Liam and Mike both just about ran into the dining room, relieved to be away from the awkwardness of trying to keep Jacob in polite conversation.

They all sat, said Grace, and began to eat. It was not lost on Mike or Fr. Liam that Jacob did not participate in Grace at all. As an atheist, he appeared to feel that he should not be put upon to pretend along with his new simpleton relatives. Mike resented his manner and attitude. He felt that polite atheists would at least bow their heads silently as their hosts prayed, instead of looking from person to person almost scoffing at them as they prayed. Fr. Liam led their Grace and Mike again bit his tongue.

Dinner began with a champagne toast to Maria for Mother's Day and for Colleen's future Mother's Day. After the toast, the platters of sliced turkey, potatoes and broccoli were passed around the table with the other side dishes.

"Colleen, your father tells me you're now looking for paralegal courses?" asked Fr. Liam, as he began eating.

"I'm still looking to find all the online choices that offer paralegal courses and degrees. I have two online schools that I can sign up for in September, so I'll be going for my degree starting then. I have to decide which one I want to go to by then."

"Very good. I'm glad to hear you're continuing on to get your degree."

"How is your parish? Any castle intrigue you have to share with us?" asked Colleen.

"Not really. It's a sizable parish but it's still a small town. Not much out of the ordinary happens besides births, baptisms, sacraments, deaths, wakes and burials. Those are what we consider business as usual," said Fr. Liam, raising his eyebrows in jest.

"That's an interesting way to put it," said Jacob smirking. Mike began to seethe as he noticed the smirk. He looked to Maria almost asking for special permission to respond, but she closed her eyes in a non-verbal "*don't you dare.*"

"How is work, Jacob," asked Maria.

"It's great. Like I've been explaining to the guys inside, we're going through a merger at work. We're taking on a lot of new clients, so I've been working crazy hours. I still go in by 8:30 in the mornings, but I'm not done until sometimes nine or ten o'clock at night. It's exhausting, but that's the business sometimes," said Jacob. "It won't be like this forever, but it is now."

"I know Mike used to have to work late on occasion and he had his busy years too. The business world has become even more demanding than when he was still in it, to be honest. I'm sure Colleen is being supportive," said Maria, smiling at her daughter. Colleen smiled at her mom but said nothing.

Dinner conversation went through lots of mini subjects. They talked about Colleen and Jacob's new apartment and the two houses they would be looking at next week. Colleen and Jacob talked about the new restaurants they had been to on Saturday nights. They even talked about a show or two they had all watched on TV. All in all, it was a happy and positive visit. Mike, true to his word, let several topics pass without sniping.

At around 2:45, on cue, Jacob said to Colleen, "Well, we better get going. They're expecting us by 3:30."

"That's right. Mom, we're sorry to leave so soon, but we have to see Jacob's mom too."

"Sure, sure. I understand. It was so great seeing you both and thank you so much for the gifts," said Maria.

As Jacob and Colleen rose from the dining room table, Maria walked with them to the front door. Fr. Liam walked with Mike behind them to say goodbye. Hugs and kisses were exchanged and off Colleen and Jacob went to see Mrs. Kessler for their second Mother's Day dinner.

After Colleen and Jacob left, they all went back to the dining room table. Mike poured them all another glass of mimosas and sat down and joined them.

"When they first came, I felt like I was rushing everyone to eat, but we just made it, so I'm glad I jumped right into action. I have to get used to the shorter dinners," said Maria as she sat down with them. Mike could tell she was relaxing now.

"Here's another Mimosa, Maria. Relax now. Everything was great."

She took a sip of her Mimosa and settled in for after-dinner talk.

"Liam, did you see the jumping knee?" asked Mike.

"I saw the jumpy knee. Did you see the sweating?" asked Fr. Liam.

"What are you two talking about?" asked Maria, trying to steer them away from troublemaking.

"Jacob's knee was bouncing like crazy when he was sitting in the living room," said Mike.

"Maybe he was nervous," said Maria.

"I thought I was imagining the sweat," said Mike to Liam.

"No, I saw the sweating. It was subtle, just across his brow, along his shirt collar. And he was showing signs of sweating under his arms. He was definitely sweating," said Fr. Liam.

"You two are terrible," said Maria. "He was a perfect gentleman."

"We didn't say he wasn't a gentleman. We just said his leg was jumpy and he was sweating," said Fr. Liam without challenging Maria.

"Why is that significant?" she asked.

"Well, usually that jumpy knee is what you see in teenagers who have too much energy and not enough activity to get rid of it. By 21, a man is mature enough to control himself. That same movement can be an indication of someone taking drugs or being on some kind of medication. Something was or is making him anxious and jumpy," said Fr. Liam looking at his brother for support.

"That's right, Maria," said Mike, in support of his brother. "Our knees weren't jumpy and neither of us are all sweaty."

"I think you two are just making trouble and over analyzing things."

"What trouble? Are we supposed to watch someone with a crazy bouncing knee and not mention it?" asked Mike, feigning outrage at a false accusation.

"This type of thing has to be discussed, Maria," said Fr. Liam, teasingly.

"So besides the jumping knee and the sweating, they looked very happy together, don't you think? I was very happy to hear them mention trying to conceive, weren't you, Mike?"

"Yes, it would be nice to have grandchildren."

"That's why we can't run up to Ocala right away. She may need me here," said Maria. "I know you understand, Liam."

"I do understand your feelings, Maria. But you two can be snowbirds too. Then you can have the best of both worlds. You could live in Ocala for maybe two to four months. Then the rest of the year, from October to Easter, you can live here with Colleen and Jacob." Fr. Liam felt like he scored two points for the team.

"That would be a compromise, Maria," said Mike.

"I should have known that you two would be lying in wait to twist my arm as soon as you got me alone," said Maria, slicing another piece of pie for both Mike and Fr. Liam. "Here, you two need to finish this because the feast has to be over for me by tomorrow."

"If you are up in Ocala, instead of only getting them for two and a half hours, you'll get them for three days every other holiday. Remember, you have to share them now with the in-laws," said Fr. Liam.

"That's true. If we did become snowbirds, it would have to be with a built-in proviso that I would be free to come down to visit her by myself. I want to still have our mother-daughter days together." She began to eat her second slice of pie.

"I would be completely fine with that," said Mike. "It's much cooler there in the wintertime. They don't have to worry about hurricanes up there either, Maria."

"It would be a relief not to have to run for our lives every other week during hurricane season," said Maria. They had been through a few very active hurricane seasons recently.

"We have an actual winter in Ocala. It's mild, but it's a season. It's 40 to 50 degrees in the mornings and evenings and it goes to 60 or 70 degrees at mid-day. You would love it, Maria," said Fr. Liam.

"I'm afraid I would lose Colleen, that she will get close to his family and I would be forgotten."

"That never happens. The grandchildren are always closer to the mother's mother. It's a law of nature," said Fr. Liam, smirking. "You'll get to be with them for long weekends, instead of two and a half hours on a Mother's Day weekend."

"You should have become a car salesman in your second life instead of a priest," said Maria.

"I'm speaking the truth. That's what priests do," said Fr. Liam. "If you had grandchildren, they would have left with Colleen and Jacob. You would have seen them for only three hours. If they come to visit you in Ocala, you would have them all day or all weekend."

"He's telling you the truth. If you stay here, you'll only get to see your daughter and grandchildren on occasion for two and a half hours. It will be disappointing. It'll be just like today. But if they visit you in Ocala, which you know they will, you'll have them overnight. You can read to them, make them breakfast and lunch, take them shopping. They'll also get the whole Christmas experience away from that atheistic atmosphere," said Mike, adding a physical shutter to the words *atheistic atmosphere*. "It's very tempting you must admit."

"Oh, I cringe when I think about the atheism. I hope she'll at least baptize the grandkids. Otherwise, we'll have to do it secretly, Liam."

Fr. Liam nodded to her. "We'll definitely baptize the baby."

"I love Jacob and I'm happy that Colleen seems happy. But when I think of the grandchildren growing up without knowing Jesus, I can't face it. It's heartbreaking," said Maria, shaking her head and dropping the peace-keeper mantle. She suddenly looked upset.

Mike put his arm around her shoulder and hugged her to him. "Now you know what prompts me to make all my snide remarks."

"By the way, you were very good today, Mike. Thank you. It was a lovely day and I appreciate you not sniping, which I know you were dying to do."

"I appreciate the notice as I had a lot of good zingers me and Liam would have enjoyed," said Mike.

"I don't want to hear them, please."

"So think about it, Maria. It's only four hours in a car. You can come down and visit them for a three-day weekend once a month if you want," said Mike.

"I like the idea of snowbirds; I'm open to that. Moving there for good, that's out of the question right now," said Maria.

"This house is too big for us anyway. We can get a three-bedroom condo or a four-bedroom condo that would be less work and upkeep. We can sell this house and get two condos, one here and one up in Ocala."

"This house is too big for us now. It was always too big, but we used to need it for entertaining and house guests. We should scale down anyway, so let's agree to get this house ready for sale. Then we can take our time looking at condos in both places. That would be a great compromise, don't you think?" asked Maria, to both Mike and Fr. Liam.

"That would be perfect, Honey. I'll start doing the odd jobs around here getting this ready for the market," said Mike, smiling at Fr. Liam.

"And I can start giving away some of the stuff we have accumulated in the 25 years we've been here. We have too much stuff right now that we won't need now that we're retired and you're no longer entertaining once a month," said Maria.

Mike kissed Maria and smiled. The brothers looked at each other and raised their eyebrows. This was an unplanned and unexpected win for them. The campaign was finally going their way. They scored a great victory with the snowbird idea.

They finished their mimosas. Maria got up from the table. She quickly sat down again. "I have to tell you two, and I hope this isn't the mimosas talking -- and I don't want this going any further than here -- but I'm a little worried about Colleen and Jacob. She keeps telling me that he's changed overnight and he's short tempered and snapping at her. She never said that before.

"Her main complaints are about him working late. But she keeps saying '*I think he's not telling me something*' or '*he's hiding something from me*.' When I ask her to elaborate on it, she can't give me anything specific that she thinks he's hiding. She thinks his working late is a reflection of his feelings for her fading. Do you think it is just her youth and insecurity?" asked Maria.

"Did you ask her what she thinks he's hiding?" asked Mike.

"Yes, I've asked her a few times to elaborate on what type of secret she thinks he may be keeping, and she says she doesn't know. He just seems to be telling her whatever he needs to in order to get her to stop questioning him. And if she asks too many questions, then he snaps at her. He's told her to stop '*bitching at him*'," said Maria, closing her eyes to emphasize the word *bitching*.

"Could he be gambling again?" asked Mike.

"I asked her if she thought he was gambling again, but she said no. She doesn't think it's that," said Maria. "I want you to both pray for her. Pray that she either finds out what he's hiding, or she realizes she's reading too much into his working late."

"I'll pray for her," said Fr. Liam. Mike just looked knowingly at Liam. He knew they would have more to say about this when they were alone in the smoking room. Mike chose not to tell Maria about hiring the private investigator, at least not yet.

The guys helped Maria clear the table and wrap up the leftovers for the week. They spent the rest of the day talking out by the pool where Mike and Fr. Liam went for a first swim of the season.

In the early evening, while Maria called her friends and family members to wish them a Happy Mother's Day, Fr. Liam and Mike sat outside at the pool table under the umbrella and had a last soda together.

"So what do you think is going on with Jacob? What do you think the jumpy knee was all about?" asked Mike.

"Like I said earlier, you don't usually see this in normal adult males. I've seen this mainly in drug addicts, when they're hyped up on drugs or need a fix. But Jacob doesn't look like a drug addict on any other level," said Fr. Liam, "so it's confusing. I don't know what to make of it. But it's indicative of something."

"No, he doesn't look like a druggie, I agree with you there. Is it possible he's just anxious about this work merger and having so much to do at work?"

"It's possible. We should give him the benefit of the doubt, I guess," said Fr. Liam.

"Did you catch his attitude during Grace?" asked Mike.

Fr. Liam said, "I did catch the attitude during Grace."

"You know, there are polite atheists and rude atheists. He acted like a rude atheist. I had to bite my tongue while you were saying the prayer," said Mike, lighting a cigarette.

"I agree. I find that most people who don't believe in God usually identify themselves as agnostics or they have a more friendly or tolerable attitude. It's only the ones who hate God that openly and loudly identify as hardcore atheists. They take delight and glee in being disrespectful towards religion. They are hard to take, but I refuse to take the bait from them," said Fr. Liam.

"You're a better person than I am. I wouldn't admit this to anyone but you, but I wanted to backhand him right at the table. Every time I meet with him, I get a lecture from Maria to not start any trouble. I then lecture myself and decide to only focus on his good qualities. But I always wind-up reaffirming how much I dislike him."

"I understand. It's hard to accept someone you don't like as your son-in-law, but you keep the peace for your daughter. You're doing the right thing by biting your tongue and keeping the peace," said Fr. Liam. "But it's just as good to express your true feelings to me because otherwise, you'll blow up one day."

In a voice just above a whisper, Mike said, "I know I can trust you. I told you about hiring the private investigator to do the credit check on Jacob. But in light of all this working-late stuff, I'm having them do surveillance on him after work too. I want to make sure he's really at work and not going somewhere else."

"That's a little extreme, isn't it?" asked Fr. Liam.

"There's talk of babies and if he's gambling again, I want to know right away," said Mike, "and my daughter has a right to know."

"It's hard to see evidence of gambling. It's not like spotting a drug or alcohol problem. But I keep thinking of Maria saying Colleen thinks he's hiding something. That could be gambling or even something else," said Fr. Liam thinking out loud.

"Exactly. If he comes back clean, I'll relax. We can both lecture one another for being suspicious of our dear son-in-law," smiled Mike. He took another drag of his cigarette.

A moment of silence passed between them.

"Do you think it could be drugs," asked Mike.

"Not street drugs. With all these hours he's working, I wonder if he and his co-employees have gotten their hands on some Adderall. It's a stimulant that's popular on campuses now. It helps people concentrate and work or study long hours. It's like a prescription level speed," said Fr. Liam.

"That could explain the jumpy knee," said Mike, blowing smoke rings.

"You still love to smoke, don't you?"

"I only smoke the two cigarettes, but I love it. I'm lucky Maria puts up with me. All her friends have told me they would throw me out."

"Temperance, moderation. That's also fallen out of vogue. We live in a world of extremes now," said Fr. Liam watching his brother smoke.

"We do live in a world of extremes, don't we?" asked Mike.

"We do. We never see anyone ten pounds overweight anymore. They're now 60 pounds overweight. We don't see anyone with one or two tattoos, they tattoo their entire bodies. Instead of having a drink or two, people start getting *wasted* as soon as they can legally drink. I can go on and on," said Fr. Liam.

"Very true," said Mike.

"I'm going to leave for home now so I can get home by nine o'clock. I'm saying eight-thirty mass tomorrow morning.".

"Are you okay driving at night for four hours?" asked Mike.

"Of course I am. I'm used to driving there at night now," said Fr. Liam.

Mike put out his cigarette. They embraced and Fr. Liam said goodbye and thank you to Maria and he was off.

132

# CHAPTER 9

### Two Weeks Later - Sunday
### Ocala, FL

IT WAS SUNDAY, two weeks after Mother's Day weekend. Fr. Liam walked over to the church at 10:15 to prepare for the eleven o'clock mass. As he crossed from the rectory to the sacristy, he met Marie-Louise on her way to church.

"Hello, Marie-Louise, how are you? Are you coming to the eleven o'clock mass?"

"Yes, I am. They asked me last week to help with the collection so I watched them carefully. I'll be helping today."

Fr. Liam detected she was a bit more engaged than normal. "I'm so glad to hear that. You'll be great. Plus, Marie-Louise, the other young women in the parish will see you helping out. It will make them want to pitch in and help around here too. We can always use more help." Fr. Liam smiled and was surprised when Marie-Louise smiled back. Seeing her smile on occasion made him question her diagnosis of Asperger's but he was not an authority on it.

"I came early so I can look around again so I'm ready. I have to make sure that I know when to go to the back of the church," said Marie-Louise, as she walked next to Fr. Liam.

"They take up the collection right after the scripture readings and right before the Offertory of the Gifts. If you look in the missal and find the page with the Offertory or Preparation of the Gifts, it will be there. Let's find another usher here and I'll make sure they guide you."

"They'll do that?"

"Sure they will do that. I'll tell them it's your first day and I want it to go well for you."

She half smiled only to herself.

As they approached the church, Fr. Liam called over another usher by the name of Gary. He asked him to make sure he gave Marie-Louise the cue when to come back to take up the collection. Gary led her into the church and showed her where the ushers stood during the mass. As Fr. Liam continued down the side of the church, he could tell that Marie-Louise was in good hands. She was a bit nervous, even a bit overwhelmed, but he knew this would be good for her.

Inside the sacristy, Alice Brennan was center stage narrating what happened at Damon Russell's funeral. About three other sacristans were leaning in as Alice was telling the story.

"He was eating a Dunkin Donut with his morning coffee, and his daughter just happened to call him. As he was talking to her, he began to choke on the donut. He kept choking and he couldn't talk. She heard him choking and not being able to regain himself. She hung up and called 911. But by the time the paramedics made it to his house, he was already dead. It happened that quickly. Can you imagine that?"

They all couldn't help their morbid interest in the story, as who could resist hearing the details of how one of their own died. But as soon as Fr. Liam walked in, everyone suddenly acted no longer interested. They all greeted Fr. Liam and went about their individual duties in getting ready to serve at mass.

Only Alice remained. "That was some funeral, wasn't it, Father?"

"You mean Damon Russell, I assume?"

"Yes, I mean Damon." Alice whispered, "I didn't know what to do or where to look when his widow tried to get in the coffin with him." Alice was grabbing her pearls, literally.

"Well, she wasn't trying to get into the casket, Alice. She was crying and attempting to put her arms around her husband for the last time."

"Not from the angle I saw her," said Alice.

"Our church is international, Alice. People bring their cultures with them into the church, especially those from outside this country. Damon's people are more demonstrative about their grief and mourning, that's all," said Fr. Liam smiling. He wouldn't admit to Alice that he too didn't know what to think when he saw Mrs. Russell loudly crying her husband's name and attempting to hug him while he was in the casket. "Most of us white Europeans are stoics at heart and we tend to suppress our deepest feelings of grief until we're alone, don't we?"

"I guess that's true," said Alice.

"He choked on a Dunkin Donut. That's how he died. It's very strange how the Lord takes people, isn't it?" asked Alice reflectively.

"Yes, it is. But I thought it was very telling how it all played out. Instead of God taking Damon when he was alone, he happened to be talking to his daughter who was able to call 911. This prevented his wife from coming home and finding him dead in the chair. The Hand of God protected his wife from the shock of seeing him sitting dead in the chair."

"I never thought of it like that, but that's true. I live alone and I worry how I'm going to go," said Alice.

Fr. Liam knew this was only a sliver of insight into what made Alice so fixated on dying and death.

"You should get one of those emergency gadgets to wear around your neck, Alice."

"I've had one of those from the day after my husband died."

"So you're ready then. We all really live in God's Hands and he will make sure you have someone to help you at the end like he did with Damon," said Fr. Liam.

"I sure hope so. See you later," said Alice as she went out to take her place in the procession line.

As he finished putting on his vestments, he was inwardly chuckling on how different his parishioners all were. They weren't perfect, maybe even a little crazy -- or was *eccentric* the right word? Or was *quirky* more accurate? It depended on the day. But they all had good hearts. He didn't miss the criminal classes he spent so much time with when he was working homicide. This was another moment where he knew he made the right decision to enter the priesthood.

## One Half Hour Later
## Boca Raton, FL

Things were going well for Colleen and Jacob since Mother's Day weekend. He worked late three nights that week but remembered to give Colleen notice in the morning. She was adjusting to the change in plans without any problems. They went out with another couple on Saturday night and Jacob was in the best of moods.

On Sunday morning, they held hands as they walked into the gym. She looked up as Jacob, smiling at her, said, "I need a good workout today with all that sitting I'm doing during the week, you know?"

"I know what you mean. I get a little bit of exercise running around on errands, but not enough," said Colleen. Jacob reached around her shoulders and hugged her close to him as they continued into the gym. She wondered, *'Am I happy that he's being nice to me or am I just happy?'* She didn't know the answer. She did know that her husband's moods were controlling her in ways that she never envisioned.

Once inside the gym they went their separate ways with a kiss as they parted.

Colleen went to the leg machines and began her workout. She glanced up at the clock and it was 10:30. This would be the time she would be at mass on any given Sunday. Since she was with Jacob she was no longer going to church. He wanted her to leave that whole Catholicism thing in her bedroom after she left her parents' house. She hated arguing about religion because it seemed to make him angry when she tried to stand her ground.

She always thought of herself as assertive. She could see that she allowed his disapproval to render her submissive. She thought back to her teenage years when she was combative with her father about staying out late and other issues. She never had a problem standing up for herself. What was it about Jacob that made her surrender without so much as a fight? Was she changing or was there something about the way he acted that caused this? She didn't know. She would have to analyze this with Marsha and maybe they could figure it out.

At the time of her marriage, she thought not going to church would be okay. She felt she could still believe in her heart of hearts, which she did. For the first time she allowed herself to think how disloyal this was on another level. Jacob could have been more accepting of her religion the same way she accepted that he had none.

As she worked her legs on the machine, she thought about having a child. What would she tell her children about Jesus? She would want to tell them about Him, of course. But would Jacob roll his eyes and tell their child that it was all nonsense? She finished up on the one machine and moved to the next.

139

She realized she should have talked to Jacob and got him to agree that his atheism didn't trump her Catholicism. She should have at least insisted that they get to learn about her religion and what she believed. They could know their father's opinion of it. That position was more of a compromise.

Knowing she should raise this as an issue now, she knew she would face his disapproval or maybe worse. He wasn't violent in any way, but he had a way of weaponizing this disapproval that made her dread doing or saying anything he wouldn't like. His disapproval was loaded with rejection and mockery. She decided she would have to pick her time and place carefully to raise the issue.

On the way out of the gym, they talked about where to go for lunch. They chose a restaurant on the Intercoastal waterway. It was May and it wouldn't be too hot to eat outdoors on the patio right on the water. It was a bit of a drive, but they took the tree-lined 18th street in Boca all the way east to the Intercoastal. Then they drove south on Route A1A along the ocean and looked at all the mansions. They pulled into The Cove Restaurant which was right on the marina.

Jacob had been checking his phone on and off all morning, even when he was working out. "I notice you're getting a lot of messages this morning. Is something up at work?" asked Colleen, gingerly.

"Yeah, there's a few deals waiting to close and we're checking in with one another." Jacob glanced out onto the Intercoastal and said, "Look at these yachts. That's the life, isn't it?"

"I guess. They are beautiful," said Colleen.

A moment of silence passed between them.

As they sat silently and waited for the waitress, Colleen said, "I've checked the mail three times this week and there's nothing. I know you said you would have the bills forwarded to you, but I don't see my cell phone bill or my insurance bill. There's no junk mail either. What's going on with the mail?"

"I put in a change of address to have it forwarded to me. I also put a no junk mail request so they stopped sending the avalanche of all that junk mail we used to get. It's a nuisance. I forgot to bring home your wireless bill. I have to remember to do that. I have it in my briefcase. Remind me at home," said Jacob.

"Okay. I hope it's not late. I'm never late on my bills. I get nervous about that."

"Don't make a big deal out of it, Colleen. I'll give you the bills at home." His delivery was exasperated for no reason. This was what she was trying to explain to her mother. He seemed to have no patience with her anymore for anything.

"I'm not making a big deal out of it. I'm just letting you know I want any bills you have today so I don't worry about them or I'm not late paying them," said Colleen.

"Oh, here we go," said Jacob, as he rolled his eyes and looked out at the boats.

Colleen looked at the menu and decided what she wanted. She hated it when he got this way. He was so loving at the gym and one little snag about the mail and he turned completely nasty.

The waitress came and they ordered their food.

"I don't want to fight over the mail, Jacob," she said.

"We're not fighting over the mail," said Jacob, now seeming more playful. "You know, it might be easier if you take $200 cash out of your paycheck and give the rest to me. I'll pay all the bills online. Then the rest of the money from your check, we'll put it into the house account we set up. Or should we open a new baby account where we start saving for all the stuff we'll need when we get pregnant. What do you think about that idea? That would prevent any more fights about the bills." asked Jacob.

"I guess that would work. I would still need to put the groceries and stuff on my debit card," said Colleen.

"I'll get a debit card for my account so you can use it. We both use our debit cards for everything anyway. We could put everything on autopilot," said Jacob smiling.

"Okay. That sounds easy and I won't have to worry about being late on paying anything."

"Exactly," he said, smiling again.

His mood was lighter now. They talked easier together as they enjoyed the views on the intercoastal. It was a beautiful sunny day. The skies were blue and there wasn't a cloud in the sky. There were boaters who drove up and docked to have lunch at the restaurant. Some of the people on the larger yachts tooted their horns and waved as they passed by The Cove restaurant.

The rest of the day was magnificent. Still honeymooners, they finished their leisurely lunch on the water. On the way back to the car, they were swinging hands together like they had just met. They went on to spend the night on the couch watching back-to-back movies. All seemed well in the world where Colleen and Jacob lived.

# CHAPTER 10

## One Day Later - Monday - 3:30 PM
## Boca Raton, FL

MIKE PUSHED THE door to Lucchi Investigations open a little too wide as he exited the private investigator's office. It was his anger. He was carrying the report he just received. Mike's blood pressure was already up as he digested what he was told by the private investigator. Jacob had a bankruptcy in his past that he had hidden from Colleen. Mike had been controlling his anger inside Ken Lucchi's office, as they were both professionals. He thanked him, they shook hands and Mike left, but his anger was rising by the minute.

Now in his car, he called his brother Liam. As happened a lot, it went to voice mail.

"My son-in-law went bankrupt already and he's only thirty-two years old. Didn't think it was worth mentioning before marrying my daughter. Call me when you can talk."

145

Mike started his car and headed home. His mind imagined how many problems a bankruptcy would cause for Colleen with her dreams of a home and having a baby. Having a husband with a bankruptcy record and a credit score of only 570 would be a problem. If she was going to have kids, they would need to buy a home. He and Maria had given them a cash wedding gift as a house down payment. That may not be enough to overcome the bankruptcy record. It was the secrecy that angered him. He knew Colleen's credit rating was excellent before she married. He hoped she was strong enough to not fall into bad spending habits along with Jacob. His worries were all over the place.

As he approached his street, he thought about this *start of a gambling problem* that Jacob was peddling as his explanation for going to GA meetings. That may be the real reason behind the bankruptcy. Either way, he was furious at the deceit.

He pulled into his driveway and then the garage. Maria's car was there so she was home. She too would be outraged by this. He shut off the car and walked into the house carrying his investigative folder. Maria was standing at the kitchen island cutting tags off new towels.

"Maria, I need to talk to you."

Maria looked at him and knew something was not right. "Is everything okay?"

"No, it's not. I need to talk to you now."

146

Maria gathered the various tags she had cut and put them into the kitchen garbage. She was watching Mike and he could tell she was trying to get a read on him. She was attempting to figure out what was on his mind. They both walked into the living room and sat down on the couch.

"What's in that folder?" asked Maria.

"I had a private investigator do a background and credit check on Jacob."

"Why did you do that?"

"I was curious about their finances now that they're talking about having children."

"And what do you want to talk about?" asked Maria, with raised eyebrows.

"He has a bankruptcy already that he never told Colleen about," said Mike.

"He did tell her about it," said Maria.

Mike stopped short feeling like he just hit a brick wall. "You mean you knew about this and never told me?" asked Mike, now angry at Maria.

"Colleen told me about it one night when she was upset but she swore me to secrecy. She was afraid you would try to stop the marriage or make too big of a deal out of it," said Maria.

"I didn't know we had secrets, Maria."

"We don't have secrets, Mike. She was hell bent on marrying him. I knew if I told you about the bankruptcy, this would have been your reaction, just like now."

"A bankruptcy is a big deal. Not only does it prove the person couldn't manage their own financial affairs, but it also proves they're completely fine with screwing their creditors and moving on. To me, it's a sign of a lowlife, a societal parasite," said Mike as he looked into Maria's eyes.

"Mike, please don't let this come between us. Please."

"You chose to keep this secret from me. So now instead of knowing before the marriage, I found out this way and now I don't trust you either."

"Mike, don't say that. You can trust me. I have no other secrets besides that one."

Mike looked at Maria and shook his head, letting her feel his disappointment.

"Was there anything else in the report?" asked Maria.

"No, everything else was clean. His credit score is terrible but it is slowly going up again. At least he has no other debt right now. I had him followed for three days and his car was in his work lot the whole week until he came out and drove home. So at least he's not going somewhere after work and telling our daughter he's working," said Mike.

"That makes me feel better. It's proof he's just working late and she's adjusting to a husband who is in a very busy period of business," said Maria.

Mike could tell his wife felt guilty about her secret. He was tempted to wrap his arms around her and tell her it was okay, but he didn't want her to think it was okay to lie or keep things from him like this.

"Okay, well, that's what I wanted to tell you."

"I'm sorry I kept it from you, Mike."

Mike walked away without replying.

## Two Hours Later - 5:30 PM
## Ocala, FL

Ryan was sitting alone in Fr. Liam's parish office as Fr. Liam was talking with his secretary outside in the receiving office.

There was a lot to discuss so Ryan hoped Fr. Liam would be on time.

When he finished, he came in and sat down behind his desk. He had already closed the door. "So how did your trip to St. Thomas go?"

"Well, some good, some not so good," said Ryan.

149

"Let's start with the good. What was good about the trip?"

"Well, my mother survived and although she kicked and fought until I literally had to peal her off of me, she wound up liking Nadia, the nurse's assistant. She did nothing but glare at her while I was introducing them. But somewhere during the check-ins, Nadia softened her up and even talked her into going to the hair salon."

"That's very good news," said Fr. Liam, "better than even I expected."

"Yeah, it gives me hope that she'll be less resistant next time. My first weekend away, she absolutely refused to have a CNA. Even though I went away anyway, I had a steady stream of guilt texts reminding me of stuff she needed when I got back. I also got the call at 1:00 in the morning claiming someone just broke into the house. That, of course, turned out to be nothing but tree branches hitting the front window."

"That's huge, Ryan. You've installed your first boundary with your mother. You've taken back some time and space in your own life."

"Yes, I have."

There was a pregnant pause between them.

Fr. Liam said, "And what about Angelica?"

"Well, now we proceed to the bad news."

"What do you mean? Was it all bad with Angelica?"

"Not all bad. But everything we've spoken about in past weeks came to life. I could see it play out right before my eyes for the first time, and I couldn't believe I didn't see it before."

"Like what?" asked Fr. Liam, sitting back in his chair and listening.

"Well, first of all, I noticed Angelica's drinking from a different perspective."

"What perspective was that?"

"I noticed that her idea of fun is drinking and partying, period. I go along with it and, I did notice that alcohol fuels my feelings for her too. I feel like I love her more than anyone in the world, but it's after about the fourth drink."

"Is that so?"

Another silent pause.

"Do you think you could have a drinking problem too?" asked Fr. Liam.

"I thought a lot about that. I really don't think I do. I tend to go along with Angelica who suggests what we do when we're together. I never seem to have any counteroffers because I'm so busy at work, I go along with whatever she wants to do.

"On the few occasions when I do suggest something else, I get voted down or worn down. I seem to be too busy to come up with any ideas for healthier things to do and I go along with doing whatever she wants. I would prefer to do just about anything now other than go out to a bar, especially where her and her girlfriends will be carrying on all night. But I wind up going along to get along. I'm not a good social director in the relationship. I tend to go along with the woman's choice. I can see this pattern in my other relationships too."

"Go on," smiled Fr. Liam. "What else did you notice?"

"Well, I noticed that when we're both sober, we don't have that much to say to one another. I think this fighting we do is a filler of some kind. We don't have much to talk about during the day, but at night, after a few drinks, that's when things come alive."

"I even broached the subject of marriage and children and I was a bit shocked by what came out." Ryan looked up but Fr. Liam was waiting for him to continue.

"I asked her if she wanted kids and she told me that she does want them but just not now. When I asked her when she would want them, she didn't give me a certain age or a specific year. She seemed to refer to some unknown time off in the future. I also asked her if she could cook for them, and she was a bit insulted but said she would be able to cook for her kids, but … "

"But what?" asked Fr. Liam.

"But she hopes that I or we make enough money to be able to have a nanny or full-time housekeeper. She can't envision working and being able to also be a full time cook and housekeeper. I do see her point in that.

"Then I asked her, what about if you could be home all day and I supported us? She said she doesn't want to leave the job market because most men dump their wives after a while. I can't remember the rest of her theory, but she had a negative view of marriage. At least that's my interpretation of it."

Ryan went on. "I realized by the end of the trip that there isn't much more than a day-to-day alcohol-fueled affair with no firm marital goals between us. We're not going anywhere definitive and I'm not even sure where Angelica wants to go. I even question whether I know where I'm going at this point. I chose Angelica and have been in the relationship for almost a year and a half. I'm shocked that I assumed so much about what she wanted. I thought all women wanted to get married and have kids.

"This is the same mistake I made with my first wife. That backfired after the fact," said Ryan "and now this seems to be headed in the same direction."

"What do you mean by it *backfired*?" asked Fr. Liam.

"Well, we never talked about children and what life was going to be like. I assumed there would be children and that we would live a pretty traditional life. I assumed everyone wanted the same things. I thought everyone had the same expectations of marriage.

"I also rushed things. So maybe she would have told me about not wanting kids if I had waited a year before getting married. But at the time, I felt that it was true love and we were meant to be together." Ryan rolled his eyes as he looked up at Fr. Liam, who was wearing a poker face and revealing nothing. He was maintaining eye contact and just listening.

"So anyway, I think Angelica may be thinking three to five years from now for children. I want to have kids soon while I'm still young. I even asked her about marriage and she said she would like to live together to see how things go. That's too tentative for me.

"The strange part is that the trip was planned to separate from my mother and bring Angelica and I closer. I expected we would fall more deeply in love, firm up our marital goals. I planned on confirming that we both wanted the same things. It's like the opposite happened. I found out we don't want the same things at all. I also feel that I fell out of love with her or I realized it was only lust and not love."

Fr. Liam nodded affirmatively, letting Ryan know he was still listening.

Ryan looked at him for feedback, but Fr. Liam knew he wasn't done.

"What do you think this means? What are you going to do?" asked Fr. Liam.

"I think it means I should end the relationship because I know it's not going anywhere. But her sister's wedding is coming up in about six weeks. I don't want to break up with her right before the wedding and ruin things for Angelica."

"Well, waiting until after the wedding is the noble thing to do," said Fr. Liam. "Waiting six weeks or so to make a decision this final is a good idea anyway, as feelings can change."

"I'm so tired of dating and looking, you know? The thought of starting over with someone is crushing."

"I do know. I was lucky and married my high school sweetheart. I was saved from the horrors of dating in the modern world. I can only imagine what this hook-up culture can do to a human psyche. I'm sure it's exhausting.

"Take the next few weeks to think about this decision, pray on it and make sure it's the right decision. This way you'll have no regrets.

"It's still good news about your mom separating from you for a weekend and being okay with a caretaker. You can free up a lot of your time with this change," reassured Fr. Liam. "You have taken back your independence."

"Yes, I do feel empowered by it. I am hopeful regarding that," said Ryan.

Another moment of silence passed. They both glanced at the clock and realized their session had come to an end.

"Now that we're done, can I ask you a professional question?" asked Fr. Liam.

"Sure."

"My niece is 23 years old and just got married about nine or ten months ago. I saw her husband on Mother's Day and he seemed anxious and jittery, sweating, not too social. To me, it looked like he was on something and my brother is worried he's gambling again. There was talk right before they were married about the start of a gambling problem. Apparently, he was going to Gambler's Anonymous to nip it in the bud is how my brother presented it.

"My brother hired a private investigator to do a background and credit check on him. The investigator found a recent bankruptcy. When I saw Jacob on Mother's Day, he appeared very nervous and was sweating seemingly for no reason. My brother left me a message earlier that his private investigator found out about a hidden bankruptcy. I haven't spoken to him about it yet, so I don't know much more about it yet.

"I dealt with street crime and murders when I was a detective. I have a lot of experience with drug addicts, drunks, the lower criminal class, I would say. Gamblers are a whole different animal. I don't have much experience with them. Have you had any cases with them? What are the signs that they are gambling and hiding it?" asked Fr. Liam.

"I've had a couple of gamblers, one of which was in a long-term marriage. He literally cut through every dollar in the family, including his mother taking a second mortgage to pay for treatment. So they are brutal on their families.

"Gamblers all have credit issues. After filing for a bankruptcy, he wouldn't be able to borrow money on his own. He would only be able to borrow from a loan-shark or companies that are in the loan-shark business. You need to check the credit of the family members around him. They start by borrowing from those around them, usually family members first. One clue is they start accumulating unpaid bills, eviction notices, phones shut off, things like that."

"Interesting. I'll have to ask my brother if he had my niece's credit checked. I'll talk to him tonight. I was just interested in your take on it because admittedly, I worked street crimes and homicides but gambling is more of a white-collar crime. Different mindset and I'm not that familiar with it."

"Today, they also have online gambling, so he could be gambling at his desk at work if he has enough privacy. It depends upon what type of betting or gambling he likes to do. People can hide this easier now with the internet," said Ryan.

"I know my niece went to Las Vegas with him before they were married. I also remember her talking about going to local casinos too," said Fr. Liam.

"Then he would most likely do the same kind of gambling. They usually have a favorite thing and they stick with it. The casino gamblers like the high life, the flash of the money. Is he a big shot kind of guy?"

"He can be, yes," said Fr. Liam, thinking about some of his brother's snide remarks about his bravado.

"Check your niece's credit. Let me know if you want me to pull a credit check on her. I would be happy to do it for you."

"I'd have to talk to my brother about that. I appreciate your opinion. I'll see if he wants to check my niece's credit."

Fr. Liam rose from his desk and Ryan stood as well. They walked out to the parish door together.

"So same time next week?" asked Fr. Liam.

"Same time, same channel," said Ryan.

"I may take you up on that credit check. Anyway, you've made tremendous progress with your mom, and it's only downhill from here."

"Not really. I'll have to go back to square one looking for a new girlfriend," said Ryan. "I'm dreading it. I hate the initial phase of dating."

"A good-looking guy like you? You'll have no trouble meeting someone new. I'm going to pray you find a nice

Catholic girl that will make life easier for you. You need a nice Italian Catholic girl who will understand your mom being from the old country," said Fr. Liam.

"Angelica is Italian and her family was once Catholic. But unfortunately, they lost the faith and now she's a Catholic-hating atheist," said Ryan.

"There's usually more to that Catholic-bashing by ex-Catholics. I mean, I don't believe in Santa anymore, but I don't go berserk when I see them in a department store, right? When I see Mormons out proselytizing, I don't lose my temper and call the cops. There's more to that Catholic sniping thing than meets the eye."

"What do you think it could be?" asked Ryan as he was holding the doorknob to leave.

"My own theory is that it's guilt over dumping their faith. Or it could be they're angry at God and the bashing is their way of lashing out. I've even thought, on occasion, that it's somehow wired into some toxic dynamic they had with their own fathers. But all the bashers seem to enjoy being disrespectful and they get some level of enjoyment out of it. Some even strike me as being stuck in adolescence and the defiance that goes along with that," said Fr. Liam. "Those are my current theories anyway; I'm still observing and mulling it over."

"That's an interesting take. Her father abandoned her, her mother, and her sisters. It is defiance when she does it and it does have a back-handing feel to it. I know I'll be chewing on that for a while. Something about it clicks together like a puzzle piece."

They bumped fists, and Ryan left.

### Three Hours Later - 8:30 PM
### Ocala, FL

Fr. Liam walked into his rectory bedroom and put his keys and a glass of water down on his night table. It was another long day, saying mass at 8:30 am, hospital visits, counseling sessions in the afternoon, and a bible study class from seven to eight-thirty. He took his Advil with the water and began undressing from another long day. He listened to his voice mail messages. He could hear the anger in his brother's voice. Glancing at the clock, it was only 9:00 and he knew his brother would still be up.

"Hey, Mike, I'm just getting home. I got your message but tell me everything that happened with the private investigator. What's going on?"

"I got the report from the private investigator today and Jacob has a bankruptcy filed about a year before they were married."

"That's never good to hear," said Fr. Liam.

160

"I assumed he never said anything to Colleen. But when I told Maria, it turns out they both knew and decided not to tell me because *I would have made too much out of it* is how Maria put it."

"Maybe they don't know how damaging a bankruptcy can be and how often the need for credit comes into play, especially for a young married couple" said Fr. Liam.

"Could be. I've been thinking about it all afternoon since I found out. It makes me livid. He acts like he's the most brilliant guy in the world and it turns out he wasn't able to handle his finances in his 20s," said Mike. "And even now he saunters around like he's God's answer to Wall Street."

"Were either of them angry that you hired a private investigator?" asked Fr. Liam.

"No, no one said anything about it, at least Maria didn't. I think she felt so guilty about not telling me about the bankruptcy, I got away with hiring the PI," chuckled Mike.

"You told me his family is wealthy, so maybe if there's a credit issue in the future, the family will help him navigate around it. People do get over bankruptcies." Fr. Liam didn't know what to make of his brother's silence in response to what he just said.

"It doesn't change the fact that he's part of the parasitic class that is completely happy to screw his creditors and move on, does it?"

161

"No, it doesn't change that. It also doesn't change the fact that he was not your favorite choice for a son-in-law. This is only a confirmation of your seeing something in him you didn't like."

"Do you think I'm wrong for judging him about it? Is that what you're saying?"

"No, I'm not saying that at all. I'm saying you were never impressed with him. You thought he was all show and no substance and this proves it. The bankruptcy is evidence that you were right and your daughter has married a guy you would not have picked for her. You're not wrong for judging him. This is proof that your assessment of him was accurate.

"There's no point in allowing anger to drain you now. There's nothing you can do with this right now, especially since Colleen went along with it. She accepted it."

"You're right about that. It really changes nothing on my end," said Mike, disappointed his tirade would end here.

"Don't let it come between you and Maria because of the secret either. If you do, he wins," said Fr. Liam.

"You're right. I won't let it come between Maria and I but I let her know I wasn't happy about being kept in the dark over it."

"You just got her to agree to being a snowbird and buying a condo up here. Don't let your quest for justice change that," said Fr. Liam.

"You're right. You're right about that. I'm going to let it go. His parents are loaded; I have some money and Colleen and Jacob will be fine. The only problem would be needing a house when she gets pregnant, so it'll be fine."

"Exactly. First world problems, as they say," said Fr. Liam.

"You're right. I'll let it go. I need to refocus on getting a handyman or two to get our house ready to sell before Maria changes her mind," said Mike.

"You want to move fast because a pregnancy announcement at this time can and will only work against us."

"That's true. I've got to jump into high gear on fixing this house."

Mike adjusted in his chair. "So that's enough about me. How are you? What's going on at the church?"

"I had another long, long day, ending with my weekly bible study. I knew a weekly bible study would be too much for me, but I had parishioners almost demanding one, so I had to sign onto it. Otherwise, they'll go to the bible study four blocks from here at a protestant church and there's no supervision at all. They gather into a room and the person with the biggest mouth is the theologian. They come traipsing back to me with all kinds of anti-Catholic rhetoric they pick up there. I have to correct them on it and point out where in the bible our teachings come from, which takes twice as long. So I figured I would just do the bible study."

"You need to take care of yourself too, Liam. You're a better man than me. That's for sure. I would have told them it was too much for me and let the Protestants have them," said Mike.

Fr. Liam chuckled at Mike's attitude.

They talked about politics for a few minutes before saying goodbye. Mike felt much better after talking to Liam. His brother had a way of re-balancing his perspective on things. He was able to let go of the bankruptcy and Maria's mother-daughter lie.

As Fr. Liam hung up from his call, he pondered whether he should have shared Ryan's advice about checking the credit rating for Colleen. He decided he would wait a few days and bring it up in general conversation. He kept thinking back to Jacob's jumpy knee and wondering whether there could be something else going on besides gambling.

# CHAPTER 11

### One Day Later - 6:30PM
### Boca, Raton, FL

COLLEEN COVERED THE Chinese food she picked up on the way home with a dish towel to keep the heat in. Jacob was expected by 6:30, so she went about setting the table for them. She looked forward to another night together. Thinking back over the last few days, she felt more accepting of his work schedule. She was getting better at going with the flow.

She heard a light knocking at her front door along with one doorbell ring. Looking through the peephole, she expected it would be Jacob but it was her mother. She opened the door and stepped aside as her mother came rushing in.

"Good, you're home. I have to talk to you before you talk to your dad."

"What's going on?" asked Colleen.

165

"He found out about Jacob's bankruptcy and he also found out that we knew and chose not to tell him. Yesterday he was mad with me and I sense he may be more hurt by you. Either way, I didn't want you to be blindsided by him the next time you two talk."

"You could have called me instead of driving all the way here."

"Your father was around me all day and I couldn't get the privacy I needed to talk to you freely. I told him I was running to the store and here I am."

"Is he really mad?"

"He's mad about the bankruptcy but he was madder at me for keeping secrets. I explained to him we were afraid he would make trouble right before the wedding. He kind of understood the reasoning, but he still felt hoodwinked. It's going to take me some time to crawl back into his good graces and recover my credibility with him, let me put it that way."

"I'm sorry, Mom."

"It's okay. In 30 years of marriage, I've crawled back into his good graces more than once."

"Jacob is coming home and I picked up Chinese food. Do you want to stay for dinner?"

"No, you have so few evenings together anymore, I don't want to take you away from each other. I'm sure he doesn't want his mother-in-law staring at him while he's eating Chinese food. Besides, Dad and I are having a frozen pizza tonight. He thinks I went over to Walgreen's to pick up Advil. That was the only excuse I could think of to get away to come and warn you."

"Here comes Jacob now. He's parking his car," said Colleen, as she looked out the living room window into the apartment parking area.

"Okay. Kiss me goodbye and I'll talk to you soon. Enjoy your night together. I'll just wait to say hello and goodbye to him."

"He looks a little mad now," said Colleen, as they both looked at him through the window.

"He looks tired and deep in thought to me," said Maria.

Jacob walked up the alleyway and was out of sight for a few minutes as he approached the front door. Colleen opened it for him.

"Oh, hi, Mom. I didn't expect to see you," said Jacob.

"I just stopped by to catch up with Colleen, but I'm on my way out again. So I'm saying hello and goodbye in the same breath." She kissed him on the cheek once for hello and once for goodbye on the other cheek. Then she kissed Colleen again before she left. "Bye. Enjoy your evening together."

"Bye, Mom," said Colleen. She closed the door and greeted her husband with a hug and a kiss.

"How was work?"

"It was busy and tiring. I'm glad to be home early tonight. I can smell Chinese food." She misjudged him. He looked angry when he was walking up to the apartment, but his mood seemed okay now.

"I still keep checking the mail on the way home expecting to see at least some junk mail, but there's nothing," said Colleen. "I guess I should just forget it, right"?

"I discontinued it, all of it. You don't need to stop there anymore. No more junk mail and all the bills come to my office where I know the mailman is not drunk or stupid," said Jacob.

"I'll stop checking then. It'll make my life easier not having to stop and check every day," said Colleen. She followed Jacob as he walked into the bedroom to undress from work. After catching up on each other's day, she went back to the kitchen to put out the food. She set up the plates and utensils at the kitchen table and put the Chinese food out for them to eat. She lit two candles and put them in the center of the table and dimmed the lights. Her mom had given her the two candle holders after she came back from their honeymoon. She told Colleen to have as many romantic nights as possible before the kids showed up. They did make for a romantic atmosphere.

Jacob came in, he leaned over and kissed her and they ate. Things felt wonderful.

## One Half Hour Later - 6:30 PM
## Ocala, FL

Fr. Liam finished eating dinner at 6:30 pm at the rectory. He went into his bedroom to refresh himself before leaving for the wake he was scheduled to attend later. As he splashed water on his face, he thought about what Ryan had told him about checking his niece's credit. He checked the clock and he had about 20 minutes before he had to leave for the wake. He called his brother.

"Hey, Mike, what's going on?"

"Nothing. I'm still stewing about the bankruptcy and being held in the dark by the two women I thought I could trust."

"I think all mothers and daughters keep the man on an as-needed basis for certain information. Don't take it so personally," said Fr. Liam.

"Yeah, I guess so, but when you catch them, it still feels like a betrayal."

"You'll live. Listen, I spoke to a friend of mine who's a private investigator. I wanted his take on what your investigator found. I hope that doesn't feel like another betrayal," said Fr. Liam, lightly teasing his brother.

"No, it doesn't. What did he say?"

"He said that gamblers very often wind up with no credit. So if they start gambling again, they may borrow from people around them. He suggested you have Colleen's credit checked. Did your private investigator do that?"

"I really don't remember. When I met with Ron Lucchi, he went over the whole report with me. But to be honest, after he mentioned the bankruptcy, I began seething and I was only half-listening to the rest of his report. I don't remember anything about Colleen's credit. I'll call him back and ask him about that. Actually, he gave me a copy of a written report, so I'll check that first. I don't think Colleen would allow Jacob to take credit in her name, but you never know. I never thought she would marry someone who was bankrupt either."

"Let me know. Otherwise, I can have my friend Ryan do the credit check."

"I'll check on my end first," said Mike.

"Listen, I have to go. I'm getting ready to go to a wake service. Let me know what you find out. If her credit is clean, he's fine. I keep thinking about his leg jumping up and down. There's always a reason for everything and I'm wondering what was causing that, you know?"

"I know what you mean. I keep thinking of him with the designer wardrobe, the Italian leather shoes, taking her out to the best restaurants, going to Vegas, driving a Jag, and now he's bankrupt. And apparently, he screwed his creditors while he was doing all of this. It's time to bring back the public stockades for people who do this kind of stuff."

"Don't pin your hopes to that one. Let me know if you want me to ask Ryan to do a credit check on your daughter. I've got to go. Talk soon."

"Okay. I'll let you know."

# CHAPTER 12

## Ten Days Later - Friday - June 1st
## Ocala, FL

IT WAS FRIDAY afternoon at 4:30 and Ryan had just finished up with a new client, a woman who wanted to find her birth mother. She was given a name and a location of where she lived at one time. This would be an easy find -- so long as the woman was still alive. He had passed the information to Linda, his assistant.

"Linda, this is a birth mother case I want you to start on. Start a preliminary search beginning 30 years ago in Brooklyn, NY. The client was told her birth mother's name was Dianne Mulligan. She has tried to find her on social media but doesn't know whether Mulligan is a maiden name or a married name."

"Okay, I'll start the search. I finished two weekly reports and they're in this folder for your signature," said Linda. Ryan signed two reports she had waiting for him on her desk.

173

"And your 5:00 appointment is here already. Mr. Jean-Francois Lenoir, the guy who owns the Lenoir Horse Farms," whispered Linda.

"And the Lenoir International Tire Company," whispered Ryan. "You can bring him in now."

Linda opened the glass door to the waiting area and said, "Mr. Lenoir, Mr. Mallardi will see you now." She led Mr. Lenoir into Ryan's office.

"Thank you, ma'am. Thank you very much."

As Mr. Lenoir came in following Linda, Ryan said, "Hello, Mr. Lenoir, have a seat right here." Ryan pointed to a chair in front of his desk and extended his hand for a handshake.

Mr. Lenoir shook his hand, sat down and adjusted his tie.

Linda said, "Can I get either of you a soda or a coffee?"

Both declined. Linda left and closed the door.

"How can I help you, Mr. Lenoir?"

"My wife passed away a few years ago and I have a new girlfriend. Her name is Tara. She's 45 years old, which is almost thirty years younger than me. I know I'm too old for her, but I'm in love with her and she's in love with me. We got married in Las Vegas two weeks ago."

"I see," said Ryan, waiting for him to cut to the chase.

174

"Tara had a long-term boyfriend for almost ten years. His name is Anthony and he's now living in Ocala."

"Where was he living before Ocala?" asked Ryan.

"Well, he was in jail for three years because of a break and entry. He's a thief, apparently."

Ryan could tell this romantic saga was making this seventy-year-old feel young and excited. He waited for Mr. Lenoir to go on.

"Now that he's out of jail, he's pressuring her to see him and I want to see what's going on between them. I would like for you to do some surveillance on her."

"What is her name and where does she live?"

"Her name is Tara Murphy and she's living with me. I have the address of the house she was renting and I believe this Anthony is now living there alone."

"I see. Do you suspect she's having an affair with Anthony?" asked Ryan.

"I'm afraid so. I caught her once, and she told me she has battered woman's syndrome and that she's still controlled by him. She wants to get away from him, but she claims she still weakens and goes to see him. He makes up all kinds of excuses why he needs her and she falls for them."

175

"I can do surveillance and videotape anything I find. Is that what you want done?" asked Ryan, as he grabbed a new client file.

"Yes, that's what I want, surveillance and to see where she goes and what she's doing when she goes out at night. She says she's going to a woman's group at church, but my son Francois has told me that she's lying to me. He doesn't like Tara."

"I see. What day and time is the women's group? We'll start with that."

"It's Friday nights at seven at Our Lady of Mercy Church. There's a second meeting on Wednesday nights, which might be a bible study, same church," said Lenoir.

Ryan wrote down the information about the meetings.

"My son Francois is a grown man, 43 years old, but he hasn't liked any of the woman I've been dating. He can't picture me with anyone but his mother, I guess."

"Well, Mr. Lenoir --"

"Call me JF. My name is Jean-Francois, but friends and relatives call me JF." JF had the slightest French accent, just a hint of it left. Ryan guessed he may have been born and raised in France but had lived in the USA for the better part of his life.

"I will need a picture of Tara. Do you have one with you?" asked Ryan.

"Yes, I have several of them here." JF passed several color photographs of JF and Tara posing by their horse stables and at a few social events.

"I will need you to text those to me," said Ryan.

"Sure, sure. I will do it now."

Ryan wrote his cell number on the back of his business card and JF texted three photographs of him and Tara to Ryan.

"Okay, JF. I'll do surveillance starting Wednesday of this coming week and we'll see what we find. How does that sound?"

"That's great. I'm glad you can start right away," said JF, without getting up.

"Linda will talk to you on the way out about how we do our billing. I'll call you with whatever I find on Wednesday and then you can decide if you want to continue surveillance at that point." Ryan had dropped a subtle hint that the meeting between them was over, but JF didn't move.

"You know, I've never felt this way about anyone, the way I feel about Tara. I was married for 30 years to my first and only wife and raised a wonderful family. I loved her very much, but when she died, I was devastated. I dated a few other women and things didn't work out. But when I met Tara, I went upside down," said JF, with a smile from ear to ear.

"That sounds very romantic. It sounds like it was meant to be," said Ryan. He wondered if that was appropriate to say to a seventy-something-year-old who claimed to be in love. He had the excitement level of a teenager.

JF went into a forty-minute monologue about how beautiful, loving, and wonderful Tara was and how much he loved her and was happy he married her. Of course, he had to get to the bottom of this Anthony controls her thing. He acted like Anthony was merely an obstacle that needed to be moved out of the way and he already had his checkbook out and was beginning the process.

Ryan glanced at his watch during the monologue and he was now fifteen minutes late meeting Angelica. But JF was on such a roll that he wasn't able to even get a hint in about having to leave.

About the fourth time Ryan glanced at his watch, JF took a break and said, "Oh, here I am going on and on about my Tara, and I'm probably keeping you. I'm sorry."

"No problem," said Ryan rising from his chair and extending his hand to shake on the closure of their meeting.

"So let me know what you find out on Wednesday. I hope this Anthony will step aside and allow Tara and I to find happiness."

"Well, that will be our goal. It was nice meeting with you, Mr. Lenoir."

"JF. It was nice meeting with you too. I look forward to hearing the results from Wednesday and Friday."

JF left the office, got into the back seat of a Jaguar and it drove out of the lot. Ryan quickly got himself together and headed out to meet Angelica. He hoped she didn't start in with him again about always being late.

He parked his car at the Horse & Saddle Restaurant. It was now about 6:30 so happy hour was well underway. As soon as he arrived, opened the restaurant door and walked in, an already-drunk Angelica started right in with him. "What the hell? I've been texting you all day! You're so busy, you can't take five seconds to respond to one text?" Her voice was louder than normal, a sure sign that she had already had a few drinks.

"Angelica, I was working against the clock all day, I'm sorry."

"You know, Ryan, there's something about us that really doesn't work." Angelica's dramatics were at a charades-game level already.

"Look, you're being really loud, let's go outside."

"No, I'm not leaving."

"Just for a few minutes so we can talk and clear the air," said Ryan as he gently pulled and led Angelica outside.

179

"We just spent a great weekend together. Let's not fight, Angelica."

They both stepped outside the bar and Ryan led them towards the parking area.

"There's something about us that doesn't work, Ryan."

"I know."

"What's that supposed to mean?" asked Angelica, now alarmed.

"I'm agreeing with you."

Silence. Ryan led Angelica over to his car. She was getting teary-eyed after he agreed that something was wrong between them.

Ryan broke the silence and put his arms around Angelica's waist and leaned her against his car. "Do you want to be together tonight or not?"

"I have to leave in like fifteen minutes. I have the bridal shower tonight. Why don't you ever remember anything I tell you?"

"I remember some of the things you tell me," Ryan said, trying to defend himself with a pleading smirk, "does that count for anything? I still remember we're going to your sister's wedding in a month. I still remember you have the reception dinner that we're going to the week before. Don't

180

I get a few points for remembering those?" Ryan said turning on the charm and kissing her every third word.

Angelica mirrored his kissing behavior and said, "You get one point each for those two remembrances, but you lose a point for forgetting about the wedding shower tonight. So you're down to only one measly good-boyfriend point." Angelica embraced Ryan and they began to kiss more deeply. Although he knew she drank too much and had little interest in marriage or kids, the alcohol did make her particularly sensual and he liked that. Every man had his weakness and Ryan's was a beautiful and sensual woman, and in particular, this one.

Ryan and Angelica had moved into his car and things got even steamier, about as steamy as a couple can get in open public. There was a lot that didn't work for them, but it wasn't the chemistry.

Angelica was dressed for the night life, not so much a bridal shower. She wore a full face of makeup and her hair was freshly blown out. "You look so beautiful, Angelica." She melted even more into his arms. She loved to hear Ryan tell her how beautiful she was. It made her feel desired and wanted. They continued kissing and embracing.

"Ryan, when are we going to move in together?" asked Angelica playfully, "I think we should move in together." She continued to kiss Ryan.

"I thought you said you weren't ready to get married," asked Ryan.

Angelica said, "But I'm ready to move in together."

"I don't want to move in together if you aren't ready to get married," said Ryan, continuing to kiss Angelica.

"What does that mean?" Angelica said pulling away from him. Her mood changed abruptly, as sometimes happened when he said the wrong thing after she had been drinking.

"It means maybe we're not ready to move in together," said Ryan.

"You were talking about marriage in St. Thomas. Now you're acting like you have no desire to even be together. All right, well, I have to go. It's time for me to go to the shower." Now she was cold again and reached for the door handle.

"Don't jump to any conclusions, okay? Let's talk about moving in together and where we're headed, and everything else, after your sister's wedding." He said this while kissing her and trying to smooth down her feathers. "We'll focus on only us then; just me and you. How about that?" he asked.

"Okay. That sounds better — but I've got to go -- look, they're leaving." Angelica gave Ryan one last kiss before jumping out of his car. She joined her friends who were already half-lit and the shower hadn't even begun. Ryan watched as the girls all went to their separate cars in pairs, yelling to each other and laughing. The shower had yet to begin, but the party had already started. Ryan could see Angelica was in her glory.

As he drove to his condo, he weighed his passions for Angelica and the reservations that became so clear to him over the past two weeks. Tonight only confirmed his love affair with Angelica's beauty and sensuality and Angelica's love affair with the booze.

Early in counseling, Fr. Liam had suggested to him that he was dressing up fornication and calling it a relationship, and that it didn't seem like much more than a sexual affair to him. Ryan danced around the remark at the time and moved on to another subject, as he wasn't ready or able to see it at the time. But he saw it now and he saw that Father was right.

Angelica had said it herself that there was something that didn't work for them. At the same time, he was so attracted to her and loved being with her when things did work. But again, he could tell that his sexuality was ruling him, not the other way around.

He still felt he would need to end the relationship after Mia's wedding. But thinking about and praying about it for two weeks was good advice, because he dreaded it. The thought of starting over and looking for another girlfriend was something Ryan didn't want to face. He already had one failed marriage behind him. The thought of starting over with someone new was depressing.

As he continued driving a thought popped into his head. He wondered if Angelica would stop drinking if he asked her to. That might change things if she did. He suddenly thought that things with Angelica could work if she were willing to stop drinking so much. Maybe after Mia's wedding they could start over without the booze. They could get to know one another in sobriety. They could do healthier things together. Maybe she just needed to let go of this teenage-party-girl thing. That might work. He suddenly felt hopeful.

A text came in about 1:00 AM and it was from Angelica. *"I love you, Ryan."* Ryan read the text but decided not to reply. He knew by now Angelica was very drunk and he didn't want to deal with her that way.

### Later That Night - 11:50 PM
### Boca Raton, FL

It was 11:50 PM and Jacob wasn't home yet. Colleen had gotten a call from Jacob at lunchtime stating that he would be very late tonight as he had to work again. He was friendly and loving on the phone, so Colleen had no problem with it. She quickly adjusted to being alone another night. She did more research on the paralegal courses she would sign up for.

She texted him at 10:30 pm. *"It's 10:30 now. Will you be working much longer?"*

*"No, I'm finishing up now."* Jacob texted back.

Another hour and twenty minutes passed and he hadn't come home yet. Her thoughts turned to worry. *'Should I be worried that something happened to him on the way home? Or did he just get caught up again and he'll be home in a few minutes?'* She didn't know how to feel or what to do.

At 12:30 in the morning, she called her mother.

"Mom, Jacob hasn't come home yet. I texted him at 10:30 and he said he was finishing up and he would be home soon. Then at ten to twelve, I called him but it went to voice mail. I texted him too, but no reply. Should I call the hospitals? Or is he just caught up? I don't know what to do."

"Has he ever been this late before?" asked Maria.

"No, never. Once he came home at 11:00 but that was the latest. But now it's twenty to one. I think I should call the hospitals. What do you think?"

"I would give him until one o'clock --"

"Wait, I just heard the front door. I think that's him. Yes, it's him. I heard him whisper my name. I'll call you tomorrow." Colleen hung up and went out to greet Jacob.

"You're so late. I called my mother. I thought I should call the hospitals. I was worried you got in a car wreck on your way home."

"I'm okay, just working late but I'm glad someone would be worried if I didn't show up." He grabbed her and swung her around in a half circle and then kissed her on the side of her face.

She could tell he had a few drinks. "Someone's been drinking. Were you celebrating something?"

"Yes, we were celebrating a great week and two new super rich clients that we signed on this week. It was a big celebration." He walked with his arm around her shoulder and she could tell he was officially drunk.

"I'm on a lucky streak, no one can stop me," he said. He pulled at his tie and loosened it enough to pull it off over his head.

"What do you mean a lucky streak'? You're not gambling again, are you?" Colleen could tell she sounded alarmed.

"No, no. That's old talk, I guess. I mean a lucky streak in business. I was the one who sweet talked and charmed these new clients into signing with us. So my bosses are very happy with me. That's what I meant by a lucky streak."

He took off his shirt and pants standing inside the closet and he needed to grab the closet hanging rail more than once. Colleen was so happy to know he wasn't wounded from a car crash that she saw the drunkenness as comical. He finished undressing and they both fell into bed. Jacob was asleep within ten minutes.

As Colleen was snuggling up to Jacob and getting ready to fall asleep herself, she heard a text come in. She looked and it was from her mother. *"Is everything okay?"*

*"Yes, all is well. Thanks, Mom!"*

# CHAPTER 13

### One Day Later - 10:30 AM
### Boca Raton, FL

ON SATURDAY MORNING after Colleen's frantic call, Maria was speculating about what would make Jacob so late. He worked for an investment company and people decided to either invest with them or not. She began to wonder if working late was part and parcel of the finance business, but she didn't know.

She called Colleen about 10:30 to talk. "What are you two doing today or tonight?"

"We're having a leisurely day at home and then we'll go out for something to eat at dinnertime. What about you?"

"Your dad is golfing this morning and we'll go out for a late lunch or early dinner too. I'm curious about why Jacob was so late. What did he tell you when he came finally came home?"

189

"They were celebrating two new clients this week and another great week of business. He was the one who talked new clients into signing with the firm, so he was the center of the celebration, so he couldn't just beg off. That's why he was so late and why he couldn't answer my texts. He had one person after another talking to him," said Colleen.

"Maybe the next time he has to work late, you and I can have dinner together and then visit him at work. We can see what goes on there after hours. What do you think?" asked Maria.

"We can do that. I've already spied on him a few times and I know his car was always there, but we can visit one night. I would love to see what it's like there in the evenings night too. I think it will be fun to do a little surveillance."

"Me too," said Maria. "It will be a little mother-daughter spy caper we can go on."

"I almost can't wait," said Colleen.

Maria could tell all was well. Colleen was like that; she wore her emotions on her sleeve and if something was amiss, Maria could spot it a mile away.

Jacob was hung over Saturday and remained quiet and withdrawn most of the day. Bustling about between running errands and house chores, Colleen noticed how unusually quiet he was.

"You seem quiet and thoughtful today, Jacob. Is there anything on your mind?"

He hesitated and looked like he was going to say something, but then said, "No, nothing. I'm just tired from work and partying last night. I'm fine."

"Do you want to stay in tonight instead of going out to dinner?" asked Colleen.

"No, we'll go out to dinner. I'll just go to bed early. You've been busy all day and I haven't helped you at all, so at least let me take you out to dinner." He glanced over and smiled at her. Then he went back to watching TV.

Colleen continued folding laundry and thought to herself, *'Why did he hesitate when I asked if something was on his mind? Why do I always think every little nuance in his behavior is evidence he has a secret? He was drinking last night, he's hung over, so he's quiet. That's all there is to it. I don't want to always over-analyze things and make an issue out of every little change in his mood.'*

She busied herself for the rest of the afternoon with a little cooking for the upcoming week as well as getting her work clothes ready for Monday.

When Jacob and Colleen were dressing to go out for dinner, Jacob said, "I need to let you know about something that just popped up from my past."

Colleen froze in place as this announcement had an ominous tone. "What something?"

"A woman from my past is getting ready to sue me for $5,000, saying that she loaned me this money and I never paid it back. So if someone comes to the door to serve papers, I don't want you to get blindsided or get scared."

"Is this your first girlfriend, Abby?" asked Colleen.

"No, it's a girl I was dating for a few months after Abby and before we met." Jacob was standing at the bathroom sink and he ran water through his hair and combed it back. "It was during my gambling phase. She offered to help me pay for my lawyer at the time and said it was a gift. Now she wants to make it into a loan."

"So what's going to happen now?" asked Colleen. She was standing behind Jacob watching him comb his hair in the mirror. She couldn't help but notice his nonchalant attitude over this gift or loan.

"She threatened to sue me and if she does, I will have to go and explain the circumstances before a court, I guess. It will cost her more than the $5,000 to sue me, so don't worry about it. Don't make a big deal out of it, Colleen. I know how you like to blow things out of proportion, so don't do that. This is nothing. I'll handle it."

192

"What things do I blow out of proportion?" asked Colleen.

"Like this, what we're talking about now. I see you looking at me like I've got a multi-million-dollar case being filed against me. This is nothing. It's fallout from a previous relationship. She's mad that I married someone else. Now she's trying to get revenge of some kind. Don't make a bigger deal out of it than it is." Jacob moved past Colleen from the bathroom and finished getting ready.

"Maybe you should give her the money back. You can take it out of the house fund. Wouldn't that be the best thing to do? This way, you pay back someone who tried to help you and she can let go of the anger she has for you."

"I'm not paying her back. I never asked her for the money. She offered the money. It was like a birthday gift. When you broke up with your last boyfriend, did you ask for all your gifts back?" asked Jacob. He suddenly recovered his energy and lunged into his debate mode.

Colleen didn't want to make a big fight out of it so she said nothing in response.

"You need to be more supportive of me, Colleen. You claim to love me, but you're taking the side of my ex-girlfriend who is suing me now. You know how that feels?"

"I'm sorry. I was just looking at it from the perspective of what would be the easiest and most fair solution. I thought we were in discussion mode, that's all, exploring all the options."

"That's not how it feels. Are you ready?" asked Jacob, now ending the discussion.

"Yes, I'm ready to go."

They walked out to the car and once outside the front door, Jacob, who used to hold hands walking to the car, walked three paces ahead of her. His manner was gruff and rejecting. Colleen could feel a stab in her heart. Something didn't feel right but she couldn't put her finger on it.

Once inside the car, Jacob immediately put on music and began to make small talk. "So what are you in the mood to eat tonight?"

"I'm not sure. I'll look at the menu and whatever makes my mouth water, that's what I'll have. How about you?" asked Colleen putting aside all that went on before for later analysis.

"I'm hungry so I'm thinking steak or even a burger. But looking at the menu is a good idea. I'm feeling adventurous too, so maybe I'll try something different." He glanced over and smiled.

Colleen smiled back. As Jacob had taken his eyes off the car ahead of them, he suddenly jerked on the brakes and said "Whoa! That was a close one."

At the same time, a gold-plated lipstick rolled out from under the passenger seat. Colleen picked it up, opened it, and wound up a used lipstick in a burgundy color. "Whose is this" she asked Jacob, frowning.

"I have no idea. It's not yours?" he asked innocently.

"No, this isn't mine. Have you had another woman in your car?" asked Colleen accusingly.

"Here we go," said Jacob, smacking the steering wheel and going into one of his instantaneous mood changes. "You know how many people I have in and out of my car in any given week?" He glanced over at Colleen who was frozen and still looking at the lipstick.

"I drive clients to and from lunch, to and from dinners, any one of them could own the lipstick. Who knows what else we would find if I cleaned out the car seats? I don't have a girlfriend, Colleen, if that's what you're thinking."

"Well, what should a wife think when she finds a lipstick in her husband's car?"

"If your husband drives clients around, your default should not be that he is cheating. It should be giving him the benefit of the doubt and assuming it was a client's lipstick."

195

Colleen looked at Jacob and back at the lipstick, but she said nothing. All her energy had drained away and she felt heartsick.

"This is another example of you not supporting me. I can't be married to someone who doesn't trust me. If you were driving lawyers from work around, and I found a baseball cap in the back seat, I wouldn't automatically think you were having an affair. I would default into thinking it was one of the lawyer's hat, that's it," said Jacob. He glanced over to see how his argument landed on Colleen.

She said nothing but noted the '*I can't be married to someone*' remark. She recalled Uncle Liam telling her that Atheists, Jews and Protestants all believe in divorce, as well as most non-practicing Catholics. This was during the time they were trying to talk her out of marrying outside the faith. It didn't work on her, but here he was threatening divorce already in their first year of marriage.

Jacob looked over waiting for Colleen to carry on, but she continued to say nothing. She looked out the front window.

"Let's not fight anymore, Colleen. The lipstick has to belong to a client and it rolled out when I stopped short and that's the end of it, okay?"

"Okay."

"Don't be mad at me, Colleen. Don't make a mountain out of this little molehill. We're on our way to have a nice

196

dinner and I don't want to fight." Jacob glanced over again at Colleen.

She could tell that he turned off his foul mood when he saw that she was wounded and silent. It was at that moment that she realized that he had learned to weaponize his personality in order to maintain control. She knew she was no match for him; she was too sensitive.

Dinner went okay. Jacob carried the weight of making small talk at dinner. Colleen participated as best she could from where she was emotionally after seeing the lipstick. Yes, it could be a client's lipstick. But tonight she knew that if it wasn't, Jacob was capable of lying to her.

The following week, Collen met with Marsha over coffee and they talked and analyzed the lipstick incident from different angles.

"Yes, it could be a client's lipstick, but it could be the first sign of cheating. Yes, you can give him the benefit of the doubt and let it go. But you should jump into close-scrutiny mode and watch him for other signs," said Marsha.

"I'm already on high-alert and watching everything he does, but he's working all the time. My mother suggested we do a little espionage one night when he is working late. We should go to dinner and then just casually stop by to see how busy the office is at night. At first, I didn't want to start spying on my husband. But now I think the next time he's working late, I'm going to take her up on it."

"I would already have a two-inch-thick dossier on him starting from the day we married, but I admit I'm jaded and distrustful of all men because of my own personal experiences," said Marsha.

"Any time we have any type of argument or discussion that arises, he says things like '*I can't be married to someone who ...*' and then fills in the blank. It's like his default is to run to the divorce courts. I always thought marriage would give me the feeling of security, but it doesn't feel secure at all."

"Not if he thinks that divorce is a problem-solving skill," said Marsha. "I think I would have been happier if I was born in late 1940s or early 1950s. Women had all the new conveniences around the house to remove all the drudgery, but you could still count on marriage. Women didn't get traded in every ten years or less like now. I was born in the wrong era. That's my biggest problem," said Marsha, as she finished up her first cup of coffee.

"Me too. I remember my father and uncle telling me that most non-religious people believe in divorce today and I needed to know this going into an interfaith marriage. I thought they were being old-fashioned or prejudiced, but now I see what they meant."

"I thought Jacob was an atheist?" asked Marsha.

"He is. I corrected them about this, but they always still think of him as having a different religion, not as having no religion. It's a pretty moot point right now, isn't it?"

The waitress came over and refreshed both of their coffees.

"What about having children? Are you still trying?"

"I am and I'm not. I'm avoiding having sex when I know I'm fertile. I don't feel secure right now. I already know I'm not one of these superwomen that can work 40 hours a week and take care of kids on my own. I wish I was, but I don't have that level of energy or confidence. I'm going to suggest we go for counseling to see if we can fix these problems."

"That's a good idea, but will he go?" asked Marsha.

"I don't know, but I have to pick my timing with him. He has to be in the right mood when I bring it up. I'm exhausted from having to tiptoe around his moods. He never seemed moody when we dated or in the first five months of marriage. I keep telling you and my mother that he has changed in some way.

"My mother thinks he has let his hair down, as all married couples do. She thinks the honeymoon is ending and we're entering the real world of marriage where there are compromises and challenges that we both have to commit to getting through."

"That sounds good on paper, but your mother thinks the men of today were made from the molds of the 1950s. That's where her theory goes completely awry. I would bet anything that Jacob will not be open to counseling. He likes to be in control too much," said Marsha.

"Well, I'm going to ask him even if I have to ask him to do three sessions as a birthday gift. How can he say no if I ask him as a birthday gift?"

"Well, maybe. I'm too jaded. I wish I wasn't, but I am."

"You're jaded now, but when you meet someone else, he'll restore your hope in men and in marriage."

"I hope so. But listening to these incidents about the rolling lipstick and the suing ex-girlfriend, I don't know. I think it could be a permanent condition."

"I admit I'm suspicious, but I'm still hopeful. I don't know why, but I am," said Colleen.

"Well, if you and your mom need any backup spying on your husband or a decoy, let me know. It sounds fun," said Marsha smiling.

"I hope someday I can look back with two or three kids and laugh. I hope I can talk about how crazy I was in my first year of marriage tailing Jacob with my mother in tow while thinking he was up to no good. I hope I'm just being paranoid and crazy, and these feelings I have are not an ominous warning of things to come."

# CHAPTER 14

## Two Days Later - Monday - 5:00 PM
## Ocala, FL

FR. LIAM HAD thirty minutes before Ryan came for his weekly counseling session. This created a perfect window to call his brother. "Hey, Mike, what's going on?"

"I'm just sitting down after taking a full carload of tools to Salvation Army. I've gotten the garage down to the essentials and that's one of the biggest jobs I needed to do to get the house ready for sale. I'm making great progress."

"Very good, very good. Is Maria still looking for condos?"

"She is. She found one five minutes from Colleen and Jacob's apartment, but I told her we should wait. If they buy a house, which they are saving for --"

"I thought you gave them house money?" asked Fr. Liam.

"I gave them enough for a down-payment as a wedding gift. They put it in a house account and they're adding to it monthly, I was told."

"Are they looking in Boca?"

"They are, but as I explained to Maria, they may need to buy in a more affordable town as the houses in Boca are outrageously expensive. They have to think of other expenses that attach to having children. I've told Maria we should buy the condo up in Ocala first, and then when Colleen settles into a house, we can look for a condo close to where she settles."

"That does make better sense. Is she going along with it?"

"She is, but I think by looking for a condo, she's letting me know she's okay with being a snowbird. But she has repeated a few times that she's not ready to move away for good, which is fine with me.

"So what's going on with you and your priest job?"

"It's a vocation, not a job," said Fr. Liam, kiddingly.

"That's what the church calls it so they can keep you busy 60 hours a week and pay you a stipend instead of a salary," said Mike. "I was onto that racket before I hit thirty."

"I think you're onto something there. Anyway, everything is great. The parish is growing. Ocala itself is growing, more housing developments are going up every day. The only thing that will make it better is when you and Maria get here."

"I'm working on Maria every day. She's cleaned out her closet and brought half of her stuff to Salvation Army so she isn't just humoring me. We're moving faster than I thought, to be honest with you."

"Listen, I have my private investigator friend coming into the office in about ten minutes. Did you ever find out whether your PI did a credit check on Colleen?"

"I did look into that, but they didn't run Colleen's credit. I asked for Jacob only and that's what they did. With Maria agreeing to sell the house, I forgot all about it. Maybe your friend can do it just to be on the safe side. Things seem to have settled down with Jacob and Colleen. Maria says besides working late, everything else seems to be going great guns. I've accepted and gotten used to the idea of the bankruptcy. I've also accepted that I have a lower security clearance than the girls, so I've let go of my anger."

"Do you want me to do the credit check or forget about it?"

"No, have your friend do it and tell him to send me the bill, whatever it is."

"Okay, I'll do that today. I'll need her social security number and address. Can you text it to me?"

"Text? You know I don't know how to text. I had a secretary and a wife for 30 years, I'm lucky I know how to use a cell phone."

"Okay. Email me or call me with the information and I'll forward it to him. I'll hire him to do it today and pass him the info when you get it to me."

"Sounds good. I get a good feeling that her credit will be fine. Maybe this gambling thing really was nipped in the bud and there's no problem. Maybe we just over-reacted to the jumpy knee and the sweating. But if I'm going to do the search, and with grandchildren on the horizon, this is the time to do it, so let's go forward with it."

"Will do," said Fr. Liam.

Ryan settled into his chair in front of Fr. Liam's desk and loosened his tie. He sat back and got comfortable. He put a bottle of water he brought along on the end of Fr. Liam's desk.

"So how are things going this week?" asked Fr. Liam.

"Things are better with my mother. She's more respectful about my schedule, more cooperative. She's stopped with the sarcastic suggestions on how to euthanize her, which I'm happy about. She's gotten attached to Naomi, the caretaker. The agency sent another woman last week in Naomi's place and my mother called the company and raised hell about it. They reassigned Naomi this week. This is the same woman, mind you, that told me Naomi was going to murder her after stealing all of her things on the first day they met," said Ryan, shaking his head.

"Your mother doesn't like change, but she does get used to it. I'm very glad to hear this. You seem much less stressed now. Do you think this made a difference in your overall stress level?" asked Fr. Liam.

"Yes, it has. I have more control over my schedule and she's working around me instead of the other way around. I used to get several phone calls a day reminding me of what she needed me to pick up after work. She would call about every thought that popped into her head, but I think Naomi is getting most of those calls now."

"Very good. And what about Angelica?"

"Well, that's another situation all together. I told you in our last session that I was going to ask her about maybe not drinking all the time and doing healthier things together. Well, at first, she seemed okay with it although she still wanted to go out on Friday nights with her girlfriends. But I get the impression that she likes to go out on the town and that's it."

"I see." Fr. Liam gave Ryan a chance to continue, but he didn't. "Do you think she's uncomfortable if she can't drink? Or does she like the excitement of crowds, music and the partying lifestyle? What is it she likes about drinking?"

"She loves the party atmosphere. Whether it's at a club, or with another couple drinking together, or even us drinking at dinner, that's when she's happiest. The forum doesn't seem to matter. The common denominator is the alcohol. She likes to have several drinks until she feels buzzed or drunk. Not really sloppy drunk, mind you, just high, playfully drunk. It gives her the feeling that she's having fun."

"Have you raised it as an issue with her to talk about?" asked Fr. Liam.

"I told her how I feel about drinking all the time. She told me that I'm the one who's changed, not her. She said that I liked to drink as much as she did and now, I'm acting like it's only her. I told her that may or may not be true, but we're at a point where we need to think about whether this relationship will go to marriage or not.

"I told her I don't want to have a party lifestyle when I'm married. I want to have a family lifestyle. When I said this, she seemed horrified."

"What do you mean by horrified?" asked Fr. Liam, tilting his head.

"Well, I raised the issue like you raised it with me. I told her that when I envisioned us married, I pictured a scene where we both worked -- or only I worked -- and we ate dinner together as a family. We had a few kids and we both worked on and took care of our home. I told her I envisioned us spending holidays with family, including my mother. That's when I got the distinct impression that this was nowhere near what her expectations were.

"She said she thought of us as more of a modern couple, working and having a nanny to take care of the kids. She wanted us to still go out with friends. She agreed that we would go to our mom's houses for the holidays. She told me again she would find it hard to work and whip up a whole domestic scene."

"Is that all that was said about the drinking?" asked Fr. Liam.

"No, we went back and forth about the drinking on another occasion. This conversation I'm relating now was about our expectations of marriage. About the drinking, she said I'm making her out to be the drinker, but she reminded me that I was her drinking partner."

"Is she right about that?" asked Fr. Liam.

"She is right about it. She is right about it. However, this is where I think it differs. I drink with friends and at parties, even when I go out to eat with her. I do like to have a drink or two socially. But I wind up drinking more than I want to in these scenarios. This is my own fault, mind you, I'm not blaming her. But I do think it is more about letting her decide what we do socially than it is my secret quest to go drinking.

"I'm also reaching an age where drinking even on a weekly basis is not fun anymore. I guess I've lost all enthusiasm for it, especially when I see that it has such an effect on us as a couple.

"I've even stopped drinking over the last few weeks to see if my sober behavior could affect the relationship in a positive way, but it hasn't. She always wants to drink and is adamant about it. I wonder if she can't stop or doesn't want to stop. She keeps telling me I'm the one who has changed, not her."

"Anything else that came clear to you?"

"Well, that's a huge difference between us. The other thing that has changed recently are my thoughts about having kids. I want to have them soon. I also believe our difference in religion is a bigger problem than I originally thought."

"In what way?"

"Well, in the beginning, she said she was an atheist and somehow, I didn't think that would be a problem. I figured as long as she accepted that I was a practicing Catholic, it wouldn't be a problem. And she did accept it in the beginning. I didn't think beyond that point. I figured as long as she accepted the difference, it would be okay.

"But after the passage of a year or so, she's not really tolerant of my religion anymore. As a matter of fact, she snipes it just about every chance she gets."

208

"What do you mean by *snipes it*?"

"When I play golf in the Knights of Columbus tournament, she tells me all the money they raise will go to defending the pedophiles. She's told me that the catholic church should pay taxes like everyone else because they just build bigger and more glamorous churches. No one remark is that bad, mind you, it's nothing that any one of us Catholics hasn't heard before. But it is the all-out campaign of intolerance, I guess is how I would put it," said Ryan.

"I see. Well, that doesn't sound very tolerant. If you have children with her, will they be Catholics or atheists?" asked Fr. Liam.

"Well, this is where I see a big obstacle. This is the core of the issue. I asked her earlier on in the relationship if she would object to having her kids be Catholic. She said no as long as she could tell them her side of things. But her side of things is more anti-Catholic than atheistic. So I don't see any way to pass on my faith married to someone who will contradict me at every turn. I see too much hostility towards my religion. I don't believe it would be possible to raise Catholic kids in that environment."

"That's a big problem. Children tend to absorb the religion of their mothers because they're usually around them more. It's important for you to know that. So if she's not willing to at least be tolerant, you need to accept this if you go forward with marriage plans with Angelica. As your priest, I need to tell you this is not a good situation at all."

"I saw little problems in the beginning when we met and fell in love, but now I see insurmountable problems. Her sister's wedding is only a month away, so I'm holding out until after the wedding to make a final decision. But right now, I don't see us making it."

"Do you think your mind was not focused on what your marital goals were when you met Angelica? How was it that it took a year and several months to come to the conclusion that all was not well?" asked Fr. Liam, gingerly.

"I can see now in hindsight I was instantly attracted to Angelica. She's so beautiful and I instantly fell in love with her. But as much as I hate to admit I'm so shallow, I fell in love with her beauty and all that I projected onto that beauty. It was lust that was driving me, at least in the beginning," said Ryan.

"Was it only lust or was there something else you saw in her?"

"I don't know. I just did what I always do and that is to project onto the woman assumptions of how she will be or what she will want. I know I did this with my first wife."

"Is it possible that your lust blinded you to other things?" asked Fr. Liam.

"Definitely. I didn't know it at the time, but I can see it in hindsight. I believed at that time that a wife was chosen by who swept you off your feet. I mean, this is the plot of every love story. Otherwise, if you're too practical, it seems more like you're interviewing someone for a wife job. So I know I was led by lust, but I'm not sure how else I should have been proceeding," said Ryan, as he looked to Fr. Liam for guidance.

"Sexual attraction is a component of choosing a spouse, an important component, but it's not the only component, nor should it be.

"If you go forward with a set of realistic marital goals, with a flexible picture of how you want things to be when you're married, you'll choose with more than lust. You'll see lust in its proper perspective. You will be ruling your lust, not allowing your lust to rule you. Does that make sense?"

"It does, but using me and Angelica as an example, how would that have played out if I was led by more than lust?"

"You would have acknowledged that you were sexually attracted to her, and that's a good start. You want someone you have good chemistry with. But you would have been focused on finding out her ideas and goals concerning marriage right from the beginning.

"You would have known three or four months into the relationship that she wasn't ready to get married or have children. You would have figured out that drinking was a favorite pastime for Angelica. You would have seen that as more of a problem much earlier on. The religious obstacle may or may not have taken time to rear its ugly head, but as soon as it did, you would have seen it as a red flag. But these other traits would have shown up much earlier.

"You would have seen a more balanced view of things. By allowing lust to overtake you, you allowed it to rule you. It blinded you and you weren't able to see much beyond your intense sexual feelings for her. As Catholics we're taught to seek the virtue of temperance, all things in their proper perspective. Allowing lust to rule us is a sin of idolatry, in the same way a gambler allows greed to rule him or her. We give one of our emotions the power to rule us; we make it our god. We should only be ruled by the one true God and His laws. And temperance is one of His laws."

"It makes perfect sense now, but I wish I woke up earlier to all this."

"Be kind to yourself. Some of this is the result of not having a father. These are the types of lessons you learn at a father's knee as you grow up, one little snippet at a time. Your circumstances were different. But you're learning about them now. Losing your dad made you a bit of a late bloomer. Better late than never, or better late than after the marriage, right?"

"Right. Not having a dad created a lot of problems for me, I guess."

"Yes, it did, but none of them are irreversible. You have put up healthier boundaries with your mother. Now you'll get to redo things either with Angelica or with someone new."

212

A moment of silence passed between them.

"Do you think things with Angelica are salvageable?" asked Ryan, reaching for hope.

"If Angelica knows she'll lose you if she can't or won't stop drinking, she may decide you're more important than the alcohol. If she knows that you can't make a life without true tolerance of your religious beliefs and a promise to raise your kids as Catholics, she may reconsider. Although the sniping is fun and she enjoys it, she won't want to lose you over it. Sometimes faced with the reality of loss, people do change."

"I've always given in to her so I can't picture her being willing to change for me," said Ryan.

"Angelica is a very beautiful woman and at her age, she is at the height of her sexual prowess. She has ruled you with it since the beginning. Now, the relationship needs to be tested. You will have to conjure up the courage to test it. Before you break up with her, you need to be ready and able to accept the consequences of that test."

"I understand." Ryan paused and looked down in thought. "Well, I have another month to think and analyze all of this. Mia's wedding is a month away, so I'll see what plays out."

"You seem very disheartened today, Ryan. Of course, coming to these realizations is never easy. But remember, you want a successful marriage. So you only want this

213

relationship with Angelica to move forward if you have a good chance to make it work. You already have one failed marriage and you don't want to sign onto another one, right?"

"That's bluntly put, but yes. I don't want another failed relationship. And I definitely don't want to be a dad who's raising kids in a divorce -- if I can help it."

"Exactly," said Fr. Liam.

"I see I've gone over my time with you about ten minutes, Father, sorry about that. I hope I'm not making someone else wait."

"No problem. You're my last conference for the day. I wanted to ask you about some private investigation work anyway."

"Oh, about your niece?" asked Ryan.

"Yes. I spoke to my brother and his PI didn't do a credit check on Colleen, only her husband. My brother wants to move forward with it. He's going to email her social security number and address to me. I think that's all you will need, right? Let me see if he sent it already."

"Yes, I will need her married name, of course."

"No, he hasn't sent it. I just spoke to him before you came in. His attentions have been diverted now that his wife has agreed to sell the house and buy a condo up here."

214

"So he wore her down and she agreed to move?" asked Ryan.

"Well, they did a compromise. They're going to be snowbirds. They'll live up here for a few months, and then they'll have a condo down in Boca too. They're going to sell their big house and buy two smaller condos."

"I'm happy for you. I know you wanted your brother closer."

"Yes, I love the parish and the area here, but I miss my brother. I'm used to being five minutes away from him. That was the only drawback to my assignment in Ocala. But now he'll be here in no time."

"Are you free on Wednesday afternoon?" asked Ryan as he looked at his calendar on his smart phone.

"Yes, Wednesday is my day off so that'll be great. What time?"

"Any time from 4PM on."

"Okay, I'll come at 4:00. I'll have Colleen's information with me. How long does a credit check take?"

"Five minutes or so. Could be ten minutes if we see anything that requires more searching, but a credit check is quick. You can see my new office," said Ryan.

"You moved?" asked Fr. Liam.

"No, but I had a professional decorator redo the waiting room and the offices. They did a great job," said Ryan. "I'd like for you to see it."

"Okay. See you Wednesday at four."

# CHAPTER 15

### Two Days Later - 1:30 PM
### Boca Raton, FL

WITH HER ATTORNEY engaged in trial, Colleen was super busy at work all morning. She didn't get to eat lunch until 1:30. She had the lunchroom all to herself and it was nice to eat and read quietly. While she was reading, her phone rang and glancing up she saw it was from a local number. She had been waiting for a call back from Rachel, her real estate agent, and maybe this was her. She picked up. "Hello?"

"Is this Colleen Kessler?" asked the man on the phone.

"Yes, it is."

"Mrs. Kessler, we're giving you a courtesy call to let you know your medical insurance payment is late. Do you wish to make a phone payment?"

217

Her heart started pounding and she shifted into panic mode. "My husband is paying my bills now, so I'll have to ask him about it. How late is it?"

"About ten days late. We make a courtesy call at 10 days late before it's submitted for cancellation," said the man on the phone.

"Please don't cancel it. I'll call my husband and have him call you. Actually, can I give you my debit card number and pay it right now?"

"Sure, that would be great."

"I need a minute to get my purse. I'm at work in the kitchen. Oh, this is awful."

"It's okay. If you take care of it today, it won't be a problem."

"I need a minute to get my debit card."

"No problem. Take your time."

Colleen reached into her handbag with shaky hands and retrieved her debit card from her wallet. She gave her information to the insurance guy on the phone and he gave her a confirmation number. After a cursory exchange of *thank yous* and *have a nice days*, she hung up. Her heart was still beating so fast. She didn't know why she went into a panic over any little thing, but she did. Her anger began to rise as she thought how close she came to having her

218

health insurance canceled, all because Jacob forgot to pay the bill.

She texted Jacob. *"I just got a call that my medical insurance was not paid and they were about to cancel my coverage. Are you paying the bills or not?"*

*"I'm paying the bills. I had it on my list of things to do this afternoon. Sorry, been too busy."*

The insurance problem was now solved so the panic drained from Colleen. In its place was frustration and anger. It was over Jacob's irresponsibility and the lackadaisical manner that he handled things that were important to her.

She went back to work preparing pleadings and motions for her attorney to sign by the end of the day. Her anger kept a continuous inner conversation going the entire time. *'I need to get him to redirect the mail back to the apartment if he's going to be late on things. If he gets mad, he gets mad. I don't want to deal with what happened today on a monthly basis.'* Of course, she played her own devil's advocate by thinking: *'This is the first time he's been late on anything. And we did just switch over to this system. Maybe I'm over-reacting again.'*

This went on for most of the day. By the time 5:00 came along, she was exhausted from the mental debate, inner reasonings, and solution ideas that were set off by the disturbing phone call.

As she gathered her things to put in her purse to leave, a text came in from Jacob. *"I'll be late tonight, so don't stop for food. I hope I caught you in time."*

She was happy she wouldn't have to face him as she still had a residual of anger that would have been hard to hide. As she walked out to the parking garage, she remembered her mother's invitation to do surveillance. This was the perfect night.

### ~ Meanwhile ~ at 4:00 PM
### Ocala, FL

Ryan met Fr. Liam at the door to his office. As Fr. Liam entered, he looked over the waiting room. It was now decorated with light gray modular tufted chairs, glass and chrome tables, and matching lamps. There was a decorative stone fountain that covered one full wall. Colorful modern art prints decorated the walls. The room had been painted a grayish blue, with a hand-painted geometric design wainscoting.

The cocktail table in front of the waiting chairs was a glass case on chrome legs. It displayed the various spy gadgets and security cameras that his company sold. Underneath the check-in window was table with various brochures of information and lists of available investigative services.

"So this is the newly-decorated waiting room. Very nice. I like the fountain," said Fr. Liam. "It looks great, Ryan."

"Hopefully, it calms everyone before they come into my office -- at least the betrayed spouses," said Ryan.

Ryan led Fr. Liam into his office and they stopped at his assistant's desk. This part of the office was also redecorated as well. "Very nice," said Fr. Liam.

"Hi, Father. Can I get you a coffee or soda?" asked Linda, Ryan's assistant.

"Hello, Linda. Oh, no, I'm fine. Thank you."

Ryan's office was also upgraded with a new design. It used to have open shelving, displaying all his cameras, tripods and other surveillance equipment. Now, two walls were covered in light-gray closed-door modular cabinetry so his equipment was now hidden. He maintained the same modular desk and chairs, but they fit much better in the new décor. All in all, his office had a much more professional look.

"It looks great, Ryan. It looks like a high-end professional office. You did a super job," said Fr. Liam, as Ryan directed him to have a seat.

Once seated, Father said, "So we're on opposite sides of the desk today."

"Yes, that's true," said Ryan chuckling and waiting to see how Fr. Liam wanted to proceed.

"Were you able to do the credit check on my niece?" asked Fr. Liam.

"Yes, I did a credit check and a few things came up, so I did a few other searches with her husband as well," said Ryan.

"That doesn't sound good. What did you find?"

"I ran a credit report and there's been a flurry of activity on Colleen's credit over the last month or two. Four new credit cards have been opened all around the same time but with different merchants. The cards all have a few thousand dollars on them already."

Fr. Liam was looking intently at Ryan, taking it all in.

"I was able to hack into one of the accounts and saw charges at the Seminole Casino in Coral Springs. That's pretty close to where her husband works."

"The question is: Did he sweet talk her into opening the credit cards or did he do this behind her back?" asked Fr. Liam as a hypothetical.

"What do you think?" asked Ryan.

"Colleen knew about his bankruptcy before marrying him. She and her mother kept it from my brother. So it's possible she went along with this and hasn't said anything about it. I don't know what to think. I just know it's not good."

"I also ran his credit and saw the bankruptcy. His credit rating is rock bottom because of it, but it is beginning to at least crawl up again. However, Colleen's credit rating is falling, as there are two late payments on the new credit cards. Her credit limit went from $7500 down to $3500, so now she's heading in the wrong direction."

Fr. Liam exhaled and looked at his phone. "I should call my brother."

"Before you do, I did find something else," said Ryan. "Jacob Kessler now has a small claims lawsuit against him for $5,000. He allegedly borrowed $7500 from an ex-girlfriend named Beverly Rodgers and he's refused to pay it back. She makes mention in the court papers that they had a romantic relationship but she ended it when she found out he was still married. He has now cut off all ties, and she wants her money back." Ryan looked over to Fr. Liam. He had his eyes closed like he was wincing. Father exhaled deeply.

A moment of silence passed between them.

"So he's been cheating on her too? They are only married nine months." Fr. Liam was shaking his head. "My brother is going to hit the ceiling."

"Do you think it was a real marriage or was he grooming her for this type of a life?" asked Ryan.

223

"I never thought about that until you just mentioned it, but it almost seems that way, doesn't it?"

"Can you tell with certainty that this relationship took place when he was married?   Maybe it before was he was married," said Fr. Liam.

"The dates referred to in the complaint are dates within the last nine months.  It appears to be when he and Colleen were first married."

"Is it possible that he married her to access her credit? Could someone be that cold, that heartless?" asked Fr. Liam.  "I'm dreading telling my brother."

"Maybe he loves her and maybe he doesn't but she should think about getting away from him, at least to protect herself," said Ryan.   "I've had other cases involving gamblers and they can be extremely destructive."

"I don't know what's worse, the credit cards or the cheating," said Fr. Liam.  "I saw my niece on Mother's Day and she seemed deliriously in love with him.  Is there a way we can find out if he's still cheating?"

Ryan looked at his computer and thought a moment or two.  "Angelica and I are supposed to go down to Miami Beach this weekend, from Thursday to Sunday.  I can switch it to go to the Boca Raton Beaches instead.  Then I can do surveillance on him if you want.  I can put a GPS on his car and check out where he goes over the weekend, from Thursday to Sunday."

224

"Let me step outside and call my brother and I'll confirm whether he wants you to do more surveillance. I sent him an email that I need to talk to him and he said he's home now. So give me ten minutes."

Fr. Liam stepped out into the parking lot and paced back and forth as he relayed all the information to his brother.

"That no good bastard. I knew he was a big phony from day one. First, the bankruptcy and now this. Colleen is running around trying to find them a house so they can prepare for having a baby and this is what this guy is up to?"

Fr. Liam could hear the anger rising in his brother. "Mike, Ryan hacked into one of the credit cards and there are charges from the Seminole Casino in Coral Springs. I know the place from working on the police force, the Seminole Indians helped us out a few times. The casino is a few blocks from where he works. It has to be him. But, like the bankruptcy, does she know about it and did she give her permission for him to open the credit cards?"

"I doubt it. Listen, I don't want to let her know I'm surveilling her husband right now without any evidence. I want your friend to follow him and see if he's still gambling and if there are any other women around. I need proof of the gambling otherwise, she may not listen," said Mike.

"You don't want to ask her first about the credit cards?"

225

"No, because there's no way to ask her without revealing that I'm looking into her husband with a private investigator again. By the grace of God I got away with my Boca PI, but she'll know this time if I ask her about specific credit cards. Based on her waving away the bankruptcy like it was no big deal, she may have gone along with opening these credit cards. I need to confront her with evidence of him actually gambling. That's the only thing she'll take seriously. This is a nightmare, Liam."

"I know. Listen, Ryan and his girlfriend were set to go to Miami for a weekend away. He's offered to go to Boca instead so he can do some surveillance on Jacob. He's going to put a GPS tracker on his car and watch where he goes."

"I thought those were illegal?" asked Mike.

"For cops they're illegal, but he's a private investigator and he plays things right up to the edge of legalities. He has untraceable throwaway GPS units. Sometimes it's best not to ask too many questions. We just want to find out what's going on." Fr. Liam waited for Mike's go-ahead.

"Tell him I want him to do the surveillance. Have him send me the bill. Actually, I have a friend who can get a room for them at the Boca Raton Resort. His girlfriend will love it. I'll pay for the hotel and his bill. I want to know for sure if Jacob is gambling and if there's another woman around."

Fr. Liam heard two or three bangs and knew it was his brother banging the phone in anger. "Relax, Mike. You don't want your blood pressure to go through the roof. Let's see what comes up. Ryan will be going tomorrow, so we'll know right away."

"God, I'm so mad. He's been cheating on Colleen, my little girl. She deserves better than this."

"Yes, she does. Let's see what comes up. If Ryan catches him gambling over the next four days, then you can tell her about it. If there's no gambling, then the issue is just the credit cards. Of course, there's the affair at the beginning of the marriage, but according to the legal papers, that's over now --"

"With the exception of paying her the $7500 back," said Mike.

"Yes, but that's not your problem. His gambling is your problem because Colleen may be too naïve to understand what this can lead to," said Fr. Liam.

"Okay. That's the plan. We'll take it a day at a time."

Liam waited to see if there was more. There was.

"Who takes out $20,000 in credit cards? That decision alone should allow my daughter to have him institutionalized as mentally insane."

"The jumpy knee could have been worry over money or even over this lawsuit," said Fr. Liam.

"I knew it was something, but I never dreamed he would do this. Colleen is trying to get pregnant. If she does, she'll be trapped with this monster," said Mike.

"No, she won't be. But listen, in four days Ryan will find out if he's gambling at the casino, at least this coming weekend. He'll be watching him for four days. We'll figure out what else has to be done after that."

"Okay. Tell him to do everything he can and send me all the bills. I've got to calm down; otherwise, Maria will know something is up," said Mike.

"Talk later," said Fr. Liam.

"Okay. I'll do a few laps in the pool to work off my anger," said Mike, before he hung up.

Fr. Liam went back into Ryan's office and took a seat.

"Okay, my brother wants to go forward with the surveillance this weekend. He knows someone at the Boca Raton Resort and he'll get the hotel room for you. He said to send him the bill for everything else."

"What did he say about the lawsuit and the other woman?"

"He took it all in, but he was banging the phone in anger. My brother has a bit of a temper, but he's focused on the gambling right now. He's afraid Colleen may have been talked into getting the additional credit cards. That's why he wants evidence that Jacob is gambling again, if he is. Of course, if he's with any other women, he wants that too. He's pretty mad, but we'll know more after you surveil him for four days.

"So do you need anything else from me, Ryan?"

"I need a picture of Jacob and Colleen so that I can know what he looks like ahead of time. I need Colleen's picture to see if he's with her or someone else."

"I have those right here. I took pictures of them on Mother's Day. Let me text you a couple of them. You've met Mike already, right?"

"Yes, he golfed with us at the Knights tournament."

"That's right. I'll text you the pictures of Colleen and Jacob."

"I've got his license plate number. He drives a Le Baron. I notice his license plate spells out 'Hi Roller'."

"What do you mean?" asked Fr. Liam.

"'H1R01R' reads as 'Hi Rolr', you know 'High Roller' as in big gambler."

"It's funny that a guy who washed out in bankruptcy still sees himself as a high roller."

## Two Hours Later - 6PM
## Boca Raton, FL

When Colleen arrived at her mother's house, her dad was finishing his laps in the swimming pool. Her mother prepared three plates of fried chicken, potato salad and broccoli. This would be the night they would drop into Jacob's office afterhours.

"We'll eat out at the pool with your father and then we'll say we're going to the mall. If we tell your father we're snooping on your husband, he'll assume the worst and just add this to his arsenal of snide remarks somehow." Colleen agreed that he didn't need any additional free ammunition. Shopping at the mall for upcoming birthday gifts would be the cover story.

Colleen greeted her dad with a big hug and kiss. He seemed happy to see her but also preoccupied. Her mother mentioned to her that since she agreed to become a snowbird, Mike had stopped moping around the house. He even put away his Summer Glen brochure.

"I didn't know you were coming over," said Mike.

"I only found out at 5:00 that Colleen was coming for dinner tonight, and I wanted it to be a surprise for you," said Maria.

"To what do we owe this pleasure?" asked Mike.

"Jacob is working late and Mom and I are going shopping at the mall after we're done," said Colleen.

"I see. Well, that sounds nice. You'll get a little mother-daughter time together. Be careful at that mall. Those places are a haven for crime."

"We will," said Maria, looking at Colleen and half smiling. "We'll be very careful."

They finished their dinner with Mike around 6:45 and decided to leave for the mall. Once inside Maria's car, they began their drive over to Jacob's office.

"We can't just drop by. We'll need an excuse," said Colleen.

They both thought a minute.

"I've got one. We were having dinner at Houston's and you mentioned to me that Jacob worked right across the street and I wanted to see his office. How's that?" asked Maria.

"I guess that'll work," said Colleen.

"We'll stop at Houston's and get a coffee to go for him; that will confirm the story. We'll tell him we decided to stop by to see his office and bring him coffee for a long night," said Maria.

"Okay. That's good. You seem good at this, Mom."

"I used to spy on your father before we were married. This brings back such memories."

"Did you ever catch him doing anything?" asked Colleen.

"No, I never did. We grew up in Fort Lauderdale and at that time, there was a big group of girls and guys who were all friends. We were all dating one or another of this big group. So we would find out where the guys were going. Then all us girls would go there and literally spy on them from behind the bushes. They used to catch us half the time, but that was the fun of it." Maria laughed as she remembered crazy times from her own youth.

"I wish I grew up in earlier times. I think those times were easier," said Colleen. "Marsha wishes she was born in the late 1940s, early 1950s. I'm beginning to see her point."

"But we had to live through the 1960s and they were turbulent times too. Every generation has its challenges. When we drop off Jacob's coffee and we see him fast at work, this will put your mind to rest about his working late." Maria glanced over at Colleen as she drove.

"I guess," said Colleen.

"Don't you think it will put your mind at ease? This is a random night that he says he's working late. We'll see how many others are working along with him, and what it all looks like there after 5:00. I know it will put your mind at rest."

As they got off the elevator on the 9th Floor, Colleen knew the way to Jacob's office from her earlier dating days. As they exited the elevator, she saw a twenty-something woman walking towards the elevator they just exited. Colleen noticed she wore the same shade of lipstick that she found in her husband's car.

When she noticed the lipstick, she locked eyes with the woman. She could swear the woman looked at her in a suspicious way. Or was she imagining it? Was this another sign of her paranoia? She glanced at her mother who seemed oblivious to this other woman. She concluded it was her paranoia.

They walked down the hallway to Jacob's office and no one else was around. His office was empty.

"No one's here," said Colleen. She walked around the office and went behind Jacob's desk. His desk was on the end of a string of about seven u-shaped desk areas. Each desk had four computer screens all linked together, classic stock-trading style. She looked out the wall of windows behind his desk area and saw his car parked in the usual spot. "He's not here, but his car is in its spot."

233

"Well, he's probably in the men's room or had to go somewhere," said Maria. "If his car is here, he's in the building. Let's sit down. He'll be right back."

At that point, a thirty-something guy dressed in a shirt and tie wandered into the office from a second doorway. He seemed startled to see strangers in the office. "Can I help you?"

"Hi, I'm Jacob's wife, Colleen, and this is my mother, Mrs. Mullens. We ate at Houston's and decided to drop by with coffee for Jacob. My mother wanted to see his office," said Colleen on cue.

"It's beautiful," said Maria. "He told us all about the merger and we wanted to see all the after-hours action, but no one is here."

Gary frowned at the remark about the merger. "I'm Gary." He walked up to them. "I work with Jacob. Nice to meet you both." Gary shook both of their hands.

"We thought there would be more people working late with the merger," said Maria, nonchalantly.

"The merger? Uh, yeah, the merger, that's right. Well, we are busy, that's for sure. That may have been in Jacob's group." He had backed up again into the door jamb area of the office and looked down the hallway towards the elevator. "Well, he may have taken a walk as he was sitting in a meeting and at his computer all day. Sometimes he just needs to get a little exercise before he finishes up his second shift, as they say. He'll be back within ten minutes or so."

"Okay. We'll wait for him. The office is lovely," said Maria.

"Can I get you two a coffee or a soda?" asked Gary, who was checking his watch and looking down the hallway.

"Oh, no, we just finished dinner. We'll just wait a few minutes to see if he comes back," said Maria.

Gary nodded, and quickly took off. As Gary walked down the hallway, Colleen could see his head was down and his cell phone was out. She wondered if he was texting Jacob or was he just going on with his life? Again, she felt she was going right into paranoia.

Colleen sat in Jacob's desk chair and Maria sat on a couch that was off to the side of the desk area.

"I expected more action with the merger talk. Gary seemed a little unsure about the merger, didn't he? Do they work in groups?" asked Maria.

"I never heard him say anything about groups. Maybe Gary isn't a trader. He didn't say what his job was." Colleen had a nervous and uneasy feeling but it all started to feel like general paranoia. She had lost faith in her radar.

"I'm going to ask him about it when he comes," said Maria.

"Are you suspicious about him not being here?" asked Colleen suddenly alarmed by where her mother was going with this.

"Not necessarily. But he did make it sound like working late was essential. And all this talk about mergers and new clients, I just expected more action, that's all," said Maria. "I'm sure he'll explain it all when he comes back. Let's not let our imaginations run wild. He'll be back within 10 minutes or so. Maybe you can call him and let him know we stopped by."

"I texted him as soon as we walked in. He hasn't replied yet."

Colleen got up from Jacob's chair and began to pace around the office. She tried to manage her anxiety.

"I see they all work in a row. The chairs and workstations are very elaborate and they seem comfortable," said Maria. "They're fancier than what I remember from watching those wall street movies.

"It's a nice office, Colleen." Pointing to an alcove with a long library table and chairs, Maria said, "This must be where he has the meetings that he talks about."

Colleen stood up and looked out the window to see if she saw him walking anywhere. "Do you think he's really walking?"

"I have no idea. We'll know in a few minutes. Why don't you call him? He may not have seen the text."

Colleen called Jacob but it went to voice mail. She didn't leave a message. He called about four minutes later.

"Hey, I just got a call from Gary that my wife and mother-in-law were in my office. What's up?"

"We ate at Houston's Restaurant and I mentioned to her that you worked right across the street. She insisted that we get you a coffee and drop by so she could see your office."

"You're so sweet. I went for a walk and I'm on my way back now. I'll be there in about 10 minutes. If I knew you were coming, I would have stayed. I left just before you arrived. We probably were moving in opposite elevators. I'll see you in a few minutes," said Jacob as he hung up.

"He's on his way. He said he left just as we came in and he'll be back in a couple of minutes."

Colleen was relieved -- at least for a few minutes. Five minutes later, the same twenty-something with the burgundy lipstick popped her head into Jacob's office. She said, "Oh, I wasn't expecting to see two women in his office. Do you know where Jacob is?"

"He's on his way back from taking a walk," said Colleen.

"Okay, I'll catch him later," said the girl.

"Who should we tell him stopped by," called Maria after the girl.

"Sandra. Sandra from down the hall. There's two Sandras that work here. He knows me as Sandra from down the hall."

Colleen got a weird feeling from *Sandra-from-down-the-hall*. She wondered whether this *Sandra-from-down-the-hall* was also the owner of the burgundy lipstick. Or was Sandra one of the many people who rode in Jacob's car and dropping her lipstick was just an innocent happenstance like Jacob suggested? Colleen was pacing back and forth in his office thinking about all of it.

Maria and Colleen looked at each other when they heard the elevator bell go off. Two seconds later, Jacob entered the room with his arms out to greet Maria first, and then Colleen.

"I just missed you. You should have texted me you were coming," said Jacob.

"We didn't think of it until we were finished eating and we took a chance that you would be in. Mom wanted to see your office, which is beautiful, by the way. This is all new since the last time I was here," said Colleen.

"Here is your coffee, it's sort of iced-coffee now," said Maria, teasingly.

"No problem. I have a microwave in the kitchen which is on the other end, and I'll be happy I have this in an hour or so."

"So how was your dinner?" asked Jacob, as he sat down on the couch next to Maria.

"It was wonderful. We decided to get together since she had a free night. It worked out well, right, Colleen?"

"Yeah, it was great. Where do you go walking, down Federal Highway?" asked Colleen.

"Sometimes. This time I walked over to another building. After sitting for a long time, I need to stretch my legs and get some exercise. When it's too hot out, I walk the buildings under air conditioning." Jacob seemed to be in a good mood.

They visited with him for another fifteen minutes or so. Maria told him all about a condo she had her eye on. Colleen had Jacob's facial expressions under a suspicious-wife's microscope. He seemed relaxed and genuinely happy to see them. Colleen was participating in the small talk her mom and Jacob were making, but she was also distracted by her own thoughts. *This all confirms that I'm officially a paranoid schizophrenic.*

As they were leaving, Maria said, "Oh, by the way, we almost forgot, there was a Sandra from down the hall who was looking for you earlier."

239

"Did she say what she wanted?" asked Jacob.

"No, she said she would stop by later to see if you were still here."

"She's probably waiting for a report or some other work that's on our list of things to do. She does clerical work here," said Jacob.

They shared hugs and kisses as mother and daughter left his office. As luck would have it, as they walked up to the elevator and the doors opened, Sandra from down the hall with the burgundy lipstick got off and walked in the direction of Jacob's office.

They got into the elevator and Maria looked to Colleen for some feedback. "So what do you think? It makes sense that he leaves and walks and that's why his car would be here. I don't see anything out of the ordinary, do you?"

"No, I guess not," said Colleen. She had not shared the lipstick incident with her mother and she didn't want to go into it now. It was all speculation anyway.

"You don't sound convinced," said Maria.

"Well, we wanted to know if he was here and he was here. Yes, that confirms that he is where he says he is." Colleen looked down at her phone. As she looked up, she could tell her mother was studying her and knew there was something she wasn't saying.

"I wonder what your hesitation is all about. I wonder if there's something going on that you're not saying, Colleen."

Colleen didn't say anything and Maria let it go.

# CHAPTER 16

### One Day Later - 2PM
### Coral Springs, FL

IT WAS THURSDAY afternoon and they were down in Coral Springs on their weekend away. Angelica was looking out the front of Ryan's car window and looking back at Ryan, not saying anything.

"It's easy, Angelica. Just drop your handbag and I'll bend down to pick it up. You hover in front of me to give me cover. His car is right over there, the white Le Baron. As we walk up to it, I'll be on your right. Just drop your handbag by the side of his car, let me bend down to pick it up, and I can slip the GPS tracker under his wheel well. So try to drop it by the back wheel," said Ryan as he and Angelica sat in his car.

"What if we get caught?" asked Angelica.

"We won't get caught. I've done this a hundred times before. But there are 50 windows in his work building, all of which look out onto this parking lot. I need a little cover and you dropping your purse will be perfect."

"All right. Give me a minute to get up my nerve," said Angelica, as she smiled over at Ryan.

He kissed her cheek and said, "Take your time."

She sat one minute looking from the car to the windows. She then impulsively opened her car door, looking braver than she felt. Ryan got out on his side and came around to her and held out his arm. She took his arm and they both walked towards the car. Once they were close to Jacob's white Le Baron, by the back wheel, Angelica dropped her purse and Ryan bent down to retrieve it. He positioned himself between Jacob's car and the car next to him. He quickly slipped the magnetized GPS tracker into the wheel well area on the passenger side of Jacob's car. He then repositioned himself and gathered Angelica's few items that fell out of her purse, stood back up, and handed her the bag.

"Job well done, Sweetheart." Ryan kissed her on the cheek.

"Did I do okay?"

"You did better than okay. I'm sure every eye that may have been watching was immediately drawn to you, so you gave me the best cover."

"You're so sweet." They walked towards the building.

"Now what do we do, Ryan?"

244

"I want to see what kind of security the building has, so let's go inside."

They proceeded into the back glass doors of the building and no one stopped them. There were no locked doors and apparently anyone could enter at will. This would be perfect when he came back Friday night.

Once they got to the main lobby, Ryan looked on the marquee and saw Sorrell Investment Group. They were up on the ninth floor. They took the elevator up to the ninth floor. Once they exited, it was possible to enter the offices and speak to a receptionist.

Standing outside the office, Ryan said, "We can go now."

"That's it?"

"Yep, I know I can access the office, so we'll watch the GPS tracker and see what happens. Then I'll plan the next move when I see if or when he goes somewhere."

They left the office complex and drove fifteen minutes east. They drove into the Boca Raton Resort and Club, which was an exclusive hotel that sat right on the Intercoastal and the ocean. As they pulled into the resort, Angelica was impressed, which was not always easy to do.

"Oh my God, Ryan, this is so gorgeous. How did you get this hotel for us?"

"Mike Mullens made the reservations. He knows someone from this place and he got the room for us. He's paid for our stay for the entire weekend. He's Fr. Liam's brother. He's the one who we're doing the surveillance for."

"It's so beautiful. I can't wait to see the pool and the beaches. This is even better than the one we picked out in Miami."

"He also forwarded a pass for you to get a spa treatment if and when I have to leave to follow the son-in-law."

"Oh my God, look at this fountain and the Spanish architecture. It's so gorgeous," said Angelica. She opened a browser on her smart phone. "I've pulled up pictures on the internet. It's beautiful. I can't wait. We're going to have so much fun, Ryan. This is so exciting."

Ryan valet-parked and a bellhop took in the suitcases. They were escorted to their room, which was a suite right on the water. They could see the marina below their balcony.

After the porter left them, they embraced and kissed. They looked out over the water. Ryan could tell Angelica was happy and excited.

"So are you trying to find out if the guy is cheating on his wife?" asked Angelica.

"They think he's gambling again. He had a gambling problem that he allegedly put behind him before they got married. But there's been some financial action going on that makes them think he's gambling again. So I'm going to be monitoring the GPS to see where he goes."

"Does he gamble online? How will you catch him gambling online?" asked Angelica.

"He works five minutes away from the Seminole Casino so he may gamble online but he may gamble in the casino too. There were charges on one of the credit cards for the Seminole Casino, so we know he at least went there once. I'm going to surveil him on Thursday and Friday to see if he goes to the casino."

"Maybe we can go to the casino too," said Angelica. Ryan wasn't surprised that she would be interested in going to a casino with all the flashing lights, the drinking, and the gambling. "We can go on Friday. If I have to go tonight or tomorrow, that's when you can get your spa treatment. If the GPS shows him moving, I will need to see where he winds up."

Ryan opened his GPS tracker to watch for any movement of Jacob's car, but it remained parked in his work lot. Angelica got settled into the room and took a nap so she would be refreshed to go out later for dinner. No surprises there.

It was a little after four o'clock when Ryan pulled into the parking lot to start surveilling Jacob Kessler. Angelica called him about four-thirty asking him what time he would be back.

"I'm going to stay here until 6:30. I made reservations at the restaurant downstairs, the one you said you liked, so I'll be back by seven. We'll have a nice dinner and we can take a nice walk along the Intercoastal if you want," said Ryan.

"I'm walking around now and they have all kinds of bars and little places where people gather. I'll find something exciting to do after dinner."

"Okay. I'll see you later then."

"I love you, Ryan."

"I love you too," said Ryan. He still felt like he was biding his time with Angelica and it was beginning to feel dishonest. He was still toying with the idea that Fr. Liam had planted in his mind that maybe if she knew she would lose him she would stop drinking. But somehow, he couldn't envision that happening. He put the issue aside and went back to surveillance.

Ten minutes later, a couple walked out of the back door of the building. The guy looked exactly like the picture of Jacob Kessler. The woman with him was not his wife but was a young attractive woman with red hair and dark red lipstick. They walked together like they could be a couple or they could be friendly co-employees; it was hard to tell. Ryan continued watching them as Jacob walked her to what turned out to be her car.

They both got into her car, which was a red Celica. Once inside the car, they talked for a few minutes. Ryan had a newspaper open and used it to disguise his looking at the car repeatedly. He remembered Fr. Liam telling him the first private investigator never saw Jacob's car move from the lot. He wondered if he went to the casino or somewhere else with this woman. He grabbed another GPS tracker from his glove box. Luckily, one was already out of the packaging.

He put the newspaper down, recorded the GPS tracking number, put the GPS tracker in his pocket and exited his car. He was four parking spaces away from the woman's car. He put his car hood up and looked at the motor from a few different angles. Then he went over to the Celica and knocked on the passenger side window where Jacob was sitting. It was definitely Jacob.

Jacob scowled at him but did not make any effort to talk to him. Ryan pointed to his car. Jacob hit the window button, but the car motor was not on. Ryan stood just in front of the hinge area of the passenger door, so when Jacob opened the door, Ryan conveniently fell down. On his way back up, he slipped the GPS tracker under the side panel of the woman's car.

"Sorry about that," said Jacob. "Do you need something?"

Ryan stood back up and said, "My battery is dead. I was wondering if you had jumper cables."

"No, we don't. Sorry," said Jacob, without even asking the woman.

"Okay, thanks anyway. I'll have to call AAA." Ryan turned and walked back to his car. He put the front hood down in case he had to leave quickly, but he continued sitting in his car watching. He went back to pretending to read the newspaper. The newspaper was from three years ago and was only a prop.

Ryan saw the couple kissing now. He wasn't positioned well enough to get a photo of them. He hoped with the two GPS trackers working, he would get another chance to catch them together.

Within about fifteen minutes, Jacob left the Celica and went into his own car. They both left the parking lot. Ryan put the newspaper back in his box of props and made a few notes in his notebook, including the make and model of the woman's car. He would do a license search on her later.

In the meantime, he went back to the Boca Resort. He and Angelica had dinner at the restaurant and they wound up at the night club for drinks. He had two drinks and Angelica had about six. When they got back to the room, Angelica was particularly passionate and romantic. Ryan, although sober, was still easily lured by Angelica. He didn't have enough to drink to completely forget about the disconnect between them. Instead, he now felt how almost addicted to Angelica he was sexually. This confirmed his doubts about everything else that had come up recently.

# CHAPTER 17

### One Day Later - 1:30 PM
### Boca Raton, FL

FRIDAY MORNING Angelica was hung-over and she was slow getting out of bed. They went out for a drive along A1A which ran along the ocean in Palm Beach County. They stopped for a late breakfast along the way and she asked for a coffee with a shot of Anisette.

"It's kind of early to start drinking, Angelica."

"Listen, I have a hangover and the shot of Anisette will help get rid of it. You were drinking too, Ryan."

Ryan chose to let it end there. He was avoiding all conflict until Mia's wedding. After the wedding, he could raise whatever issues needed to be raised.

They finished their breakfast. After two coffees with two shots of Anisette, Angelica did make a full recovery. Her energy and excitement seemed to return and things felt better. They began their drive back to the resort and Ryan stopped by a roadside vendor along the way. He bought a bouquet of flowers. He gave them to Angelica and said, "These are for you, Angelica, because you are so beautiful, but …"

"But what?" She took the flowers into her hands and started arranging them in the bouquet. "But what?"

"But I may need to borrow them during my surveillance."

"What are you going to do on the surveillance with flowers? I want to come with you today."

"Really? I thought you hated coming on surveillance with me. I have a feeling because it's Friday that he and this woman will either go gambling or they'll go somewhere else. It may be a longer night of surveillance. If nothing happens, we can go to the casino in Coral Springs. How about that?" asked Ryan knowing she would be up for a casino.

"That's great. I love casinos. Is it just a small casino or is it the size of the ones in Las Vegas?" asked Angelica.

"I have no idea, but once you get inside, they all look and sound the same."

Ryan was ready at four o'clock but Angelica was still putting her makeup on. She was dressing for a casino because that would be their destination after the surveillance. Ryan had tracked both GPS units on and off all day, and both cars were stationary in the workplace parking lot. Angelica was finally ready to leave at 4:30. It would be a late start, but based on Thursday, they didn't leave the building until six, so he should be okay.

As Ryan came close to Jacob's office building, suddenly the GPS for the red Celica began to move. It went four blocks away and pulled into what appeared to be the area of the Casino. Ryan was unable to get an exact reading as he was driving in traffic.

At the next light, he examined the GPS tracking app and, sure enough, the Celica had pulled into the casino. The car was now stationary. This meant she may be staying at the casino, not just dropping someone off.

Ryan switched his route to go directly to the casino. He did pass Jacob's employment parking lot. His car was still stationary in his usual space.

"Where do my flowers come into play?" asked Angelica.

"I didn't expect this woman's car to leave work and drive directly to the casino, so I won't need them now. She left early tonight and has gone to the casino. If he's not with her, then I'll have to use the flowers to go roaming around his office. But I believe we may have gotten lucky."

"Do you love me, Ryan? I feel like you're pulling away from me lately," said Angelica.

255

"Everything is fine, Angelica. It's fine. I've just been extra busy with work." Ryan could feel Angelica looking at him. He glanced over and smiled. He petted her hair gently. "Everything is fine, Angelica."

He pulled into the casino and drove the parking lot looking for the red Celica. He found it in five minutes. He parked as close to it as he was able.

As he turned off the car, he turned to Angelica. "Okay. So here is the initial plan. We'll go into the casino and we'll need to walk the entire place until we find the woman who owns the red car. Her name is Sandra Sinclair. She has red hair, blue eyes, is about five-four and thin."

"Do you have a picture of her?"

"No, this info is from her driver's license, plus I saw her from a distance in the parking lot yesterday. Her hair is not kind of red, it's really red, like neon red. If you see her, you'll know it's her."

"What happens when we see them?"

"I'll tell you our next move when I figure out where they are and what they're doing. If they're just gambling, and there are other people watching, we'll join the group. If there are no watchers, then I'll have to orchestrate something else, but we'll have time to plan. I'll either whisper to you, or I'll gently guide you with a little push as to what we do when, okay?"

"Okay. This is exciting," said Angelica with a smile.

Once inside the casino, they made their way through all the slot machines and over to the blackjack tables. As they passed through the glittering, blinking slot machines, against the backdrop of sparkling gold lamé wallpaper, Ryan could see Angelica was in her glory. He also noticed that every male eye screeched to a halt and landed on her as soon as she came into view. There was no sneaking around with her. She captured all the attention in the room.

Sitting at one of the busier blackjack tables, Ryan spotted both Jacob and Sandra, the redhead. "There they are, don't be obvious."

"I see what you mean by the really red hair. It's dreadful," said Angelica.

"There's a few people behind them. I have a button camera on, so I need you to stand behind him while I meander over on the side where I can photograph them sitting together. You call me over after three or four minutes. Then I'll come behind them and if he wins, you clap and say *congratulations*. Act a little drunk, but not too drunk."

"I could use a drink to make it authentic, Ryan."

"Let me get a few pictures first, and then I'll get you a drink."

They both got into position, and Ryan began taking snapshots with his button camera. Sandra was touching Jacob's face and hair. She seemed like she was the one pursuing him, but he was lapping it up like a dog who was never pet before.

Ryan got photos of Jacob sitting at the gambling table and placing bets with his chips. After another twenty minutes, he got Jacob kissing Sandra on the mouth after a sizable win.

Ryan and Angelica had walked away and they were at the bar now getting drinks.

"Did you get enough pictures?" asked Angelica.

"Yes, I did. I would like to get video, but my video body cam is in the car. Once the drinks come, I need you to keep an eye on them from here. I'll put on a body cam and a different shirt and get video of them kissing, if I can." He left to get his body video camera.

Angelica took her and Ryan's drinks and walked back to Jacob's gambling table. As she approached from the side of the table, Jacob caught her eye. She thought maybe he was onto her and Ryan as he was holding her gaze. But within two minutes, she could tell he was giving her the eye, trying to get some flirtation going. She half smiled at him. He continued looking at her in between watching the game.

Suddenly, she got nervous because she wouldn't know what to do if he started talking to her, especially in some flirtatious way. She walked behind the next table to disengage from him. She kept glancing over his way occasionally as she waited for Ryan to return.

Ryan came back and looked in the bar area but didn't see Angelica. She approached him and caught him off guard. "Stop walking. Here's your drink. Let me tell you something. After you left, I walked over there and he caught my eye. He started flirting, so I left and came to watch over at this other table. He's already cheating on his wife, and now he's looking to double-time his mistress. I don't know if I should go over there again."

"You'll be with me. He won't do anything with me there. Let's go over. Just don't look at him. I want to get some video of him gambling and if I can get him carrying on with Sandra, then we'll be done. We'll have the rest of the weekend to ourselves."

Angelica hooked her arm through Ryan's arm and they walked behind a table or two and then again behind Jacob. He won another hand of blackjack. Sandra kissed him and he kissed her back, all right on video.

"You're on a streak," said Ryan to Jacob from behind the gambling table.

"Yeah, finally. I'm on a roll right now. As soon as I start losing, I'm walking away."

"That's the smart thing to do," said Ryan, as he looked over at Angelica.

They hung around for another few hands and after getting three kisses on video, Ryan had more than enough for Mike Mullens.

Ryan and Angelica sat at a blackjack table of their own for about ten minutes before Angelica wanted to go to the slots. They spent a while at the slot machines where Angelica won $50 and then lost it.

They enjoyed the rest of the night both at the casino and back at the hotel. All clarity was still leaning towards breaking up, but Ryan was holding onto the idea of sobriety for dear life.

# CHAPTER 18

### One Day Later - 12:00 PM
### Boca Raton, FL

SATURDAY MORNING Angelica went for her spa service and Ryan sat on the balcony of their room overlooking the marina. It was noon and Ryan sent a text message to Fr. Liam to call him if he had time to talk, that he had information about Colleen's husband.

Less than five minutes later, Fr. Liam called and could tell right away that it was not going to be good news. "Did you see or find out anything?"

"Yes, I did unfortunately." Ryan gave Fr. Liam a minute to brace himself. "He left his job with a woman by the name of Sandra Sinclair, in her red Celica. They both went to the Seminole Casino and were playing blackjack."

"So he is gambling. That's not good," said Fr. Liam.

"And he was kissing the girl he was with, so I believe he's having an affair too."

"When you mentioned he went with a woman, I had a feeling. My poor niece will be devastated. They're only married nine months. He couldn't be faithful for a full year?"

"I think she was groomed for this marriage," said Ryan.

"What do you mean?" asked Fr. Liam.

"Well, you told me they only dated for a few months before they got married. Now he has opened credit in her name. He borrowed money from another woman, who claimed she didn't know he was married when she loaned him the $7500. That seems to indicate he was still gambling the entire time. Plus he was involved with another woman as well. Maybe Colleen was set up for this marriage all along," said Ryan. Once it was out, he hoped he didn't overstep the line by suggesting this.

"That's interesting. I know my brother gave them $20,000 as a house down payment for a wedding gift. Maybe Jacob knew this early on. Maybe he felt that there would be no downside to marrying her no matter how long it lasted," said Fr. Liam.

"Gamblers usually get used to leaning on the credit of the people around them. Unfortunately, they're also known to pull in unsuspecting women," said Ryan. "I wish I had better news, Father."

"It's the truth. He's cheating and he's gambling. I'll call my brother now. It's Saturday afternoon and he may be by himself. Thanks, Ryan. I wish it was better news too, but at least we know the truth about what's going on."

"Yes. I'll have a formal report with pictures and video available for you on Monday. Let me know if you need it before then."

"Thanks again, Ryan."

As he hung up, he knew tell Fr. Liam had a hard call in front of him.

## Thirty minutes later - 12:30 PM
## Ocala, FL

The light of day cascaded into Fr. Liam's rectory bedroom window. During the day, his bedroom had a peaceful feel to it. It was only at night that it took on a dark and gloomy atmosphere. It had been decorated by his predecessor from religious gifts he received throughout the years. The whole room had the feel of a Catholic gift store. The single bed had a plain missionary-style headboard. There was one small matching night table. As a widowed family man, it resembled a young child's room. But priests were single men who slept in single beds. He was still adjusting to the change in lifestyle.

He kept everything as it was when he moved in with one exception. There used to be a small bankers' desk lamp on the nightstand with a 60-watt bulb. The low light created a gallows' atmosphere. Fr. Liam replaced that lamp with an adjustable arm lamp that took up to a 150-watt bulb. Now he could read and see more than shadows.

The crucifix above his bed was a beautiful art piece that Fr. Liam recognized as South American. They were masters at painting the crucified Jesus in various shades of suffering.

The room had parquet flooring with a chevron design. The center of it was covered by a handmade beige carpet that was on Fr. Liam's list of things to replace.

He sat on his bed and called his brother.

"Hey, Liam. How are you?"

"Are you alone or with Maria?" asked Fr. Liam.

"Alone right now, but Maria is just out at the store. Why? Have you heard anything?"

"I heard from Ryan today about Jacob."

"Did he find out anything?"

"Plenty. Are you ready?" asked Fr. Liam, giving his brother a chance to brace himself.

"He's gambling. He caught him gambling?"

"Yes, he was gambling at the Seminole Casino in Coral Springs and . . ." hesitated Fr. Liam.

"And?"

"And he was with another woman who he was kissing. Ryan has video and pictures from all of it. The woman's name is Sandra Sinclair and apparently, she works with him."

"Oh, no. Colleen will be devastated."

Fr. Liam waited.

"That bastard! He couldn't be faithful for a year? They're newlyweds, for God's sake."

Fr. Liam heard the phone banging again. He waited until his brother was back on the line. "Colleen will be devastated.

"Who does this? What kind of a marriage is this?" asked Mike, still shocked but more angry.

Fr. Liam could tell Mike had expected to hear about the gambling, but the cheating caught him off guard. He knew his brother was overwhelmed with the extent of deceit. "It seems to me -- and Ryan was the one who suggested this -- that she may have been groomed for this marriage in order for him to get ahold of her money or credit. You need to find out from Colleen if the $20,000 wedding gift is still around," said Fr. Liam.

"Wait until I tell Maria. She'll be sick over this, especially with the cheating. When Colleen has complained about Jacob, Maria has been his greatest advocate."

265

Fr. Liam expected to hear his brother rant and rave, but he was quiet like the wind had been knocked out of him.

"What do you plan to do now?" asked Fr. Liam.

"I'll talk to Maria about it first. We'll have to tell Colleen what we found. She's trying to get pregnant. She needs to know about all of this. I pray to God she's not already pregnant."

"Let me know if you want me to come down there," Fr. Liam offered.

"Listen, I'll need the pictures and the video. I'm not sure how Maria will want to proceed with this. But we'll need to show Colleen proof because she'll automatically think we're being prejudiced or too harsh with him again," said Mike.

"I don't think so this time, Mike. I'll ask Ryan to send you pictures and the video if he has it ready now. He's still away and won't be back in his office until Monday."

"This is awful. All I can think of is how wounded, how brokenhearted my daughter will be. Between you and me, I hope she leaves him."

"You may want to point out to her that she may have been groomed for this marriage. But, of course, you shouldn't tell her that in the first discussion."

"I just heard Maria pull into the garage. I'll talk to her now. I'll let you know how it goes. Please pray for me --

266

pray for all of us. I'm sick to death over this." Mike hung up.

Fr. Liam prayed for all of them, especially for Colleen. She was still young and excited to be married and looking forward to starting a family. He knew within one day she would feel like she walked off the side of a cliff.

Maria came into the kitchen and put two bags of groceries and a bag from a big box store on the kitchen island. Before Mike went out to greet her, he checked his email and the pictures had not yet come through from Ryan.

Mike walked into the kitchen. "Did you go for a swim yet?" asked Maria.

"No, I didn't get a chance to swim. Listen, I need to talk to you about something."

"Oh? Is something wrong?" Maria put her fruit and vegetables from the grocery bags into the refrigerator. Mike could tell she was trying to read his mood. He knew she could tell something was up.

"Where do you want to talk?" asked Maria.

"Are you done putting everything away? This is going to take a good ten minutes or so."

"Everything else doesn't need refrigeration. Let's go in the living room," said Maria.

"Let's go in the bedroom," said Mike.

"Okay." She turned very serious right before Mike's eyes.

He took her hand and led her into their bedroom. He sat down on the bed and she sat next to him. "You're scaring me, Mike."

"I found out that Jacob is gambling again at a casino in Coral Springs," said Mike.

"You did? How did you find that out?" asked Maria.

"I hired a private investigator to follow him, do surveillance on him."

"That was a couple of weeks ago," said Maria.

"No, this was another private investigator that Liam knows. He's younger and told Liam that gamblers tend to use the credit of the people around them. He suggested we do a credit check on Colleen, which I had him do." Mike could see Maria bracing herself.

"There are four credit cards that have been opened in Colleen's name in the last two months. Ryan hacked into one of them and saw charges for the Seminole Casino in Coral Springs. That's the casino that's close to his job."

"Oh, my God. Okay, so he's going to have to stop gambling again and go to those Gambler's Anonymous meetings," said Maria. "Colleen said he stopped going with all that was going on at work so --"

"There's more," said Mike.

"More?"

"Yes. A woman is suing him in small claims court for a loan of $7500 that she made to him when they were dating. They dated until this woman found out he was married," said Mike.

"Ah," gasped Maria. This was the first actual sound of alarm Mike heard from her. "This couldn't be someone he was seeing in the last nine months," said Maria, as she shook her head.

"Yes, it is. The dates of the loan in the court papers are dates during his marriage to our daughter," said Mike.

Maria burst out crying and covered her face with both hands. Mike knew she would be upset. He wasn't even halfway through Jacob's marital crimes and Maria was already in tears. He decided to take a break.

He wrapped his arms around Maria and held her close. She cried for a few minutes but he could tell she was attempting to get her composure back. "What are we going to do?"

"We'll have a family intervention with Colleen. That's what we have to do," said Mike. "They're trying to get pregnant and she needs to know about this first."

"She's going to be heartsick. They went to see one of the houses together this morning with the real estate agent."

Maria grabbed for tissues from a tissue box on her nightstand and sat back down. She wiped her eyes and sat speechless.

"Do you know if Colleen and Jacob put the $20,000 that we gave them for the house somewhere safe? Did she mention to you where it is?"

"Yes, she said they put it in a joint account that they nicknamed *the house account*. They were adding more monies into it for nursery items as well."

"Let's hope he didn't gamble that money away," said Mike.

"I don't think she would let him do that. That would have caused a big fight. I'm sure that would have made its way into one of our discussions, so let's hope that money is safe for them."

Mike heard his phone beep indicating he received emails. Ryan forwarded three pictures of Jacob kissing Sandra. He also sent a link to a password-protected page on his website that had the raw video uploaded and ready to view. Mike read the email and showed the pictures of Jacob kissing the other woman to Maria.

"Oh my God, Mike, is this the woman he borrowed the money from?" shrieked Maria.

"No, that was another woman. This is a new woman he's cheating with. She's a coworker of Jacob's –"

"Maybe this was taken before he was married, while he was in his gambling stage. Where did the PI get the photos? Maybe he found them online and they're old," said Maria, in full denial.

"He took them last night at the Seminole Casino in Coral Springs. He went down to Boca with his girlfriend to do the surveillance and caught Jacob leaving the job with this woman. He followed them and caught them gambling and Jacob kissing her. He's caught red-handed, Maria."

"How can this be? How can he do this? They're not even married one year," cried Maria.

"I want you to listen to me, Maria. I want you to calm down and listen to me."

Maria calmed down and waited for Mike to begin.

"He claimed bankruptcy before he met Colleen. You told me his parents paid off some of the bankruptcy in order to get him through this. He met Colleen during this payoff period. They only dated three months before he started talking marriage. It's possible he groomed her for this

271

marriage, knowing it would be a disposable marriage. In the meantime, he could get ahold of her credit, maybe get this house money, and continue his life of gambling and carousing."

Maria had her hands covering her nose and mouth and she was shaking her head negatively trying to ward off what Mike was saying.

"I believe he loved her, Mike. He loved her and she loved and loves him." Her brows knit together and her eyes were closed. She was in a defensive position, like she couldn't accept his suggestion that a plan this sinister could have been done to their daughter.

It took Mike a few minutes to figure out how to enter the password to log into Ryan's website page. Once on the page, he clicked on one of the three videos. He shared the screen for he and Maria to view together. They watched as Jacob hooted and hollered about winning. Right before their eyes, they saw him kiss Sandra on the mouth. She was cheering him along the entire time and draping herself all over him.

The next video was from the side of the table looking onto them. This time Jacob lost the hand but Sandra kissed him on the cheek. He reached over and kissed her on the lips again and turned and waited for the next deal.

Before Mike was able to click on the third video, Maria stood up and said, "I've seen enough. He's not even the same person. His personality is completely different there.

Who is he?" She left the room and went into the bathroom. Mike knew she needed a moment to absorb the shock.

She was in the bathroom for a good five to eight minutes. There were only sniffles and silence. Mike knew she was absorbing the shock and her mind was wandering everywhere. She came out, composed herself and said, "We should tell her alone, without Jacob first. Don't you think that would be best?"

"Yes, I do. Call her and tell her we want to talk to her by herself," said Mike.

"She'll ask me what we want to talk to her about. What will I tell her?" asked Maria.

Mike thought a minute and said, "Tell her it's about the future."

"That will make her very suspicious."

"Maria, it's best if she braces herself a little bit when she comes here, so don't worry about her being a little suspicious. There's no easy way to tell her any of this."

"You're going to have to do most of the talking, Mike, because I'm going to break down as soon as I see her heart break, which it will."

"I know, Maria. I'm not looking forward to this, but she needs to know who she married before she gets pregnant."

"What if she's already pregnant?" asked Maria.

273

"We'll cross that bridge if and when we get there.

"Call her now and ask her when she can come over by herself," said Mike.

While she and Mike still sat on the bed together, Maria called Colleen and acted as nonchalantly as she could. "Your father and I were talking this afternoon and there are a few things we want to go over with you concerning the future. We'd like to talk to you alone, without Jacob. Can you come tomorrow maybe?"

"About the future? What do you mean? About a future grandchild?" asked Colleen, excitedly.

"Well, we don't want to give too much away on the phone. So just let us know when you can come by yourself." Maria was holding her breath.

"Okay, well Jacob is here, so I can come tomorrow. What time are you going to be home from mass?" asked Colleen.

"We can be here by 12:45. Do you want to come over at 1:00?" asked Maria. Mike was leaning into Maria's phone trying to hear both sides of the conversation.

"Yeah, I can be there by one. But I'm dying to know. Can I come now?"

"Now?" said Maria out loud to see what Mike thought. He nodded his head affirmatively.

"Yes, now would work. Come now," said Maria.

"Okay, I'll be right over," said Colleen.

Maria hung up and said to Mike. "She's so excited. She thinks it has to do with the future grandchildren, like we have a gift for her. I can't face this. She's coming over right now."

"There's no easy way to do this, Maria. Tomorrow would be just as hard. Actually, we both would have been dreading it the whole time, so now is better. Just brace yourself for the hardest parent-child discussion we've ever had. Pray that all will go as well as can be expected." They both paced around waiting, both silent in prayer.

Colleen hung up and said to Jacob, who was sitting on the couch with her. "They want to talk to me alone, and it's about the future. I think they have grandchildren on their minds. They must have come up with something about a future baby. I can't wait until tomorrow so I'm going to find out what it is now."

"Do you think they'll give us money for the future baby?" asked Jacob.

"I don't know. Either money or a big crib or something. I don't know what they could mean by saying *about the future* but I'm about to find out."

"Okay. Are we going to eat in or out tonight?" asked Jacob.

"Well, are you still tired from working and drinks from last night? We can stay in and have hamburgers and fries," said Colleen, as she gathered her handbag and pulled out her keys.

"Yeah, that'll work . I'll see you later, Honey." He smiled at her.

"See you later. She bent down and kissed him and he kissed her back." He smiled again like all was well.

Off she went to find out what surprise her parents had in store for her about the future. As she drove the familiar route to her parents' house, she tried guessing around a future baby. Was it a nursery decorating package of some kind? Was it a college fund? That must be it, a college fund; that would be something they would discuss about the future. She felt assured it would be a college fund they wanted to set up. She thought about how blessed she was with such doting and generous parents.

Mike opened the door as he saw Colleen exit her car. She was smiling ear to ear as she entered. Mike could tell she was reading them and they did not match her level of excitement.

"Have a seat, Colleen," said Mike, as she entered their house.

"What's going on?" asked Colleen, now only half smiling. She walked into the living room and saw her mother sitting on the couch. Her mother didn't look at her.

"There's no easy way to tell you what we have to tell you right now, Colleen."

"Is one of you sick?" Colleen blurted out, suddenly alarmed.

"No, we're not sick. Have a seat, Colleen," said Mike.

Colleen sat on the tufted chair across from the couch and placed her handbag down by her feet. She crossed her hands on her lap but never took her eyes off her parents. Her smile was now gone.

Mike and Maria sat across from her on the couch. Maria looked at Mike to start. "We've found out that your husband was at the Seminole Casino last night, so he's gambling again," said Mike. He waited to see her reaction.

"Oh, no. I asked him a week ago if he was still going to the Gambler's Anonymous meetings. He got really mad and told me he was too busy with work to keep going. He's

277

supposed to go to the meetings every week. I guess this is a slip then."

"Did you open four credit cards in your name recently?" asked Mike.

Colleen frowned deeply and said, "No, why? What's going on here?"

"I had a feeling Jacob was gambling again. When I saw him on Mother's Day, his demeanor was off and he seemed nervous and anxious. So I had a private investigator do a credit check on you and Jacob. He found four credit cards taken out in your name in the last month or two. They were opened on or around the same day," said Mike.

"Well, I didn't take out credit cards in my name, so that has to be identity theft," said Colleen. Mike could see she was extremely nervous at the prospect of having credit opened in her name. But she also lapsed right into denial. He was thinking about which avenue he should go down first.

"What does this have to do with the future?" asked Colleen.

"Well, I believe that Jacob opened those credit cards in your name, Colleen."

"Jacob would never do anything like that. You're wrong." Colleen looked over to her mother and Mike could see a look of betrayal register on his daughter's face.

278

"There's no easy way to tell you this, Colleen."

Maria said to Mike, "Show her the pictures from Friday night."

Mike showed Colleen the first picture of Jacob sitting next to Sandra from work at the blackjack table with chips in front of him. He was smiling at Sandra. Colleen walked over and sat next to her father.

"Here's the first picture of him and his co-worker Sandra . . ."

Colleen looked at the picture and looked closer. It was the same woman she and her mother had passed in the hallway when they were in Jacob's office. That burgundy lipstick was unmistakable.

". . . and here he is after he won the hand." Mike flipped to the next picture which showed Jacob kissing Sandra on the lips.

Colleen covered her face, much like her mother did earlier, and began to cry. "Oh, no, I knew something was not right. I knew he was different." She looked up at her mother who had moved across from them as her and her dad looked at the pictures. "I kept telling you that he was different, that I felt that he didn't love me anymore." She again covered her face and cried.

Mike put his arm around her and she leaned in against his shoulder. "I can't believe it. He has a girlfriend. He's cheating on me behind my back. I just left him and he's acting like nothing is wrong, like he's so happy."

Maria came over and knelt in front of her as her father held her. "You gave him the benefit of the doubt, Colleen. You tried to compromise and it turned out that your deeper feelings were correct. He was cheating on you," said Maria.

"Can you text me that picture of him kissing that girl?" asked Colleen who was now getting angry.

"I don't know how to text, but I can forward the email from Ryan to you. That, I know how to do," and he did, although it took a solid five minutes.

Once retrieved from her dad, Colleen texted the picture to her husband with the caption *'Working late with clients, ha?'*

She sunk into the couch and went speechless for a few minutes. Mike determined she was between shock, grief, and anger.

Mike waited several minutes before he broached the very delicate subject of the house money. "Do you know if the house money I gave you is still in the bank?"

"I don't know. He stopped the mail from coming to our apartment. He said the mailmen were getting all the mail screwed up and he had everything re-routed to him at work. He's been paying all the bills and I transferred money to his bank last week. This was going to be our new system."

"That's probably how he opened the credit cards in your name without you knowing about it," said Mike.

"I still don't think he would do that," said Colleen. "That's criminal and I don't believe he would do that."

Mike dropped it. He assumed Jacob gambled away their savings before he started with the credit cards. Only time would tell. The only focus today was her broken heart.

Colleen read aloud Jacob's response: *"'I'm sorry. I got drunk and I shouldn't have kissed her.'* That's his response."  Colleen seemed insulted and depleted of all energy. She went from shock victim to angry wife every few minutes. Mike and Maria remained quiet.

"What am I going to do?" asked Colleen.

"There's one more thing. There's a lawsuit against him in Palm Beach County in small claims for $5,000. It's by another woman who claims she had a romantic relationship with him until she found out he was married. She loaned him $7500 and he hasn't paid her back," said Mike.

"He did tell me about that. That's an old girlfriend from before we were married. She gave him money and now wants it back," said Colleen.

"Well, the dates of the romance and the loan that appear in the court complaint are during your marriage to Jacob," said Mike without emotion. He showed her the form that was on Ryan's website page.

281

Colleen looked at the formal complaint. The dates of the romance and the loan did occur right after her marriage. She absorbed it quietly and said, "He lied to me about that too. I guess our whole marriage has been a lie." She cried again.

For the next four hours, Colleen absorbed the shock of finding out her whole marriage was a lie on Jacob's side. She reviewed the pictures and the videos from the casino at least once or twice. She cried through each review.

Mike and Maria tiptoed around her and gave her the space she needed. She went back and forth from crying to venting anger. They both knew she needed to express both to absorb the biggest shock and disappointment of her life. Mike had a lump in his throat the whole time. He could tell Maria was sick with grief but was keeping it together for her daughter.

Colleen stayed overnight. She and Jacob texted back and forth for the rest of the day and evening, but they were all about ending the marriage. She shared the website link with Jacob. Once he saw the videos himself, he threatened to sue Mallardi Investigations for a violation of his privacy. He made himself the victim in it.

Jacob finally called her at eleven o'clock Saturday night. "Colleen, look, I had a gambling slip and I got drunk and wound-up slobbering over a woman that I work with. Your parents are pressuring you to divorce me only because they never liked me to begin with. Every marriage has rough patches, Colleen. Don't leave me," said Jacob.

"You've been cheating on me since the beginning of the marriage, Jacob."

"I have not. Who told you that?"

"The lawsuit complaint by the ex-girlfriend that you told me about, this was not someone from your past. You lied to me. This was a woman who had a romance with you during the dates we were married."

"She's wrong about the dates. Dates are easy to get screwed up. This is an ex-girlfriend, Colleen."

"I don't know what I'm going to ultimately do, Jacob, but I'm not coming home right now." Colleen hung up.

This confirmed how easily the lies popped right out of his mouth. Her whole financial life was now behind a cloak of darkness since he re-routed the mail. She had no idea how much money or debt there was. Looking back over everything, she could see how he planned the mail switch. Her father was right. He probably did open the credit cards in her name.

She was scared about the financial side of things, but she had no energy today to deal with it. It was eleven o'clock on Saturday night and there was nothing she could do about it now.

Her father walked by and poked his head in the living room. "You can sleep in your old room, Colleen."

"I know but I'm somewhere between my old self and the married woman I thought I was, so I'm going to stay on the couch."

"I understand," said Mike.

"What am I going to do about the credit cards and the other gambling stuff?" asked Colleen, looking up at her dad.

"We'll make an appointment with my lawyer Lee as soon as he can see you. He'll help you navigate your way through all of this."

"Okay. That's a plan. Thanks, Dad. You know, when I came over here, I thought you and mom had either set up a college fund for the future baby or you found a nice crib or something. I never dreamed what was in store for me."

"There will be children, Colleen. There will be a college fund. There will be a nice crib, but just not with this bastard."

"I knew that was coming," said Colleen, half smiling. "I guess with what he has done, you deserve a few minutes to gloat and vent. I should have listened to you and mom; you were right about him."

"It's okay. Sometimes we all choose the hard way to learn our lessons. It'll be okay. You're not alone. Good night."

Good night, Dad. I love you."

"I love you too, Sweetheart."

Within five minutes, Colleen dropped off to sleep from sheer emotional exhaustion.

# CHAPTER 19

### One Day later - 11:00 AM
### Ocala, FL

AFTER SAYING MASS AT 11:00 Sunday morning, Fr. Liam tried to be mentally present for his parishioners. He stood outside the church speaking to everyone on his receiving line. His mind kept drifting back to last night's conversation with Mike about how devastated Colleen must be. Apparently, she and Jacob had fought on the phone a few times, but she walked outside to the pool area for privacy. Mike peeked out a few times and could only report on her level of fury; he gave it a ten out of ten. He heard her muffled yelling and crying and when she came back into the house, she seemed furious.

Colleen was staying with Mike and Maria until she decided what to do because there was a chance she was already pregnant. She would know for sure in a few days.

Fr. Liam finished up his last greeting when the church door flew open and Marie-Louise came marching out of the church. She seemed to have a direction already in mind.

"Hello, Marie-Louise. Thank you for helping us today with the ushering. I saw you did a great job."

"Thanks." She stood and just looked.

"I wanted to ask you something --" said Fr. Liam.

"Right now?" asked Marie-Louise alarmed.

"It doesn't have to be now, no --"

"Because the other ushers have asked me to lunch and I have to go with them," she said, as if her appearance was mandatory.

"Oh, that's great. Go ahead. Have a good lunch." Fr. Liam smiled as he waved and Marie-Louise carried on walking to the parking lot. He hadn't received any further suggestions in his poor box in the last three weeks. This confirmed the ushering involvement was good for her. Marie-Louise continued walking off to her car. It gave Fr. Liam a good feeling knowing that the ushers had included her in the lunch gathering. This would also be good for her.

Fr. Liam walked back towards the sacristy and saw Alice Brennan sitting by herself on a bench outside the church. "Hello, Alice, how are you today?"

"I'm okay. No funerals this week," said Alice.

"None? What about the other churches in the area?" asked Fr. Liam smirking. "There's got to be at least a few baby boomers who died." He sat down next to Alice.

"I've tried the Protestants but they don't have enough mingling for my taste. Too much eulogizing, and you know most of the time most of what they say in a eulogy isn't even true," said Alice. "I mean it respectfully, Father."

"You prefer to work the crowd --"

"Exactly. That's why I only do the Catholic wakes and funerals. Although the Lutheran's still have a nice formal service."

"You've got to stop giving this death stuff so much energy, Alice," said Fr. Liam.

"I can't help it. My mind is always thinking about death. My death, other people's death. When people talk to me, I wonder how they will die. I worry about how I'll die."

"We're not supposed to be overly focused on death, Alice. We all have to die and none of us knows how it will happen."

"That's not true. The ones who have cancer, they know that they're going to die," said Alice.

"Well, they think they will die, but many people today go into remission and then they don't die, do they?" asked Fr. Liam.

"I think you have me on a technicality there, but you know what I mean. At least if you go from a painless cancer, you get to prepare," said Alice.

"Is that how you want to go?"

"Either that or die in my sleep -- only because I have a phone service that checks on me every morning at ten. If I don't answer, they call my two kids," said Alice.

"Well, I hope you go that way too," said Fr. Liam. "But try not to keep obsessing about it. It's not good for you."

"I saw a show on TV one time. There was a guy who was a hoarder. He buried himself in his house with all kinds of junk, newspapers, magazines, just trash really. He was also obese. He died from a heart attack, but no one knew. The only way they found him was that he stunk up his neighborhood. When the cops got there, they found him and he was half eaten by maggots and flies." Alice raised her shoulders with a dramatic grimaced look and continued. "Can you imagine dying like that?"

"This is why you shouldn't keep thinking about this, Alice. These are very morbid thoughts. You're tormenting yourself."

"I know. I must confess that I've always had a fascination with death and I'm not sure why."

"When was the first time you were shocked by a death?" asked Fr. Liam.

"When I was in kindergarten. A classmate of my older brother had gone for a ride with an uncle in his new convertible. They were in a terrible accident and he was decapitated. I'll never forget it. I kept seeing him in my thoughts all the time, picturing him without a head. I wasn't able to let go of it."

"That's probably where this all started. You were too young to even hear about something like that."

"I never thought about it, but I think that is where it started. After that, I remember hearing about people dying and thinking at least they weren't decapitated. Of course, the hoarder who stunk up his neighborhood was worse than the decapitation, don't you think?" asked Alice.

"They're both horrible ways to go, but I agree that at least the child was found and buried by his loved ones. The other guy's death was more horrible because, not only did he die alone, but he wasn't even missed by anyone. He wasn't found until nature made sure he would be found."

"Yes, I guess. I was more focused on the maggots. I'm sorry I pulled you into my morbidity, Father."

"It's okay, Alice, it's part of the job. Think about happier things today, okay?"

"Okay. Here's my friend. We're going to lunch. You're welcome to join us."

"Not today, Alice, but thanks for thinking of me. Have a great lunch."

Alice scurried off to have lunch with her friend.

## Three Hours Later - 2:00 PM
## Boca Raton, FL

The waitress delivered two double margaritas as Colleen and Marsha got through their *hellos* and *how-are-yous*. They were at their favorite Mexican restaurant for commiseration drinks. Marsha was drinking to having survived being cheated on by her husband. Colleen's drink was to help absorb the shock of finding out her husband was cheating and gambling behind her back.

"I wish we were here to celebrate something happy, Colleen, but we'll toast to better days ahead for both of us," said Marsha. They clinked their margaritas in a toast.

"Yes, better days ahead. Although, I now have to navigate through a lot of complicated legal entanglements. I talked for ten minutes to my father's lawyer this afternoon before I came here. I hit a brick wall when he started talking about holding criminal charges over Jacob's head for the credit cards. But at that point, I got sick to my stomach, so I told him I can't talk about that yet," said Colleen.

"What do you mean *criminal charges*?" asked Marsha.

"Jacob opened four credit cards in my name and he ran them up. I never gave him permission to do that. It's fraud, even though he's my husband. He swore he didn't do it for the first three phone calls I had with him. I told him the PI can get voice recordings from at least one of them because they were opened over the phone. That's when he confessed."

"How did he get them to open one on the phone?" asked Marsha.

"He responded to those mailings that invite you to get credit in the mail. My father said that when you have a great credit rating, like I do -- well, did -- they just about push them on you. Jacob's very clever. He's very charming. Mind you, neither one of us could have opened a credit card on the phone, but he did."

"I can't believe he did that. But I still can't believe my husband cheated on me in the first year of marriage either," said Marsha. She took a big sip of her margarita.

"I took this marriage so seriously, wanting everything to be perfect. Jacob seems to have not taken it seriously at all. To him, it was more like a boyfriend-girlfriend connection with a wedding. Do you know what I mean?"

"I do. I don't think a lot of people think it's that serious anymore," said Marsha. "I know you're terribly disappointed, but how are you feeling otherwise? Like do you feel like you'll be okay?"

"It's too soon to know. I feel like an accident victim. I was driving to my parents' house expecting to be presented with a baby's college fund and I smashed into a brick wall. Now I'm wounded and wandering around trying to get my bearings. That's how I feel. It's all too new for me to get a read on whether I'll be okay or not."

"Well, you'll get over the shock in a week or so. Will you go back and live there with him?" asked Marsha.

"He's sleeping with another woman. He claims she's not his girlfriend, that he got drunk and got sloppy with her and I'm making a big deal out of it. But I've seen video of him kissing her and he was acting like they were in love. Plus, he wasn't that drunk."

"Wow, so a PI found all this out. I need a PI to flush out these online dates I go on. These guys tend to pad their resumes. I could make a call and have the PI do a rundown and then I could see up front what I'm getting myself into," said Marsha. "I like the way that sounds."

"How is Gregory, by the way?" asked Colleen.

"I've seen him twice now and I was able to let go of the old pictures and he's very nice so far. I'm guarded because I'm jaded, you know, in general, nothing having to do with him. I'm still holding back, like I'm waiting for the shoe to drop. He claims he's looking for a serious relationship that will go towards marriage. But how do I know those intentions are not 15 years old like his pictures?"

"Only time will tell, I guess." Colleen took another sip of her margarita.

"It's probably too soon for you to think about dating," said Marsha.

"I'm thinking about finding a cabin in the woods away from all of civilization, so I don't think I'm there yet," said Colleen.

"What about entering the convent? That could be a good rest." asked Marsha.

"No, they have to get up at the crack of dawn and they can't wear lipstick, so that's out of the question. But living in the woods like a mystic or an anchorite, that might work," said Colleen.

"If things don't work with Gary, maybe we can do it together. We'll have two separate huts and share campsite chores," said Marsha.

"My Uncle Liam asked my father if he thought I was -- quote -- *groomed for marriage*. What do you think he meant by that?"

"Groomed for marriage? I know they groom young girls for the sex trade. They groom children for pedophilia abuse. Maybe he thinks your husband set you up for marriage to get some financial benefits."

"Do you think he's suggesting that Jacob never even loved me? Because I think he did," said Colleen. "I'm hurt that he would even suggest that."

"Ask him about it. As a priest, maybe they have another definition for what it means. I agree that Jacob did love you. I even find it hard to believe he could have been interested in another woman. He always acted crazy about you," said Marsha. "I would let that remark go. It's too ethereal and open for interpretation for everything you have to deal with right now."

Colleen stirred her margarita.

"What are you going to do regarding work? Are you going back to living in the apartment with Jacob?"

"I have to go back tonight to get my clothes for work. I don't have plans that far in advance. I'll see what happens when I go home tonight," said Colleen.

"Do you think you could forgive him and still go forward?"

"I don't know for sure. I still love him, but I keep telling myself he's not who he holds himself out to be. I was married to a person who doesn't exist.

"I do feel like marriage is supposed to be sacred and here I am leaving at the first sign of trouble." Colleen frowned in confusion.

Marsha nodded. "I left right away because I was too crushed. I was too emotionally devastated. Some women do stay and fight, but I didn't have the emotional strength or energy. I was too crushed. My mother told me I was too heartbroken to fight."

"I can relate to that. I've been sleeping every few hours since yesterday when I found out. I do feel like I was hit by an emotional truck.

"The only positive thing that happened is validation of my suspicions. I felt something was wrong between us for a while, maybe a month or two. I felt like he didn't love me anymore, even when he acted like he did. I started to think I had mental problems, that I was paranoid. Now at least I know I detected something was off and my perceptions were correct. So I no longer think I'm mental."

"How are your parents taking this?"

"They're being very supportive. I know my dad well and he's probably dying to gloat about being right about Jacob, but he is containing himself. He hasn't gloated at all – well one tiny gloat. He's being so good. I know one day he will let loose and go on a full tirade, but he hasn't done it yet."

"In all honesty, he was right about Jacob, so he's entitled to a few minutes of gloating. I mean, you have to give him his due," said Marsha, smirking.

"I guess, but not now. Even you said Jacob was never going to grow up, that he was too dependent on his parents," said Colleen.

"I did tell you that because he is a spoiled brat."

"The same thing could probably be said about me though, so I didn't pay any attention to it," said Colleen, half smiling.

"Being pampered and sheltered is different than being spoiled. You're pampered because your mother could only have one child. But your dad has been equally tough on you to stand up on your own two feet. I remember him forcing you to go to school when you got bullied that time. He was the counterweight to your over-doting mother," said Marsha.

"That's true. I am more responsible than Jacob. Of course, some of his problems are due to the gambling addiction. I told my father a while ago that it was a disease; he rolled his eyes and scoffed," said Colleen, chuckling.

"He's got a point. If he didn't gamble so much, maybe he wouldn't have gotten addicted to it. It's hard to say. You love him and you still want to give him the benefit of the doubt."

A moment of silence passed between them.

"Marsha, when I thought about this coming summer, I pictured myself announcing my pregnancy, buying a house, decorating the nursery, all good and wonderful things. I had a school picked out to continue my studying in September. Instead, everything exploded in one night of gambling and cheating. The disappointment of what has happened is the worst. I keep thinking of what I was anticipating and what actually happened to me," said Colleen. Her eyes filled up with tears.

"Coming out to get a drink was supposed to cheer you up, so don't go down that road. You were victimized and you didn't deserve it," said Marsha, building her up.

"I know fifty percent of marriages don't work, but I was determined not to become a statistic, you know?" A single tear ran down Colleen's face.

"I know. Most people hope for the best when they get married, Colleen. You didn't do anything wrong."

She had started crying a little and Marsha handed her a napkin from the table. She also lunged into some work talk to give Colleen a dose of normalcy. This did rescue her from this dark corner she inadvertently walked her into.

"Do you want to go away this weekend, to get your mind off things?" asked Marsha.

"My parents are going up to Ocala to look at a condo for them to buy. They already found a buyer for their house just by word of mouth. They're now jumping into high gear. I think I told you they're going to be snowbirds. Of course, this was all predicated on Jacob and I becoming parents soon. But I'm going up with them for that very reason, so I don't have to sit home and think about what happened to me."

"That's good. It'll be good to get away."

The commiseration drinks came to an end after they finished the one drink, as they both had to drive home.

As Colleen walked alone to her car, she reflected on how much life can change on a dime. A terrible feeling of insecurity came over her. She felt less sad, but now she felt scared to be alone in the world.

### Seven Hours Later - 9:00 PM
### Ocala, FL

Fr. Liam set aside the book he was reading for the last hour and called his brother. "How's everything going?"

"As well as can be expected. Colleen stayed over last night. When she went back home today to get some work clothes, she ran into Jacob and they started to have it out," said Mike.

"What does '*started to have it out*' mean? Are they just fighting about the cheating?" asked Fr. Liam.

"It's hard to piece together what's actually going on. One minute she is blurting everything out in tears to Maria. In the next minute, she leaves and doesn't say where she is going. Neither of us know what's going on," said Mike.

"Is he asking her to forgive him?" asked Fr. Liam.

"Well, yes, he is, but apparently, he's still lying about the other woman. He admits to cheating with the woman in the casino but says she's nothing to him. He's still maintaining that the woman suing him is from before they were married. One minute he's asking her for forgiveness. The next minute, he's telling her if she stays with her parents, to take all her stuff with her. They're all over the board."

"What about the credit cards, does he admit to taking them out in her name?"

"He admits to two, but two he says he knows nothing about. Colleen knows he's lying. I believe that's the real reason she hasn't gone back. Maria and I don't want her to go back. He's too untrustworthy."

"I hope she doesn't go back too. I don't believe he sees marriage as a lifelong commitment. There'll never be any security there for Colleen," said Fr. Liam.

"Exactly. Pray that it will work out the way it's supposed to work out," asked Mike.

"I will."

"Listen, we had a couple come up to us after church asking to see the house. They heard from our neighbors that we're getting ready to put it on the market and they want to buy it. So we want to take advantage of this. They have kids and the school system is great in our area. They have to settle in by August, so we've moved into high gear. Can you believe it?"

"That's great. I take that to mean the doors are all opening for you to come up here," said Fr. Liam. "That makes me very happy."

"If I find something this weekend, I'm going to buy it. I'll have to shuffle some money around to make it happen, but that's easy enough. This could be the weekend we pick the condo or the house. We're keeping everything kind of quiet around Colleen so this doesn't add any more emotional drain on her. Those are Maria's words.

"By the way, Maria and I want to get her out of town for next weekend, so she's coming up to Ocala to look at the condos and houses. See if there's anything going on in town that we can do together as a family," said Mike.

"Okay. I'll check out the papers and ask around. Hang in there. I'll keep you all in my prayers. Love you, Mike."

"Love you too, Liam."

# CHAPTER 20

### Six Days Later - Saturday 6:30 AM
### Boca Raton, FL

IT WAS A WEEK AFTER her marriage fell apart. Colleen was on her way up to Ocala with her parents as they looked for a house or condo. She kept going over and over the comment about being groomed for marriage by Uncle Liam. She wanted to talk to him about this because she thought he was suggesting her husband never loved her. She was angry about it but it went deeper than anger. She needed to know where he was coming from when he said it. She wanted it to be face-to-face so she could read his manner and demeanor.

During the drive, her parents engaged in all kinds of small talk, steering clear of anything about Jacob and the marriage. They went on and on a bit about Summer Glen, which was the over-55 community her father had chosen. They talked about all of the lifestyle amenities: an indoor heated pool, outdoor pool, woodworking center, craft center, dog parks, jogging trails. It was never ending. It

303

sounded to Colleen like a retirement community with an attached day care center for the aging.

She didn't feel much like small talk, so she was as polite as she could be with her parents for a while. She finally told them she couldn't talk anymore. They looked at each other alarmingly, but they continued to talk among themselves. Maria went over the questions she wrote down for the real estate agent. They were both a bit nervous as they had already sold their house. If they could swing it, they would move at the end of the month. They never expected to jump into such a short timetable, but they didn't want to miss out on a cash sale for their home.

They stopped for a quick coffee and bagel after arriving in Ocala. They were scheduled to meet Uncle Liam at his church before going to Summer Glen to meet the real estate agent. After parking the car in the church lot, they walked to the parish office. Noticing they were a few minutes early, they all walked over and peeked into the church. Pastor McCarthy, Liam's predecessor, had a flair for design and artwork. The church was beautiful. There was artwork on every wall which told the story of the bible from the Old Testament to the New. They all walked around looking at everything.

On their way to meet him, Fr. Liam was already walking towards them. He wore a big smile. He embraced and hugged them all.

"Your church is beautiful, Uncle Liam, it's so big," said Colleen. It still felt new seeing Uncle Liam dressed as a priest. Colleen knew him her whole life as her uncle, the homicide detective, married to Patty, his high school sweetheart.

"Yes, it's a beautiful church. There's a school attached. The rectory is behind the parish hall here, and we have a Eucharistic chapel in the back. There's also a small library over here." Fr. Liam pointed out the various sections of the property. "We even have a few meeting rooms in the back there, so it's like a small campus. The previous pastor raised this up from nothing."

"It's gorgeous. We went into the church and the artwork is unbelievable," said Maria.

"Yes, he had an eye for aesthetics, that's for sure. So are we still on for lunch today?" asked Fr. Liam.

"Yes, it's only 10:30 now so we're going to Summer Glen to see two houses now," said Mike, who had his brochure with him. "Do you want to come and see?"

"I'm meeting with Deacon Bob who needs to talk to me about something personal in about 30 minutes. So I'm on for lunch, but I'll pass on seeing the house right now."

"Can I talk to you now about some things?" asked Colleen to her uncle.

"You don't want to come and look at the house?" asked Mike.

"I want to talk to Uncle Liam about something personal," said Colleen. "I've seen the brochure a thousand times, Dad."

Mike seemed surprised but said, "Okay, no problem. We'll be back to pick you both up for lunch." Colleen could tell her dad was suspicious as he looked from her to her mother to see if there was some kind of non-verbal communication going on. Maria seemed surprised by Colleen's request too. They waived and went to Summer Glen.

"Do you want to have a walk around the church property and talk? Or do you want to go inside and sit in my office?"

"Let's walk," said Colleen, as she crossed her arms over her chest. Fr. Liam, dressed in a full-length Roman cassock with his white collar, walked beside Colleen, with his hands behind his back. He turned to look at her and said, "What would you like to talk about, Colleen?"

"I want to talk about something my father told me you said about my marriage. You asked him if he thought I was groomed for marriage. What did you mean by that?"

"Well, the private investigator -- who has more experience working with gamblers than I have -- he was the one who told me that gamblers usually borrow money from those around them. He told me we would need to check

306

your credit to see if he was gambling. He went into detail about how gamblers begin to borrow money from those around them. We did run your credit, and that's where we saw the credit cards." Fr. Liam looked again at Colleen.

"I know." Colleen walked closely to Fr. Liam at a meandering pace. She looked down at the pavement.

"So once your credit came up with these four credit cards, the private investigator asked me, '*Do you think your niece was groomed for this marriage?*' Fr. Liam looked again at Colleen and she looked back.

"I said, '*I don't know. I never thought about that.*' So when I talked to your father, that was still very much on my mind. For some reason, it was stuck in my mind from the moment the investigator asked me. Remember, Colleen, I've only been in Jacob's company a handful of times. I don't know him that well."

"So you don't think I was groomed for the marriage, you just wanted to know what my dad thought?" asked Colleen.

"I wanted to know what your father thought, yes."

"What did my father say?" asked Colleen. The slight wind had blown her hair into her face, and she pushed it back.

"He said he didn't know either."

Colleen said, "Huh." They both walked several steps in silence.

"You met Jacob and he was talking marriage within three or four months. He was under parental pressure to stay on the straight and narrow because he got himself into financial trouble by gambling. Your father told me you helped him get a car loan for his present car because his other car was taken into the bankruptcy." Fr. Liam hesitated but Colleen kept walking and looking at the pavement. Her brows slowly knitted into a frown.

"You got married and then he borrowed $7500 from a woman who claims in court papers that she had an affair with him. She said she broke up with him when she found out he was still married."

Colleen's frown remained steady.

"So it appears that his need for money was ongoing. I question his recovery in Gamblers Anonymous. It sounds like his recovery was all show for his parents."

Colleen glanced up at Uncle Liam but didn't speak.

"Then he comes to Mother's Day dinner and he's acting nervous and strange. So your father and I wanted to find out if he was up to no good. We both thought maybe he was gambling or something. After all, you're trying to get pregnant. Your father wouldn't be doing his job if he wasn't looking out for you, Colleen."

"I know," said Colleen.

"Then we find out that, yes, he is gambling. And he also has another woman that he's kissing in public while wearing your wedding band," said Fr. Liam. "Both of us were shocked about the other woman. We thought he may be gambling because he seemed anxious and nervous. Neither of us expected to find out about other women."

"So you think I was groomed for marriage, that he never loved me?" asked Colleen. Fr. Liam felt her bracing herself for the truth.

"I don't know actually. It could be more complicated than that. Being an atheist, what could marriage mean to an atheist? A legal agreement, I guess. It's certainly not a sacrament to him. I don't believe atheists believe anything in life is sacred, at least that I'm aware of. So he may have had a more casual understanding of what marriage was to begin with."

They turned the corner and came to the front of the Eucharistic chapel and Colleen stopped.

"This is the Eucharistic Chapel. Did you want to go in?" asked Fr. Liam.

"No, I want you to continue." They continued walking around the campus.

"In today's world, civil marriage is nothing more than an unenforceable civil contract. That means that if either of you want to end the marriage, it doesn't matter what the

309

other person wants or says. One person can turn the key and end it. No one can hold someone into a marriage.

"You can hold him into your apartment rental contract. The law will make him honor that contract. There could be technicalities involved, but the law would enforce that contract. Not so with a marriage contract." Fr. Liam looked at Colleen and she was taking everything in.

"So I'm not sure if you were groomed for marriage or not. I do believe you didn't date long enough to really get to know one another. We now know he gave in to cheating twice in less than a year. You must admit there's no security in that kind of a marriage. Wouldn't you agree?"

"I would agree. But I hate the thought of being groomed for marriage because it makes me feel like I was stupid and he never loved me," said Colleen, as she began to cry. She stopped walking and covered her face with both hands.

Fr. Liam embraced her and held her while she regained herself. "Colleen, you're an honest person who believed everything your husband said to you. There's nothing to be ashamed of. If you were groomed -- which I'm not convinced of -- you didn't do anything wrong. You trusted a man who held himself out to be someone who loved you and wanted to marry you. Every woman in the world trusts the man who is courting her, for lack of a more modern term. You have nothing to feel bad or guilty about. You did nothing wrong."

"I believe he did love me. I felt lately that he didn't love me anymore, and it turns out he did have a girlfriend. So I know what being loved feels like and I know what not being loved feels like. I know he did love me, so I don't want you to think that, about the grooming."

"Okay. I was leaning over to the *'atheist marriage as an adventure theory'* anyway," Fr. Liam said. He smiled and put his arm around her shoulder as they continued walking.

"What do you mean by *as an adventure*?" asked Colleen.

"Well, as Catholics, we see -- we're supposed to see marriage as a sacramental vow you take standing before God and all your family and friends. You're publicly proclaiming your love for each other. There's also an expectation that children will be born of the marriage. Both families will attach to you and the children you produce from it. Your family and his family become an extended family for the children born to the marriage. We believe this vow and this marriage is sacred, which is why the church raised it to the level of a sacrament."

"So atheists don't believe marriage is sacred," said Colleen.

"Well, if someone doesn't have a sacred or sacramental view of marriage, what could it be to them? Like I said earlier, it could be a legal contract. They could see it as a financial arrangement or even a business deal. Or some might see it as an adventure or a romantic whim. Do you see what I mean? Some people today refer to their first marriages as their starter marriage, the way you refer to your first house purchase. And with all the hoopla that surrounds American marriages, a lot of people see it as a romantic adventure. So I'm giving Jacob the benefit of the doubt, that he at least thought it was an adventure."

Colleen half smiled.

"I mean what else could it be to a person who doesn't believe in God or doesn't believe anything is sacred?"

"Nothing. He obviously didn't even think it was a main adventure because he had two other side adventures since we got married."

"Exactly." Fr. Liam hesitated a few moments. "You need to marry someone who thinks of marriage as a sacrament or at least that it's sacred," said Fr. Liam.

A moment of silence passed and all that could be heard were their footsteps on the cement sidewalk.

"Are you mad at me for having my private investigator friend look into this for your father and me?"

"I was mad but I'm not anymore," said Colleen. She relaxed her arms and put her hands in the pockets of her long tunic she was wearing. Fr. Liam could tell she was less defensive.

"Why did God let this horrible thing happen to me?" asked Colleen.

"It's only horrible when you look at it a certain way. It's horrible in the sense that you were shocked and hurt over this. You found out your husband is a cheater, a liar, and a gambler -- on a slip at the very least. The shock of that is horrible. But I see this as a Divine Rescue," said Fr. Liam.

"A Divine Rescue? How's that?" asked Colleen, stopping and looking up towards her uncle.

"Well, you were on the brink of getting pregnant with Jacob. Unbeknownst to you, he was cheating on you and stealing money behind your back. He would have been the father of your child. You would have been in a completely different situation if you found out about this after you were pregnant. So I should more correctly refer to this as a Just-In-Time Divine Rescue. The Lord reached out and saved you in the nick of time. He prevented much more disappointment, and the shattering of all your dreams," said Fr. Liam.

"My dreams are all shattered, Uncle Liam."

"This illusion shattered. But what was behind this illusion was a nightmare disguised as a marriage. It's shocking and disappointing. But you'll recover from this.

In the same way that you were whisked out of danger in the nick of time, the Lord will whisk in the right husband for you also in the nick of time. You'll meet him in time to have your children. You need a guy who wants to have a life-long sacred marriage. Someone who wants a family

313

and who thinks that love, devotion, and loyalty are valuable traits."

"You're right, I guess. The thought of dating anyone new feels overwhelming. I can't even envision being ready to date anyone."

"Of course you can't now. You're brokenhearted. You've been betrayed. You need to heal and grieve this loss. But you will love again. I'm sure of it."

"You're sure of it?" Colleen smiled.

"Absolutely, positively sure of it. Otherwise, there wouldn't have been any reason for the rescue," said Fr. Liam.

"Here's Deacon Bob that I have to talk with. I'll be about ten minutes. We can continue when I'm done." Fr. Liam embraced Colleen and held her close. She hugged him back. He could tell she felt much better and the air had been cleared between them.

"What are you doing with that young pretty woman, Fr. Liam?" kidded Deacon Bob.

Fr. Liam laughed and said, "This is my niece, Colleen. I was just thanking her for setting me straight."

"You know what the gossip mill is like in this place? They'll be talking about Fr. Liam hugging that pretty girl all week," kidded Deacon Bob.

"That's all I need," said Fr. Liam, going along with the joke.

"Uncle Liam, I'm going into the chapel until my parents show up."

"Okay. We'll come and get you."

## Later That Day
## Ocala, FL

Mike and Maria looked at three houses in Summer Glen, and she picked the one she wanted. The big kitchen won hands down and she was filled with the excitement of finding their summer home. She made sure she reiterated to Mike that this was only their summer home. Even though Colleen's life had flipped upside down last weekend, she still felt Colleen would need her going through the divorce. Mike said whatever he needed to say to get Maria to sign the contract of sale along with him. He would finally be closer to his brother again and that was his mission.

They finished up with the real estate agent, made notes about the dates of closing and their move-out date, which was only thirty days away. As they drove to meet Fr. Liam, she discussed their plans.

"We'll get it done, Maria. We have all day every day, a minimum of forty hours a week. We already cleaned out a lot. My whole garage is ready to be packed. Don't worry," said Mike.

"I'll call the moving company and have them send two guys who can help us pack. This way, I can oversee that everything goes into boxes that are organized and marked. Then we can unpack at a slower pace when we get up there," said Maria.

"That's a plan. We'll pay for some young muscle to help us."

They picked up Fr. Liam and Colleen and all proceeded to the restaurant for a celebratory luncheon. On the way, they took Fr. Liam and Colleen on a tour to show them the house they just purchased. They drove past all the amenities and Mike pointed out the different pools, gyms, woodworking building, miniature golf, and the main eighteen-hole golf course. Fr. Liam could tell his brother and Maria were excited and that made him happy.

As they were seated in the restaurant and drinks were served, Maria showed Fr. Liam pictures of the house room by room.

"It looks as big as your old house," said Fr. Liam.

"The kitchen is big, that's the one I picked. But it's only two bedrooms, two baths but has a nice, enclosed Florida

316

room that we can make into a semi-third bedroom, if needed. Look at all the closet space in the kitchen," said Maria, excitedly.

"Yes, I see, a lot of cabinets." Fr. Liam looked at Maria and then to Mike. In one look, Fr. Liam knew that neither he nor his brother cared about the cabinets, but they were glad they would be living close together again.

As they looked over their menus, Fr. Liam closed his as he knew what he would order. "So what do you think about the Ocala area, Colleen?"

She looked up from her menu. "It's lovely, very country-like. Their community is beautiful. It's all very exciting." She gave a half smile and went back to her menu.

Maria and Mike both went to the restrooms leaving Fr. Liam and Colleen alone. He could see she was being a good sport for her parents, but she was still brokenhearted. She was still dragging herself through life as he knew she would for the next month or two.

"Have you decided what you will do regarding your marriage?" asked Fr. Liam.

"We're going to get a divorce. He's still lying to me and I can't look at him anymore. I feel like he's a stranger, a person I don't know. I put a deposit on an apartment on Friday after work, so I'll be moving into my own studio apartment in July."

317

"I see. So you and your parents will be moving. Maybe you can come up on the weekends while you're still grieving," said Fr. Liam.

"Maybe. I'm seeing a counselor and she's helping me. I'm only living a day at a time," said Colleen.

"That's a good idea. It helps to have someone to talk to. I'm praying for you, for whatever that's worth to you."

Colleen just looked at Fr. Liam and didn't know what to make of that remark, but she was too depleted to get into it.

"I just can't get over how different everything is in such a short period of time. Two weeks ago, my parents were talking about becoming snowbirds and cleaning out their house. I was talking about getting pregnant and buying a house. Now, my marriage exploded, I found out my husband is cheating on me, and my parents have sold their house without even putting out a for sale sign. And now they'll be moving four hours away. How can this be?"

"Some changes in life are orchestrated by us and some changes come into our lives seemingly without any effort on our part. It just means that fate is repositioning everyone."

"I don't like where fate pushed me. I don't like it at all," said Colleen.

"I understand. Someday you'll see a silver lining in this dark cloud, but not for a while. But you will see that this all had to happen for a reason," said Fr. Liam.

"I guess," said Colleen, as her parents came back to the table. Fr. Liam knew she was not convinced.

They all spent the rest of Saturday and Sunday together in Ocala touring the area and catching up with Fr. Liam between his various church responsibilities. Colleen was distracted on a surface level, but she had a constant inner dialogue and quandary playing in the background. It all had to do with her broken marriage and the financial horrors she was about to face in the coming months. She was only able to drift in and out of the running conversation between her parents and Fr. Liam.

# CHAPTER 21

### Over the Next Month or so
### Boca Raton, FL

MIKE AND MARIA went home and both jumped into high gear. They had the movers come within a week to help them pack. Mike was assigned to picture duty. He wrapped each one with brown paper, towels and cording and stack them in one corner of their house. He also agreed to pack all their Christmas and holiday decorations. Maria packed her dishes with foam wrap and specialty dish boxes. Everything else would be packed by the movers when they came for four days before moving day. They had less than one month to get it all done.

The same movers moved Colleen into her own studio apartment in Boca Raton. She formally separated from Jacob. It turned out that Sandra from down the hall was his girlfriend and they decided to be together. Like Marsha had suggested earlier, Colleen was officially traded in. She was happy to get away from Jacob who had taken to treating her like she was yesterday's news.

She decided not to press charges against Jacob about the credit cards because she knew he would lose his job if he was indicted on theft charges. She couldn't bring herself to do that to him. He also promised he would take over the debt that he incurred.

Her lawyer started negotiations right away so he could use the pressure of filing criminal charges to sort out the division of marital debt. The $20,000 house money account had only $1,200 left in it and no baby fund was ever set up. It all disappeared as Jacob slipped back into gambling, which happened right after they got married and co-mingled their funds.

Colleen's lawyer pointed out that the house money began to disappear right after the honeymoon was over. Colleen kept thinking back to Fr. Liam's comment about being groomed for the marriage. She held onto denial about it for as long as she could. However, the disappearance of the house money and the credit cards taken out behind her back pointed to more sinister motives than she liked to admit. As much as she hated to think she was so naive, she wound up feeling like just *'another woman with some money'*. She could see more clearly how this was in line with his gambling behavior.

As someone who was never late on a bill, this was all new to Colleen. At first, she was horrified by the financial mess she was in. But after many talks with the lawyer Lee, she soon accepted that he would help her navigate through it. She turned everything regarding the debt and the divorce over to Lee. Her only remaining role was to field Jacob's calls, as he was still asking her to take him back -- probably when the new girlfriend wasn't around. He also asked for money to get his creditors off his back, but she hung up on those calls.

As she climbed into her new bed in her new apartment, she prayed that God would help her navigate through this financial mess as it all felt beyond her. She was happy that the whole Atheism vs. Catholicism thing was over. After her conversations with Fr. Liam, she was determined to only marry another practicing Catholic. She vowed to never be talked out of her faith again.

Fr. Liam anxiously awaited his brother's arrival and went about his parish life as normal. He kept an eye out for Marie-Louise. She had started cracking down in her own way with those who would put their money into the basket and not pass it. With her index finger and a stern frown, she made sure they all passed the basket as they should. There was only one more suggestion put into the poor box. She wanted Fr. Liam to tell people to stop faking putting money into the collection basket. This seemed to really rub her the wrong way. But the other ushers graciously included her in their after-church lunches and Fr. Liam saw this as an improvement in Marie-Louise's life. Even her Uncle Francois commented on how committed she was and that her whole life now revolved around her job at the church.

Fr. Liam asked Alice Brennan to help out by leading a rosary when he was going to be late to a wake one night.

323

She reluctantly agreed to it, only after Father explained that it took place at the end of the mingling period. Once she knew it wouldn't cut into her working the crowd and her own investigative work, she was happy to do it. So with this little limitation, he considered Alice a new volunteer.

Angelica's sister Mia's wedding was only a few weeks away. Ryan was still biting his tongue with Angelica. He was secretly rehearsing his speech about getting sober or having to break up. He didn't hold out much hope that Angelica would go for it, and it was his only hope. It was also the reason he thought the speech itself and its delivery was crucial. The thought of starting over again with someone new was still more depressing than being in a relationship to nowhere.

Life was busy but stable for all of them. All their lives went on without incident … well, for a few weeks anyway.

## THE END OF BOOK 1

# NOTE TO READER

Dear Reader:

Thanks for giving your time to read this story. I hope you enjoyed it.

As a new fiction author, reviews are very helpful to me. If you enjoyed this novel, I'd be so grateful if you would leave a review on Amazon.com.

I love to hear any feedback about the book and enjoy interacting with my readers, so please feel free to email me at rshannon@readfirstchapter.com.

Thanks again!

R. Shannon

# AKNOWLEDGMENTS

I would like to thank Geneveve Mallardi, my 101-year-old Aunt Gen, who graciously agreed to read my books. She passed away in March of 2022, just a few days before her 102nd birthday. She was a great help to me. She was also great fun and I'll miss her!

I would like to acknowledge my advance readers and editors who are invaluable to me.

I would also like to acknowledge and thank three retired police detectives who graciously answered some police procedural questions: Fred Thomas Roberts, Jr., a retired police lieutenant, Ernest Hemschot, a homicide detective and prosecutor, and Don Kettredge, a retired police officer, who helped with police procedural questions that were invaluable in writing the books.

I would also like to thank the Ocala Police Department and Field Training Officer Anthony Medeiros, who allowed me to go on a "citizen ride-along" and patiently answered many, many questions.

# ABOUT THE AUTHOR

R. Shannon's novels are Catholic and Christian friendly and feature an ensemble of interesting characters. The stories are written in a slice-of-life style with light humor, biblical morality and heart.

She was born and raised in New Jersey and has lived over 20 years in Florida. When not writing, she is coding web design and contributing to a new author blog. Be sure to sign up at www.readfirstchapter.com to get notice of new and/or early releases.

If you would like to sign up for a weekly newsletter with ebook sales, deals & steals, as well as advance reader copies, please sign up here.

She loves to interact with readers, so if you enjoyed the book, please feel free to email her at rshannon@readfirstchapter.com.

R Shannon Author Page: amazon.com/author/rshannon

# OTHER BOOKS BY R. SHANNON:

## RYAN MALLARDI PRIVATE INVESTIGATION SERIES

Book 1: Groomed for Marriage
Book 2: Beware: Things Are Not Always as They Seem
Book 3: Missing: Caught Red Handed
Book 4: Forewarned but Unheeded

## NEWPORT VAMPRIE ROMANCE SERIES

Book 1: Darius - A Vampire Story -
Book 2: Repossession of Ciara -
Book 3: The Art of Sabotage -
Book 4: Distrust - A Vampire Story of Love & Freedom

## JACK NOLAN DETECTIVE SERIES

Book 1: Murder in the Sanctuary
Book 2: I Know Her Eyes

## WHAT'S NEXT ON YOUR READING LIST?

Read a sample of Book 2 of the Mallardi Private Investigation Series:

***Beware – Things Are Not Always the Way They Seem***

# CHAPTER 1 (Book 2)

### Friday, December 14th – 12:00 PM
### Ocala, FL

THERE WAS NO OMEN nor any premonition about what was to happen to any of them. The weather gave nothing away, as it was another mild day in December in Ocala, Florida. It was sunny, seventy-something degrees with an occasional cool breeze.

The season dropped no clues as it was two weeks before Christmas and things in the church were busier every day. Fr. Liam always looked forward to the exciting and joyous holiday season. No one in the women's group seemed to sense anything in the air either. They went about decorating the church for Christmas and there was only excitement in the air.

One could say Fr. Liam's life was calm and happy, although he did still feel a pinch of loneliness every so often. His wife had died five years earlier and he still carried around a lonely heart. The loneliness came upon him only when he had the time to think about it, which was mostly at night.

He hoped that was about to change as his brother and sister-in-law were preparing to move into town. Their house was being prepared to put on the market. Their chosen retirement community, Summer Grove, was only five minutes away from Fr. Liam's rectory. This would be Fr. Liam's last Christmas without family. That was the plan anyway.

As Fr. Liam looked out the window of the parish office. He saw the gentle sway of the beautiful oak trees that lined the church property. Catching up on the never-ending paperwork of his parish, it was almost noon already. He waited for the arrival of Ryan Mallardi, a young parishioner whom he helped through the annulment of his first marriage. Fr. Liam had earned a counseling degree at night school long before they had online classes. He was quite popular with the younger men in the parish, as he had been a Fort Lauderdale cop for 30 years before becoming a priest. He always had a crazy story or two to tell.

GROOMED FOR MARRIAGE

Leading up to early retirement from the police force, Liam Mullens had entered the deaconate program in the local seminary intending to become a parish deacon. He was in his last year of studies when his wife Patty died from ovarian cancer. In one moment of time, the calling to become a deacon morphed into becoming a priest. In some strange way, he felt the door to the priesthood open for him.

A call came into the rectory office and Juanita's first whispered words were "Oh, I'm sorry to hear that. Where will the wake be?"

Juanita was Fr. Liam's secretary since he was assigned to Our Lady of Mercy Church four years earlier. The parish was surrounded by predominantly retirement communities filled with aging baby boomers. There were about twenty five percent younger families, but mainly boomers. Over the last few years, that generation was dying out in droves and Fr. Liam was doing at least one wake and funeral a week. On occasion, he had as many as three.

When the call ended, Fr. Liam asked, "Who was it, Juanita?" He stood up and went to her desk which was outside in the parish office receiving area.

"It was Geraldine Regan. She was in Marion County Hospital with pneumonia, and she died an hour ago. She'll be laid out in Kramer Funeral Home. I have the dates here. They want a mass on Wednesday morning followed by a burial ceremony. I'll call one of our deacons to do the wake."

331

"Geraldine was suffering with her breathing for a long time, so now she's at peace," said Fr. Liam.

"She'll be free of that grandson Bill who has been nothing but trouble for her. She had to take out a home equity loan on her house to get him out of jail last year. She was a nervous wreck after that. When I see him around town, I get so mad."

"What were his charges about?" asked Fr. Liam.

"Drugs, theft. Meth, which is the worst of the lot, I hear," said Juanita, as she shook her head disparagingly. "Poor Geraldine. She's in a better place now."

## Same Day - December 14th
## 4:00 PM - Four Hours Later
## Fort Lauderdale, FL

Late in the afternoon, Gladys McElroy heard a loud banging outside her new neighbor's apartment. She lived in the Tivoli Apartments in Fort Lauderdale for at least ten years and knew many of the residents. The family who moved next to Gladys was only there for about three months. No one saw much of them. The mother came and went with groceries, always walking quickly, and never making eye contact with anyone. On occasion, the neighbors heard yelling and what sounded like domestic problems coming from their apartment. Gladys didn't know anything about them, not that she didn't try to find out. They all kept to themselves.

The banging got louder and louder. Gladys considered this an invitation to open the door, as did other neighbors, and go out and watch. She saw a man about 65 years old banging on her neighbor's door and shouting, "Kaufman, I know you're in there. Open up. I want my money." He appeared to be a normal person by his dress and appearance, but he was red in the face. He was as angry as a man could be. He continued banging and repeating the same mantra over and over. Inside the apartment was only silence.

Gladys slowly approached the angry man hoping to find out more about what was going on. "Can I help you, sir?"

"I'm looking for Barry Kaufman, the stockbroker thief who stole my money, all of my money," the stranger said. He banged again, from anger, which Gladys could feel from a foot away.

Suddenly a police car pulled up and two Fort Lauderdale police officers approached the angry man. At first sight of the officers, the man lunged into a long tale about this Kaufman guy having stolen his money. Apparently, Kaufman was fired from his job and he was here to get his money back. He wasn't waiting until some lawsuit settled. His story was long and rambling and peppered with expletives. The cops told him to lower his voice, but they let him vent for a couple more minutes.

One of the police officers began shooing all the neighbors back into their apartments -- for safety, of course.

The other officer, as deliberately as he could, said, "I'm sorry, sir, you cannot continue to bang on the door. Mrs. Kaufman, who does live here, was the one who called us about a man banging on her door. If you continue to bang on the door, we'll have to arrest you for disturbance of the peace."

"So, he gets to steal almost a million dollars from someone and that's it, I'll see you in court?"

"Sir, what is your name?" asked the officer.

"Martin Silver. I invested with his company. He was assigned to me as an expert investor and he stole money from my account. The company can't reach him. No one else is moving on this. I found him myself after paying a private investigator."

"Sir, we are happy to meet with you at the police station. You can file a criminal complaint against Mr. Kaufman if a crime has been committed."

"I've already filed a complaint. I've been told by the prosecutor that there's a warrant out but they can't find him," said Martin Silver. "I've tracked him down here. He lives here. He should be arrested." Both policemen said nothing.

"You steal from the wealthy, nobody cares," said Martin Silver, now gesturing with his arms and hands, acting for his audience.

The shooing police officer wasn't doing very well. All the neighbors went into their apartments but kept their doors open and continued to watch.

"I cannot tell you whether that is true or not, sir, but you will still have to stop banging on this woman's door. She has told us by phone that her husband has left her, and he doesn't live there anymore. Why don't you come down to the station and file a complaint? If you have proof that he still lives here, and he has stolen from you, we will be happy to arrest him."

"Oh, great. It took me two weeks to find this bastard here," said Mr. Silver. "By the time I fill out the complaint, he'll reinvent himself again and take off."

"I'm sorry, sir. Like I said, we are happy to make a report for you, but you have to stop banging on their door. If you have proof of a crime, we will proceed and put out a warrant for Mr. Kaufman."

This was all Gladys was able hear. She was finally just about physically pushed back into her apartment by the one cop and the door closed by the second officer. She then watched through the apartment window. The two police officers slowly escorted poor Mr. Silver into the parking area. She could see Mr. Silver's frustration and anger as he went on and on to the police officers in the parking lot.

335

Pacifying and diffusing the public was now part of the officers' job duties. The cops let Mr. Silver carry on for another five minutes venting, before all three of them left.

# CHAPTER 2 (Book 2)

**December 23rd**
**Almost two weeks later**
**Fort Lauderdale, FL**

IT WAS THE START of Christmas week in Fort Lauderdale. The Intercoastal was littered all day with boats and yachts of every size and kind, all filled with residents and tourists alike. From party boats to single day cruises, the waterways were busy from early morning to sundown. As the sun went down in early evening, the same waterway became almost deserted. The local restaurants and bars filled up with the same tourists and residents. Christmas week was a busy time in Fort Lauderdale. It was a frenzied combination of out-of-state vacationers and locals. Everyone was anticipating and preparing for the holidays.

By eight o'clock, it was as dark as midnight on the Intercoastal. A slight purring of a single boat engine could be heard on the water. It made its way into an alcove hidden from the shoreline. Once it turned into the alcove, the boat's lights went off. The boat slowed to a crawl but continued forward for several minutes in the dark. Then the engine shut off.

Two minutes later, an anchor splashed into the water and began to sink. The only other sound was the slight rocking of the boat in the dark but calm waters of the Intercoastal.

Inside the boat, on the floor, the body was wrapped in a new tarp purchased at a home store. Next to the body were two fifty-pound bags of river rocks and two rolls of duct tape.

The murderer unfolded the tarp which now contained a small pool of the victim's blood. The body was still dressed in shirt and trousers. He wrapped duct tape around the pant ankles and sleeve cuff endings. He tore open the river rock bags and stuffed rocks inside both legs of the victim's pants. His hands shook more than they had ever shaken before. His actions were frantic and awkward. He hadn't expected to feel such panic.

As he stood once or twice during the process to wipe sweat from his forehead, he could tell this scene had novice written all over it. His plan was hatched in the state of frenzy and his inexperience showed. At this point, he had no choice; he just kept going. He would have to make it work.

After stuffing the pant legs with rocks, he abruptly stopped. It just occurred to him that he had to get the body, once stuffed, over the boat wall. He should have thought this before putting in any rocks. But again, he had to keep moving.

Before stuffing the upper shirt area, he dragged the body into position onto the back wall of the boat. This way, once he added more rocks, he only had to push the body overboard. It required every bit of his strength to hoist the body up onto the boat wall. He could feel the strain in his lower back.

He finished stuffing the pant legs and shirt with river rocks. He put on extra pieces of duck tape around the victim's neck. With the little energy he had left, he pushed the body into the water. As he watched the body hit the water, he could tell the neck area didn't look secure at all. He hoped the rocks in the pant legs would be enough to keep the body submerged at least until he could get away.

Like the anchor, the splash of the body sounded twice as loud against the silence of the deserted Intercoastal. He watched as the body sank. The last part of the body to go under was the back of the victim's head. Even in the moonlight, he could see the bloody bullet hole in the lower cranium.

He threw what was left of the rocks overboard next and pulled up the anchor. He started the boat, turned around, and slowly and stealthily returned to the marina.

# CHAPTER 3 (Book 2)

### Friday, February 1st
### 4:30 PM - Approximately five weeks later
### Fort Lauderdale, FL

BUSINESS AT Levitt & Cohen Financial Services was bustling. The market was up and the sales force were high-fiving each other as the market closed for the week. Several of the salesmen were mulling around and showing off at the reception desk where the two prettiest girls, Sarah and Kim, answered phones and greeted investors. It was Friday afternoon and close to five o'clock. Several of the younger traders were planning to go to happy hour to celebrate another market win. On the surface, all looked copacetic.

David Baker, one of the firm's private investigators, had finished speaking with Mr. Levitt, the head partner, behind closed doors. He left and nodded goodbye. He weaved his way through the celebration around the reception desk. He spoke to no one as he left.

341

Mr. Levitt exited his office. He quietly walked to his partner's door, knocked lightly, opened the door, and entered Mr. Cohen's office. At the sight of Levitt, suddenly the party atmosphere at the front desk subsided and everyone disbursed.

Levitt and Cohen were partners and business owners for fifteen years. They had been good and successful years together. Neither of them was expecting what had recently happened. The staff was not aware of what was going on under the facade at Levitt & Cohen.

Once the door closed, neither partner sat. They stood; Cohen behind his desk and Levitt in front of it. "I just spoke with David Baker," said Marc Levitt.

"What's going on?" asked Cohen, knowing by Levitt's expression that it was not good.

No louder than a whisper, Levitt said, "They just found Marty Silver floating in the Intercoastal. He was shot in the back of the head and weighed down with some configuration of duck-tape and rocks. They are in the process of notifying the family."

"He's the one who filed the FCC complaint against Kaufman, isn't he?" asked Cohen.

"That's the one. You know what this means for us, don't you?"

342

"It's going to be all over the papers and there's going to be blow back and more lawsuits," answered Cohen.

"Exactly. I've called everyone and the lawyers are coming in the morning, and we'll figure out what to do next. They're bringing in a PR company for damage control starting tomorrow." Levitt shook his head.

A moment of silence passed between them.

"Kaufman was the last person I would have thought would have gone this bad," said Marc Levitt shaking his head.

"I knew he couldn't be trusted," said Cohen.

"You don't trust anyone, Bernie," said Levitt.

"Now you know why," said Cohen, as he dropped down into his chair and swung around and looked out the window.

Levitt walked casually out of Cohen's office. The celebration around the reception desk was over and staff members were packing up to leave for the weekend.

Levitt went into his office and sat at his desk. He thought about what the next several weeks would bring: newspaper articles, sensational headlines, screaming clients, paranoid clients, and nasty clients. They would all be worried that they would be the next victim. No amount of assurance that the thief was gone would stop it. They would all assume their money was already gone. Fear could make people crazy.

Levitt and Cohen were trying to keep the mood up in the firm, but they were both laden with worry. Kaufman and the money he stole were nowhere to be found. If he was already out of the country, Levitt knew he was smart enough to land somewhere that would not extradite to the US.

The authorities traced some of this money through about four different transfers which cut off in Panama, where it was now stuck in legal limbo. Their private eyes were working with local detectives in Panama, but they hit a dead end. They had not found any trace of him there. There was now a legal standoff between the embassies and the banks. At least a large portion of the money in Panama was still there.

While working at the firm, Kaufman was known as extremely bright, daring and shark-like. The younger traders all looked up to him. He had a big personality and was the center of attention most days. Apparently underneath this intellect was a criminal mind. He first slowly embezzle monies from Levitt & Cohen. Then he moved onto stealing from their clients.

Levitt knew Kaufman would reinvent himself and hide the money in a way that no one would be able to find him. He had an extremely calculating mind. Levitt just hoped, this time, he was wrong about him.

Marc Levitt was holding his head between his hands, looking at his desk. He was absorbing the last report of the investigator. Thoughts of the private investigator bills, the legal bills, the newspaper articles, the frightened and screaming clients, the financial losses all seeped into his mind. He knew he had no choice but to take things one day at a time. He would need to trust the lawyers, investigators, state attorneys and SEC investigators. Hopefully, they could at least get back the lion's share of the money.

Levitt had liked Kaufman. He paid him very well, promoted him, and even protected him from a few disappointed clients. He treated him like a family member. Aside from the legal and financial storm that he faced, Levitt felt betrayed and heartbroken.

Bernard Cohen felt only hatred towards Kaufman. He never trusted him. In this moment, he realized why Cohen had built a wall around himself. Although Cohen had to deal with the same financial and legal fallout from this, he didn't feel the sting of betrayal or the heartbreak Levitt now felt. Maybe Cohen had a point.

Click below to go to Book 2:

Printed in Great Britain
by Amazon

28937956R00195